SHADEHAUNTER

SHADEHAUNTER

A
REALM OF KAHR'ANIS
ADVENTURE

R. J. XANDER

251 SF

SHADEHAUNTER
Written by R. J. Xander
Copyright © 2025 R. J. Xander
ALL RIGHTS RESERVED

Cover design by Studio 251.
Cover images used under license from Shutterstock.com.

Published October 16, 2025

ISBN (eBook): 979-8-9906096-4-8
ISBN (Paperback): 979-8-9906096-5-5

251 SPECULATIVE FICTION
P.O. Box 551
Gloucester, MA 01931

TABLE OF CONTENTS

TRAVELER'S GUIDE TO THE KAHR'ANIS PLAINS
(Believed to have been created by Landon Quilson,
Honorable scribe and Liberator of Kahr'anis.)

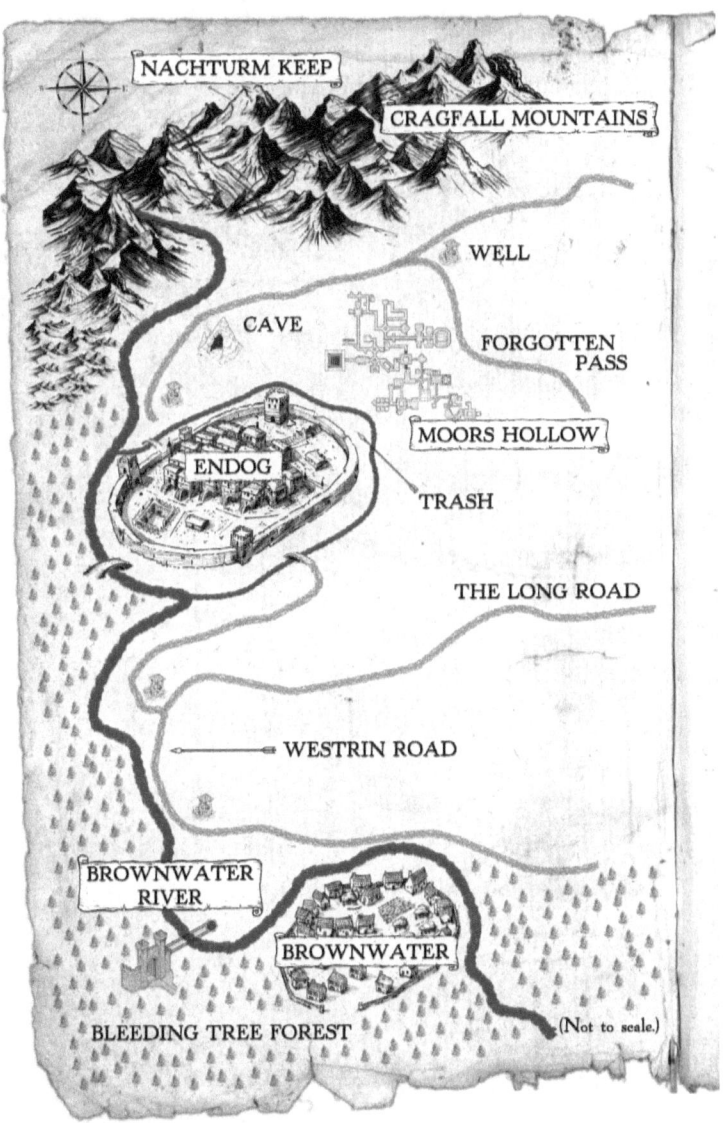

"Woe be the fate of any soul caught where light doesn't shine, for the wraith's power over the darkness is absolute."

Excerpt from the *Grimoire of Shadows*.

PART I

THE REALM OF KAHR'ANIS

1 KAHR'ANIS

Landon Quilson flicked a mosquito off his arm, leaving a smear of viscous blood behind. He hated when the red stuff oozed out of his body, so he reached into his back pocket, pulled out a bit of old cloth, and wiped it off. Landon was not ignorant, like most Muckluckers in his village, having been born the son of a scribe. He knew hot blood coursed through his veins with every heartbeat, but he believed with unerring certainty that it should remain inside, hidden from view.

After returning his arm to a less leaky state, Landon used the same rag to dry his sweaty brow. Cutting wood was hard work, and even though it was early in the morning, he'd already been at it for hours.

When people bothered to ask him why he was so conscientious about his job (a quality not common in these parts), he imagined responding with something quippy, like *the early bird gets the worm* or *the sooner I start, the quicker I finish*, but he never did because neither was true. It didn't matter how early he got to work or how much wood he chopped; there was always another pile of logs. Wood meant fire. Fire meant light. And light meant safety. Therefore, after sneaking a glance to make sure his arm had stopped dribbling, he stuffed the cloth back into his worn trousers' pocket and swung the axe again.

Throughout recorded history (not to mention long before recording was considered a profitable venture), people visited places for trade, vacation, or left the house in a huff and decided never to return. Some of the exotic destinations they sought out boasted rare cuisines, expansive vistas, manufactured goods, renowned artists, or simply had a vacancy at a decent pub where your throat wasn't likely to be slit in your sleep.

The Kahr'anis plains were none of those places. In fact, the valley was so forgotten by time that the Anisens didn't worry about days, months, and years. They were all the same as far as they were concerned, from the moment they became aware that such inconsequential trivialities existed to the instant they exhaled their final breath.

It was true that the mountains surrounding the valley might have been considered sight-worthy if the people on the plains could see them through the haze, but they couldn't, so they didn't think about it. And although the woodcutter dutifully went to work every day when he woke up, he never saw a sunrise. That would have required the murky sky to permit light to pass, which it rarely did.

So, without even so much as a fleeting thought about beautiful vistas or what time it was, Landon sighed as he lifted another log off the pile.

No one knew why the stifling air over Kahr'anis hung like a damp rag on everyone's face. Old timers insisted it hadn't always been this way, but no one had direct knowledge of it ever being different. Most folks attributed fantastic stories of blue skies and clear running water to the overindulgence of drink because that concept was entirely incomprehensible to them.

Of course, there were plenty of people who had other opinions on the matter. Some suggested the air was cursed, whilst others insisted it was the land. Those who'd been there long enough knew neither was the case. Living in Kahr'anis was the curse, and death was the only blessing for those who dared try it.

Now and then, a wayward traveler from outside the valley stumbled onto the plains, but they rarely stayed. And if they did, it certainly wasn't of their own volition. The lucky ones were fitted for a casket. The rest were left to the scavengers.

However, the dangers of the plains paled in comparison to the looming terror of Nachturm Keep, where the sorcerer *Volgreth the Shadehaunter* lurked.

Far to the north, the bleak Cragfall Mountains jutted ominously out of the plains, their jagged peaks shrouded in unnatural clouds. No one dared climb those mountains, for every step on the unstable rock formations and steep cliff faces easily led to a deadly plunge. Rocks tumbled unpredictably, and mudslides swept away both those who'd fallen and those who hadn't. Consequently, whether it was due to the shadow of Volgreth's magic, the mountains' wrath, or whispered stories told by candlelight in taverns across Kahr'anis plains, people wisely kept their distance, for fear of venturing too close and meeting an untimely demise.

That being said, it wasn't the weather, the mountains, or even the terrible Unwrought Tower sticking straight up from the center of Nachturm Keep like a misshapen tumor of rock that weighed on people the most. No. Their fear was more tangible than that and much closer to home.

Volgreth had the frightening ability to emerge from the shadows whenever he wished. This aspect of his thaumaturgy ensured he was always at the forefront of everyone's minds, influencing every moment of Anisens' meager lives. It would be a sad day for any child who scared someone by jumping out at them. There was nothing funny about jumping at shadows because the shadows were just as likely to jump at them.

The only protection Anisens had was to compulsively burn anything and everything they could get their hands on. The result was that flames burned wherever a shadow might exist. This added to the murkiness of the thick air and left soot marks on anything that didn't move, including many a blackened face. In case of emergencies, folks on the plains carried bundles of sticklike dips or small tallow jars with lids and a flint. One couldn't be too careful where the Shade-haunter was concerned.

As for their indoor living arrangements, it wasn't unusual for homes to have two passably inhabitable spaces: one for sleeping and one to stockpile candles. The smaller room was originally intended to be a privy of sorts, but everyone agreed candles were far more important than privacy.

For Landon's part, he lived far from Volgreth, Cragfall Mountains, and Nachturm Keep in what Anisens referred to as the arse end of the realm: the impoverished village of Brownwater. It was the only town on the so-called wrong side of the river (the Brownwater River, to be precise), meaning it was on the forest side, not the plains side.

Except for the ferry barge, the only way to cross from Brownwater onto the vast Kahr'anis plains was to travel north to a bridge near the border town of Endog, but that was too many miles to the north for most people. Therefore, those who were unlucky enough to be born in the village usually stayed there indefinitely, idling their lives away and, sooner or later, adding to the mud under their feet.

With a determined grunt, the woodcutter swung his axe again, tossing the bifurcated wood into what he generously referred to as a cart. It wasn't much more than a few old boards and two large wheels made from planks he'd nailed together and sawed into a reasonably circular shape, but it was what he had. And since he had to pull the thing himself, he was careful not to overburden it.

Landon's sharp features stood out against the ramshackle cart and the village's higgledy-piggledy homes. Whereas his chiseled muscles appeared strong and willful, the rest of the town looked like it hadn't done an honest day's work in generations. Most of the world-weary roofs sagged so much that people had to bow their heads in supplication to the town's ungodly hovels when they entered or exited.

Passersby would have been hard-pressed to believe Brownwater hadn't been abandoned if it weren't for the people milling around or sitting on rickety stools. A great many people lived there—too many, by all accounts—but that was the way of things in villages.

Clunk! Another piece of wood hit the ground.

Reinier, Landon's wolfhound, cocked a golden eye, but when their animal mind registered nothing of interest had happened, they went back to sleep. The waist-high dog had been Landon's companion as long as he could remember, a gift from his mother when he was a lad, and they hadn't been seen apart since. Some said it was unnatural for a dog to live that long, but the woodcutter brushed off their remarks as jealousy.

"One more log for the pile," Landon muttered, rubbing his eyes with calloused fingers. "A breeze would be nice, for once," but no breeze wasted its time blowing through the Realm of Kahr'anis, let alone Brownwater.

Taking a break from woodcutting, Landon removed his jerkin and dunked his head and muscular torso into a rain barrel, splashing water on the ground. He didn't wear a shirt because he felt it restricted his movement. And when you were a woodcutter, having control of your movements was the difference between having feet or not.

Using his hands to slick back his black hair, Landon stretched his weary back.

Reinier woofed.

"Yes, much better, my friend."

His muscles cooled, Landon put his jerkin back on, and leaned on the handle of his axe.

"You know what, Reinier? I was thinking we should get out of here. What do you say to that?"

The wolfhound lifted his gray head, cocked it to one side, and plopped it back down on the ground.

"Yeah, you're right. Brownwater is where I was born, and Brownwater is where I'll stay. Besides, many people are worse off than me. I've got my dad, a house, and a job. Even a dog."

Reinier made a sound that might have been a woof if he'd lifted his head.

"Hey, that's not fair. Woodcutting is honest work," Landon said as if he understood *Woof*. "Take old Farny. He has to clean the latrines. There's nothing honest about sifting through the feculence for unfortunate souls who fell in, hoping to find a coin or two in their pockets."

Reinier whined and put a paw over his nose.

"No kidding. But I don't plan on doing this for the rest of my life. Dad used to be a scribe afore his eyes went. I'd like that. I'm getting pretty good at my letters, but he says there isn't work for scribes anymore. Not since the landslide closed the pass."

Reinier got up, stretched his unusually long legs, and leaned against Landon, who scratched behind his ears.

"Yeah, you're probably right. We've got each other."

The pair surveyed the trees surrounding the village to the south, east, and west, and Landon's shoulders sagged. Bleeding Tree Forest was another reason no one left Brownwater. Even from where he stood, the acrid scent of the poisonous sap weeping from the bedeviled woodland made Landon's eyes water. No one apart from the enigmatic forest mystics dared cut a path through its warren of tangled vines, and few animals called it home.

Not one piece of wood he cut came from that accursed place. The truth was, Landon didn't know where his boss got the wood, and he was smart enough not to ask. He had a job.

That job provided a valuable service to Brownwater and put food on the table. That was all he needed to know.

Turning back to his work, Landon picked up his axe. *The wood don't chop itself,* the boss man's voice said in his head. Landon knew what he meant was that the wood wouldn't get chopped if Landon didn't do it. The boss man certainly never lifted a finger unless it was to extricate the cigar from his mouth and swear—not that it was a real cigar, of course. What little tobacco was carried by travelers would have sold at far too high a price for anyone in Brownwater. No, he just rolled up anything he got his hands on and set it alight.

Startled by a sharp scream piercing the air, the bundle of wood under Landon's arm slipped from his grasp, scattering like kindling across the ground.

2 BROWNWATER

Reinier growled.

"What is it, boy?" Landon asked, kneeling with one hand on the dog's back. The other reached for his axe.

Together, they listened to the sounds of abject terror coming from the village.

Reinier barked, spurring Landon into action. Together, they ran toward Brownwater.

The closer they got to the center of town, the clearer the sounds of chaos grew. Panicked shouts filled the air, punctuated with screams of pain and cries for help as buildings burst into flames. The village was so awash in fire that Landon had to take the long way around.

As he ran, he noticed something peculiar: no one was trying to put out the fires. It was like they wanted the town to burn. In fact, he knew they wanted it to burn because he saw Old Man Munshun intentionally set his home ablaze.

"What in the valley are they doing?"

Then, the truth was revealed: Leering Ones.

Both he and Reinier skidded to a halt. That's why Brownwater was burning. It was the Muckluckers' only defense against the evil that had beset their village.

Everywhere Landon looked, he saw the Shadehaunter's emaciated army of undead monsters stalking the winding, muddy paths that served as roads in Kahr'anis' southernmost settlement. He was horrified by their sunken faces and gaunt skin stretched tightly across their wicked bones. They wore nothing more than old rags that barely covered their hideousness.

No one knew if Leering Ones were grotesque bastardizations of people or if they'd been made to look that way by Volgreth's twisted magic, but it didn't matter. Either way, they represented the purest form of the sorcerer's villainy, and that was all anyone needed to know.

As Landon stood there, shocked by the appearance of the monsters, one of the Leering Ones turned toward him. The woodcutter's breath caught in his throat. Where the creature's eyes should have been, two hauntingly hollow voids—deep, impenetrable holes—stared at him. Landon felt drawn to it. He even stepped toward the creature, but Reinier changed his master's direction by head-butting the woodcutter in the side.

"What was that?" Landon asked, trying to shake the buzzing sensation out of his head. "And why are they here? What could Volgreth possibly want with Brownwater?"

Everyone felt the unease that descended on a place when Volgreth's gaze lingered too long and what it meant: certain doom. With a wave of his hand, the sorcerer could unleash his corrupted army, a nightmarish horde of monsters twisted by dark magic. But what could the Muckluckers of Brownwater have done to upset the Shadehaunter? The thought was maddening to Landon...unless it was as simple as delighting in the torment of Kahr'anis' most insignificant people. Why else would Volgreth waste time with Brownwater? It's not like anyone would mourn Brownwater if it were wiped from the earth.

Rage at the senselessness of it all filled Landon, and he cursed, vowing revenge for the sorcerer's treachery.

Reinier growled, ready to defend his master from the approaching unholy threat, but Landon had no intention of risking the loss of his faithful companion today.

Holding his axe at the ready, he said, "Stay close, boy. We need to get home. Then, we'll hunt the evil of Cragfall Mountain together. Understand? Home!"

The wolfhound barked and took off.

It would be impossible to express the level of trust Landon had in Reinier, which is why he followed the animal's path without hesitation.

The smoke made it hard to breathe, and the heat of the flames burned the woodcutter's face as he charged through the mayhem. Time and time again, grasping hands reached for him from between fiery timbers, but he deftly leapt out of the way.

"Father, I'm coming!" he yelled, his voice weak against the screams and intensifying flames.

Suddenly, Reinier doubled back and ran straight into Landon, knocking him to the side. If the wolfhound hadn't interceded, a Leering One would have grabbed Landon, and that would have been the end of the woodcutter.

"Thanks, boy! We're almost there!"

As they rounded the last corner, Landon's worst fear was realized. Between them and his house were at least eight Leering Ones, and its thatched roof was sending jets of fire into the air.

"No!" the woodcutter screamed, charging toward the monsters. He swung his axe wildly, but they dodged his unskilled attack.

Reinier had more success, clamping his powerful jaws onto one of the creature's forearms. With a sickening crack, the brittle bone broke, but the Leering One didn't appear to notice, continuing to move toward the woodcutter, dragging the enormous wolfhound behind it.

"Father! Father!" Landon called as he crashed through the front door and plunged into the burning house. Embers stung his exposed flesh, and he instinctively grabbed a wet towel from the basin and wrapped it around his head.

He was too late. On the far side of the room, the only family Landon had left was slumped on the floor in a pool of blood. It looked like his father had used a poker from the fireplace to defend himself, but a Leering One had wrested it from his grasp and driven it deep into his chest.

"Why?" Landon shrieked, adding his voice to the pained villagers' cries. "Why?" The humble woodcutter collapsed to his knees. He was utterly alone. "I failed you, Father."

Something grabbed him, and Landon whirled around, thinking he was being attacked, but it was Reinier. The powerful animal had hold of his jerkin and was dragging him toward the side door.

"I can't leave him!" Landon yelled, but Reinier refused to let go.

As Landon's feet crossed the threshold, the roof collapsed, making it impossible to retrieve his father's body and trapping several Leering Ones inside. The distraught woodcutter ripped the towel off his head and threw it to the ground. Then, the pair scrambled through the village, not knowing where to go.

Reinier ran ahead, barking loudly.

Realizing where the dog was leading him, Landon stopped. "We can't go to the forest. It's too dangerous."

But when he turned to change direction, it was obvious they couldn't get to the river either, being blocked by countless rows of the unholy beasts. So, with no other choice, he followed the wolfhound south toward the dreaded Bleeding Tree Forest.

A Leering One covered in flames stumbled out of a building, and Landon ran faster. Everywhere he turned, more Leering Ones appeared.

Though they jerked like puppets on strings when they walked, they moved surprisingly fast, and Landon had to work hard to avoid being ensnared by their skeletal fingers.

One lunged for him, and Landon made to swing his axe but realized he wasn't holding it anymore. He must have dropped it in his home. "Reinier!"

The dog leapt at the monster, knocking it to the ground, but more came.

"This isn't working. There are too many of them," Landon yelled, frantically searching for a way out.

Acting on instinct, he grabbed Reinier's collar and directed the dog across the dirt road. When they reached the other side, he threw himself against a rain barrel, forcing it away from a downspout. Luckily, though the air was damp and the ground was muddy from whatever people dumped outside their huts, it hadn't rained in quite some time, and the barrel was empty.

He toppled it over and rolled it down the road. Several Leering Ones went down with a resonant and rather satisfying thunk! Then, without warning, the creatures stopped moving, threw their heads back, and shrieked at once. Reinier jumped on Landon, knocking him to the ground and covering his master's head with his furry body.

With great effort, Landon extricated himself from the suffocatingly heavy animal. The woodcutter's head spun, and his ears rang, but he managed to reach his feet. All around him, people lay collapsed on the ground, making them easy prey for Volgreth's monsters.

Reinier had saved him from the worst of the Leering One's wails, but the woodcutter still couldn't think straight. Acting on instinct, he pulled on the dog's collar, but Reinier didn't move.

That's when Landon realized the shrieking beasts had struck down the wolfhound. Paws were good for many things, but they did a poor job of covering one's ears.

"Hold on, boy," Landon said, lifting the heavy dog off the ground. "I'll get us out of here."

The woodcutter moved as quickly as possible toward the forest, past the woodyard, through the farmlands that surrounded the village, and over the low boundary wall. But just as he was about to escape, a Leering One shambled out from between the trees, barring the way.

3 SORIN

Landon struggled against the urge to lose himself in the Leering One's gaze. But why not? He was tired, and he could find stillness in the darkness forever.

"Wake up! It's a trick!" a commanding voice broke into his thoughts.

"Father! Is that you?" Landon yelled, pulling back from the precipice. "Father, I'm here!"

But no, his father was gone, and this voice sounded different. Older. Wiser.

Landon was racked by indecision. He knew looking into the creature's empty eye sockets meant certain death, but diverting his gaze was equally dangerous, as the weight of the wolfhound across his shoulders prevented him from running fast enough to escape. Unable to see a way out, he stood there, paralyzed.

Then, a thought came to him. Maybe he could use the extra weight he was carrying to his advantage. Steeling himself against the impact, he prepared to bull-rush the creature. The instant before he charged, an arrow whizzed through the air.

The Leering One twisted around with the force of the blow and crumpled to the ground.

The gorge rose in the woodcutter's throat as he watched the monster's essence seep out of the dead carcass, first pooling on the ground and then congealing and rising into the air in front of him. It attempted to wrench itself into a cohesive form, but a rare shaft of light penetrated the gloom above Kahr'anis, bathing the wraith in its golden light. Unable to escape, the creature was torn asunder, leaving nothing but ashes drifting to the ground.

Freed from danger, Landon spun around.

A young man carrying a bow called out as he ran toward him. "Not bad, eh? Dropped it from fifty yards. And you're welcome, by the way," he said, stooping to re-tie the long, crisscrossing strips of leather that held his shoe in place.

"Huh?" Landon asked, more than a little confused.

"For saving your life."

"I had things under control."

"Sure you did." The archer's peasant garments hugged his wiry frame almost as if they were a size too small. They came replete with a thigh-length beige tunic, a leather belt, and beige trousers. All in all, they weren't that different from Landon's, though the woodcutter wore a leather jerkin tied in the front, not a shirt.

What puzzled Landon was that archery—not the everyday need for survival but the art of regal competition—was reserved for nobles, not peasants or laborers. Sure, anyone could make a bow if they found a yew tree, and plenty of people had small crossbows at hand, but a weapon like the one this archer carried was decidedly not a peasant's weapon, not by a long shot. It made Landon question whether the archer was who they claimed to be. Then again, he'd proven himself helpful, and that deserved some amount of recognition if not respect.

Completing the picture, the young man had curly dark hair with bright eyes that revealed his quick wit. Across his chest were two leather straps: one held his quiver tightly to his back, and the other was a simple messenger bag at his side. Landon had seen carriers use bags like that before, but he'd never understood the appeal. A piece of burlap and a bit of rope were enough for him.

"Nice shot," Landon said, shifting uncomfortably.

"I guess," the archer said with a knowing grin. "But I could have hit that thing at a hundred yards as easily as fifty."

"You may need to if more head this way."

Sorin looked across the fields toward the burning town. "I can shoot far, but not that far! My name's Sorin. What's yours?"

"Landon." Not wanting to be rude, he added, "Thanks."

"Think nothing of it. I did the world a service getting rid of that abomination."

The woodcutter agreed. He didn't know precisely what a Leering One was, but the fewer that walked the earth, the better.

"I don't mean to pry, but do you always go around with a wolf on your back?" the archer asked, retrieving his arrow. "Doesn't it slow you down?"

"He's not a wolf. And no, of course not. He's hurt."

"I see. Then, let's get him out of here, and us too, while we have the chance."

Regaining consciousness, Reinier whined, and Landon lowered the wolfhound to the ground. "Easy, boy," he said, smoothing the dog's wiry fur.

Reinier looked at his master and, remembering the danger, forced himself unsteadily to his feet. He sniffed the air and growled.

Sorin nodded. "Smart wolf."

"He's not a wolf!"

"Could have fooled me. Now, can we please leave?"

But when they turned toward the forest, all three hesitated, coughing as the forest's dank innards exhaled its acrid air around them.

Gnarled branches stretched as far as the eye could see in a wide arc around Brownwater, and a tangled canopy of misanthropic vines loomed menacingly overhead. Like every story told about the realm, the things people whispered about Bleeding Tree Forest were filled with misery and death.

No one knew why the trees bled. On the surface, they looked like any other tree: poplar, oak, maple, and anything else you could name. However, it didn't matter what genus or species they were; they all leaked poisonous black ooze.

As a lad, Landon had mistakenly chased a rabbit into the forest. He'd managed to escape with his life, but the rabbit hadn't been so lucky. The fate it suffered was most assuredly worse than what it would have faced from the boy.

Landon wasn't able to describe what he saw that day, not that anyone had ever asked or wanted to know, but from that time forward, he'd vowed never to risk its dangerous paths again. Now, he'd have to break that promise, and he wasn't happy about it.

"You all right?" Sorin asked, slapping the woodcutter on the back.

Landon flinched. "Don't you smell that?"

"What? The putrid scent of weeping trees that rot any flesh that touches it?"

"That's not helpful. There's no telling who we'll meet in there."

"Or, what…" Sorin said under his breath.

All three turned to look at the Kahr'anis plains. No one ever wanted to stay there, but now that it came to it, they didn't want to leave it either. Struck with indecision, they stood there, hovering at the forest's edge.

Then, far across the planting fields, several Leering Ones appeared around the side of a burning farmhouse, and the decision was made for them. Rushing along the treeline, they skirted the forest to find a path, but there were none to be seen.

Reinier saw movement in the weeds ahead and nudged Landon.

Without saying anything, the woodcutter changed direction and stepped between the trees. "Stay close."

"Trust me, I have no intention of wandering off," Sorin answered, his usual humor stifled by the oppressive atmosphere.

"I wasn't talking to—" Landon started to say, but decided to let it be. Staying together was good advice, whether you were a person or a dog.

When they left the plains, the sounds of chaos in Brownwater faded into the distance, suppressed by the dense forest. Woodlands were supposed to be noisy places filled with calling birds, chirping frogs, and an incalculable number of bugs, but here, there was nothing but the faint gloop of sap sliding down tree trunks and plopping onto the root-covered ground.

Reinier rubbed his nose with his paw and whined again.

"I know, boy. It's disgusting," Landon said, his voice muffled by the arm he'd clamped firmly over his nose and mouth.

"Wait," Sorin whispered, touching Landon's arm. "I see a path."

Landon looked in the direction of Sorin's finger, but the *path* was a bit of an overstatement. *A place where they could fit between the trees* would have been more accurate. However, seeing as the woodcutter had no intention of chopping his way through the sickening undergrowth, he nodded. "I don't like the look of it, but it might be our best bet."

But before they moved, Sorin moved his hand to Landon's chest. "Wait."

"What's the matter?"

"It's a good place for an ambush."

"Great."

Sorin shrugged. "Keep your eyes peeled. I don't want one of those things flanking us."

The power of suggestion is a potent thing, and instantly, every stick and vine looked like Leering Ones' arms reaching for them. The deeper they moved into the forest, the more oppressive it felt, almost as if the trees were moving to block the way behind them. Landon focused all of his attention on not losing sight of the path.

Equally uncomfortable with the situation, Reinier's fur stood on end, making him look like an oversized walking scrub brush.

"If one of those things is in here with us," Landon whispered, "we'll never see it coming."

"I will," Sorin said with more confidence than Landon felt. "Hold on. What was that?"

"Are you messing with me?" the woodcutter said irritably.

"No. Listen."

Reinier's ears perked up, and then he ran.

"Wait!" Landon called after the wolfhound, but he was gone.

Sorin nocked an arrow. "So much for stealth."

"What did you hear?" Landon asked.

The archer slowly moved his head, attempting to get a fix on the sound. "Moaning. There it is again."

"Are you sure? I don't hear anything."

"Trust me. I've got the hearing of a bat."

"How would you know?"

"Shh."

Reinier appeared from behind a tree and barked.

"What is it, boy?" the woodcutter asked.

The dog barked a second time and disappeared again, leaving Landon no choice but to follow.

"Hey, wait. You don't know what's out there," Sorin said, standing his ground, but since remaining there alone wasn't an option, he put the arrow back in his quiver and followed his new companions. "Great. It didn't take long at all for us to do something stupid."

4 THEA STARHEART

Reinier's whines led them to a small clearing not far off the path, and when they saw what was at the dog's feet, they gasped. A woman was lying on the ground, and she wasn't moving. Her golden hair was a tangle of leaves and dirt, and her flowing white robes were torn and stained with blood. Around her neck, a skillfully carved tree hung limply on a thin cord, and on her feet, she wore leather sandals, the straps of which wrapped around her calves almost up to her knees.

"Who is she?" Sorin asked, being careful not to disturb her.

Landon didn't respond. He was too busy wincing every time the woman took a labored breath. It pained him to see her arms and legs splayed out at such odd angles, almost as if they'd been frozen in a frantic pose as she tried to escape her attackers. "Who could have done this?" he asked himself, but deep down, he knew the answer. Leering Ones. And if that was the case, it begged the question: Are they still here?

Reinier barked, breaking Landon out of his trance-like state. Shaking off the cobwebs in his mind, he scanned the forest for any sign of the evil creatures. Nothing, yet.

"Look," Sorin whispered, getting down on his hands and knees. "She's awake."

The woman returned the archer's gaze, but the blue-gray color of her eyes seemed to fade as her strength waned. "My name is Thea. Thea Starheart. My Light…" she whispered in a trembling voice. "…is your Light."

Sorin brushed a few damp strands of hair away from her face. "Shh. Save your strength."

"I was ambushed…Volgreth's creatures…my faith saved me."

The archer turned to Landon. "She's a cleric. We need to help her."

"Obviously, but how?" the woodcutter asked a little irritably. No one had helped his father. Then, feeling horrible at having such a selfish thought, he said, "Sorry."

"For what?"

Landon coughed. "Nothing. Um, I don't know how to help her. There's nothing but evil in this place."

"There's Esslla, the Forest Mystic."

"You aren't seriously suggesting we seek the Bleeding Tree Witch's help, are you?"

"She's not a witch," Sorin scoffed, though the tone of his voice didn't carry its usual confidence. "I've heard stories that she has unrivaled healing powers. I guess you'd have to, living in here. Besides, what choice do we have?"

Landon knew Sorin was right, but he didn't have to like it. The woodcutter had never turned away from someone in need, and he wasn't about to start now, even if it meant trusting the witch. He only hoped she was the good kind of witch because if the bedtime stories he'd been told as a young lad were true, the bad kind was not to be trifled with.

Thea turned her head. Barely managing a whisper, she said, "No. I must turn to my faith for healing. No witches."

"You're too weak to heal yourself," Sorin said, gently placing a hand on her shoulder. "Let us help you."

Thea's face grew paler, and she winced in pain. She obviously wanted to say something else, so Sorin leaned closer, but she lost consciousness before the words passed her lips. The gentlest puff of air brushed the little hairs on his ear when she exhaled.

"We need to hurry. She doesn't have long."

Crossing his arms in front of his chest, Landon said, "I'm not saying we're not going, but explain to me how we're going to find the mystic. This place is worse than a rabbit warren. I don't even remember how to get back to the village."

"I don't think that will be a problem."

"How's that?"

"They say she finds you," Sorin replied, rubbing the back of his neck.

"That doesn't sound ominous or anything."

Reinier whined softly, and Landon stroked the wolfhound's head.

The archer put up a finger.

Landon stopped moving. "What is it?"

"I don't know."

A mysterious melody made its way to their ears.

"Where is that coming from?" Landon asked.

Sorin shook his head. "Are those words?"

Reinier lifted his head and howled along, but was quickly silenced by the woodcutter. "Not now, boy."

The wolfhound obeyed his master's command but cocked a discontented eyebrow. He liked to sing.

The melody grew louder, and the words became more distinct. *Analarn ma-nanalee alstin poru'um ma-alstu.*[1]

There was movement in the undergrowth nearby, and Landon stiffened. "I don't like our options, but hanging around here will surely invite trouble. Let's go."

---

[1] A-nuh-larn mah-NAH-nuh-lee AHL-stin poh-ROO-OOM mah-AHL-stoo.

"At least Esslla knows we're coming," the archer said, nodding in the direction of the song.

"That's what I'm afraid of."

"Here. Help me carry her. You're the one with big arms."

Landon took this as a jab. Laborers like him were always getting made fun of as being all muscle and no brain, but that wasn't the case for him. Sure, he liked playing head ball. But as the son of a scribe, he'd learned to read long before most of the people in Brownwater, not that it was difficult to do. Most people born in the village never read a word in their lives, but he had, and one day, he hoped to copy ancient texts, like his father had.

Comprehending the sour expression on the woodcutter's face, Sorin added, "Hey, I didn't mean it that way. I don't have anything against muscles, but there are muscles," he said, pointing at Landon, "and muscles," pointing to himself. "I could use your help."

Landon snorted. Long ago, he'd learned that being bulky didn't mean a person was stronger than someone else. Besides, the archer's arms may not have been as lumpy as his, but they looked like they could lift an ox. Plus, Sorin was far lighter on his feet, which was always good in a fight.

Turning his attention back to the task at hand, Landon got the dog's attention. "Reinier."

The wolfhound's ears perked up.

"Warn us if you sense anything."

The wolfhound leapt in front of them, nose and ears at the ready.

Step by careful step, they threaded their way through the oozing trees. More than once, Landon wished he had four legs like Reinier. Then again, when he'd woken up this morning, he never could have imagined that by lunchtime, he'd be traipsing through Bleeding Tree Forest with an archer from beyond Brownwater's borders, carrying a cleric barely clinging to life.

Not for the last time, he longed for the simplicity of what he now grimly thought of as his past life—one where he woke up in the early morning, splashed his face in the rain barrel, downed a cup of whatever he could afford at the tavern, grabbed his axe, and spent the day chopping wood.

He'd hated that life, trapped in the nowhere town of Brownwater, but now that it was gone, he understood the appeal. It was certainly better than running from Leering Ones, and he really wished he still had his axe.

"Psst," Sorin said.

"Huh?" Landon asked, looking up.

"Enough daydreaming. Watch where you're going."

"Oh, yeah."

The perpetual twilight of the forest, coupled with the mass of black roots covering the forest floor, made the trip take much longer than Landon would have liked. Then again, as they moved deeper into the forest, he couldn't help but ponder Sorin's words: *They say she finds you.*

5 THE FOREST MYSTIC

Thea's eyelids fluttered open. She was in an earthen room lit by untold numbers of candles of every conceivable shape and size. Most had been placed on top of older spent candles, leaving cascades of wax frozen in time as they pooled on flat surfaces, flowed over edges, and dripped down long candlesticks and candelabras. Once her eyes adjusted to the flickering light, she noticed arcane trinkets scattered about the place —glass vials filled with colorful, and sometimes sparkling, fluids; carefully bundled dried herbs dangling from the ceiling; and countless wood carvings of animals.

"Where am I?" she asked, her voice hoarse and barely audible. Clearing her throat, she tried again, but no one answered. She was alone.

Beneath her, a makeshift bed, covered with piles of soft furs, cradled her weak and battered body. Moving hurt, so she made herself as comfortable as possible and collected her thoughts.

Before waking here, she'd been traveling south along the Westrin Road when she'd happened upon a village on the wrong side of the river. She'd just taken the ferry across the Brownwater when one of the ramshackle huts burst into flames.

Sensing the presence of evil, she'd lit a candle and prayed for protection, but before finishing, a searing pain had pierced her thoughts, and she'd run. With nowhere else to go, she'd headed into the forest but was ambushed by a group of Leering Ones. Her spell had saved her from the worst of the creatures' attack, but she was struck from behind, and everything went dark.

Thea felt beneath the furs. Her robes had been removed, and her wounds had been cleaned and dressed.

Then, the rest of the story came back to her, and a feeling of dread overwhelmed her. Two men had taken her to the Bleeding Tree Witch to be healed. That meant the unthinkable: she hadn't been healed by her faith but by a witch!

Thea fought back waves of anguish. Wrapping her fingers around the wooden talisman she wore, she prayed with all her might for forgiveness. But here, in this strange place under the ground, she felt disconnected from her world of faith, and her soul was wracked with uncertainty.

"Focus, Thea. The Light will not abandon you," she told herself, but her hands trembled as she searched for comfort. "You must understand from whence you came to understand where the path will lead."

Taking a deep breath, she pushed herself up. Her body protested, but she refused to take no for an answer. Once she reached a sitting position, she hiked up the furs to keep herself covered and opened her eyes. With all her might, she willed herself not to fall over as the room spun around her.

The potion bottles and other mysterious relics looked familiar somehow, but also hinted at something dark that she didn't like. When the room stopped moving, she said aloud, "Light of my Light, why have you forsaken me?"

A candle on a rough-hewn wooden table sputtered to life. She took it as a sign and bowed her head in supplication. When she raised her eyes again, she saw that the table was cluttered with alchemical tools, smoldering with a forgotten experiment.

Ancient leather-bound tomes lounged haphazardly on shelves collapsing under their weight, and iron pots simmered over several fires, burning in odd-looking stone fireplaces. The smell wasn't unpleasant, but it wasn't comforting either.

The more she saw, the more uneasy she felt. A wave of dizziness overtook her, and she leaned her head on the wall. Suffering trials was part of her faith, but she worried about what this particular trial might entail.

The door creaked open, and she started. The two men who'd brought her here entered—one stood quite tall and wore a simple jerkin, and the other, who was shorter and wirier, wore tight-fitting clothing. Thankfully, they didn't look evil. Quite the opposite. They were both clearly relieved she was awake and sitting up.

The smaller one with curly dark hair rushed over to her and instinctively moved to place a hand on her leg, but hesitated. She did not encourage him.

Thea studied the young man. By the look of his bow and quiver, he appeared to be a noble archer—one of the regal competing class—but his clothing spoke of the peasantry. It was a perplexing dichotomy.

The taller man kept his distance. "We were worried you wouldn't make it."

His body looked strong and weather-worn from a lifetime of laboring outdoors, but his intense brown eyes told a different story. They were thoughtful, intelligent eyes that held much sorrow and something else: anger. This man had suffered greatly but had yet to come to terms with his loss. That could be an asset or a liability. She would do well to keep that in mind.

An oversized dog with stiff, gray hair placed its head on the bed beside the cleric and whined.

"Reinier, here, was worried, too," the tall man added.

Thea loved all of the Light's creatures and instinctively moved her hand for the wolfhound to sniff it. Then she scratched behind the dog's ear. His back leg immediately moved, and she laughed despite her condition.

"Well, Reinier," she said, "we've been introduced, but who are the rest of you?"

"Oh, yeah. Right," the roguish archer said, pointing to himself and then to his companion. "I'm Sorin, and he's Landon. We were chased into the forest by Leering Ones—" Thea sucked in a breath, and he whispered, "My apologies. I didn't mean to upset you."

The woodcutter pulled a wooden stool over and sat down. "We've all had a difficult day, but you're safe now. Rest easy. No harm will come to you here."

Thea didn't look convinced. "Your faith is commendable, but how can you be sure?"

Before Landon or Sorin responded, the air in the room changed, growing heavy with power. At first, the sensation frightened her, but then Thea realized this power didn't feel malicious; it felt...

A soft glow emanated from the doorway as the Forest Mystic entered the room, her graceful form radiating with an ageless beauty. She had deep green eyes that held the wisdom of the centuries, and her silvered hair cascaded down her back nearly to the floor. It was streaked with glittering colors, shimmering as she moved. She wore simple yet elegant robes made with natural fibers, dyed in rich, earthy tones that blended seamlessly with her surroundings. This gave off the impression that she would be good at hiding if she wanted to, which was probably how stories of the invisible Bleeding Tree Witch had started. "I am Esslla. Daughter of the Light."

As she spoke, the Forest Mystic traced a circle on Thea's forehead with her third finger.

"Esslla," Thea gasped, struggling to bow.

"You know her?" Sorin asked. "Are you a witch, too? I thought you were a cleric."

"Shh! Don't be rude. Esslla's no witch. She's a High Priestess of my order. You need to bow your head."

Taking the cue, both Landon and Sorin lowered their heads.

"I just thought she was a nice old lady," Sorin said out of the side of his mouth.

"Be at peace, child. You are safe," Esslla said, her lilting words forming a gentle melody in Thea's ears.

Through the mystic's touch, the cleric was shown that Esslla spoke the truth, and the cleric was at peace.

"But how are you here?" Thea asked. "The stories say you ascended in the last age of the world and joined the Light."

Esslla chuckled but didn't offer an explanation. Instead, she prepared a cup of herbal tea. "Clerics do have vivid imaginations, don't they?"

"What's the difference between a cleric and a mystic?" Sorin asked Landon.

The woodcutter stared back blankly.

"I am but a simple *Disciple of Life*," Thea said. "In time, I hope to become a *Blessed Healer*, channeling the Light to do good in the world. *Mystics*, or High Priestesses, have transcended channeling and have become one with the Light."

Landon and Sorin wondered what they'd gotten themselves into, but were also relieved Thea wasn't mad at them for bringing her here against her will.

After Esslla handed the cup of tea to Thea, she ushered the men out of the room.

"Hey, why does he get to stay?" Sorin asked, pointing to Reinier.

Esslla gave him a knowing smile and shut the door.

• • •

"Child, *rise*," Esslla instructed.

Thea was magically lifted out of the bed and gingerly placed in a standing position.

Reinier, who looked like a pile of fur lying on the floor, walked in circles to get more comfortable.

Thea was surprised to find she had enough strength to stand, or maybe that was the spell, or the tea. She felt awkward leaving the comfort of the warm furs and vulnerable, being completely naked except for the bandages covering her injuries and the talisman she wore around her neck. Part of her faith required that she accept who she was, inside and out, but she struggled with the latter. Unlike her sisters, who rarely put on robes except when they went into the world, she didn't like to put herself on display so plainly. Esslla didn't appear to notice her discomfort.

The High Priestess' touch was gentle but firm as she guided the weakened cleric to a soft chair.

Being schooled in the lore of the ascended, Thea knew Esslla could only be seen if she wanted to, and she asked, "Why did you reveal yourself to us?"

"You have lost your way, child."

"But I am devoted to my faith."

Esslla raised a hand. It was Thea's time to listen, and she quieted.

"Do not dwell on the missteps of your past, for it will prevent you from walking in the Light."

Thea was used to her teachers speaking in riddles, but she wished Esslla had been a little more specific. For example, which missteps in particular was she talking about? Thea could think of several possibilities. Instead of voicing her concern, Thea said, "I will walk in the Light, but I must regain my strength first."

"That, my child, is already done."

Thea realized she no longer felt weary or sore. "Thank you, High Priestess."

Esslla nodded before opening a wooden chest. It looked weary from countless years of service. Inside, there was an array of neatly folded robes and garments.

"Your body is but a vessel, no more or less important than an old clay pot. It is your spirit that concerns me," the priestess said, returning with a set of pristine white garments embroidered with intricate patterns in gold thread.

She deftly enrobed the cleric and blessed her. What Esslla said next took the cleric by surprise.

"There is no shame in straying from the path, only choosing not to return to it."

Thea blushed. It was like Esslla had read her mind. Wait, had she strayed?

"We are all connected in the great tapestry of life," the High Priestess continued. "You may seek comfort and healing from others beyond your faith, but be careful, the dark is, by its very nature, hidden."

"Then how will I know it when I see it, if it is disguised?"

"Pray to the Light, and in time, you will be able to see into the dark no matter where it exists—even into the hearts and minds of men and beasts where the darkest of the dark often resides."

Thea took a breath, allowing Esslla's words to penetrate the recesses of her mind. But that didn't mean she fully understood them. She planned to pray for clarity once she had a moment alone.

Esslla smiled and went about her business, humming a pleasant tune.

Thea bowed her head. "Thank you. I will honor your wisdom and strive to guide those who walk beside me in the Light."

"May the path of Light always begin at the tips of your toes."

• • •

The door creaked open, and Thea stepped through, followed by Reinier.

Sorin's jaw dropped open.

The cleric's presence filled the candlelit room with an aura of serenity. Her long, golden hair was woven into a single loose braid and adorned with purple flowers. The bright white robes Esslla had given her glowed with the purity of her faith.

Landon stood sheepishly off to the side, clasping his hands and looking at the floor. "You're so beautiful. Oh, I mean... different. I didn't mean to offend."

"Beauty is never offensive," Thea said, "but it is not always visible on the outside."

"Well, I'm not afraid to say it," Sorin said, staring at the cleric. "You're stunning!"

"It is the radiance of faith," Thea explained.

"Whatever it is, I'm impressed."

Landon cleared his throat. "What he's trying to say is that we're glad you're all right."

The soft clink of glass punctuated their conversation as Esslla puttered around her home, tending to this and that.

"Where are you headed?" Thea asked, returning to discussing matters most pressing. While she listened to the woodcutter's answer, she kneeled before one of the candles and prayed.

For his part, Landon was shocked by the question. He hadn't had much time to think about that sort of thing. "I don't know. My father is dead, and my home and village have been destroyed. I'm certainly not going back because there's nothing left for me in Brownwater."

Before Thea had the chance to ask the archer about his plans, the sound of clinking glass stopped, and everyone, even Reinier, turned toward the High Priestess.

Her green eyes glimmered in the flickering candlelight. "Child, it is not enough to show interest in Landon and Sorin's lives; you must honor their kindness."

Reinier barked.

"Yes, you, too, Reinier," the mystic added.

Thea looked puzzled. "But how?"

"You must accompany them on their quest."

"I won't deny that we need help, but we aren't on a quest," Landon said. "We entered the forest to escape the Leering Ones and only happened on Thea by chance."

"Did you, now?" Esslla asked in a soft, melodic tone.

Sorin cocked an eyebrow. "Are you saying we were supposed to find each other?"

"I'm not saying anything other than none of us can claim to know the mysteries of the Light."

"I certainly don't," Sorin said, fidgeting uneasily.

"When I questioned the Light," Thea said, "it did not cease to shine. When I lost my way, it did not cease to guide me. And when I fell, it gave me the gift of you, Reinier, Landon, and Sorin. For that, I will be eternally grateful, but that does not mean I fully understand my place in this world. To learn that, I must seek the path of the Light and follow it, no matter where it leads."

Sorin shifted uneasily. "I'm not sure I like the sound of that. I can deal with things I can see or hear, but this mystical stuff is too much."

"Don't be disrespectful," Landon said, worried about upsetting Esslla, but there was no need.

The High Priestess chuckled as she returned to puttering. "I feel the same way sometimes."

"Tell me, Esslla, is this the quest I have been searching for?" Thea asked, trying to grasp the full meaning of the mystic's cloaked words.

"It is not for me to say. Be patient, child, for in time, the Light reveals all."

"Will it reveal dinner?" Sorin asked. "I'm famished."

6 THE QUEST

Later that night, Landon stared at the candlelight flickering against the trinkets strewn about the room. Candles were a necessary ward against the feared Shadehaunter, but they also lent an eerie glow to everything their light touched. As he lay awake, unable to sleep, Esslla's words echoed in his mind, but what use were his calloused hands against mysticism and magic?

"What troubles you?" Esslla asked, appearing beside his bed. She held a vial filled with a shimmering liquid in her hand.

"Is that for me?" he asked.

"If you want it."

The liquid inside seemed to move of its own accord, glowing enough to illuminate the palm of Esslla's hand, but not bright enough to cast any shadows.

"Will it help me understand?"

"It may, and it may not," she said noncommittally. "I can only show you the way, not walk the path for you."

Landon wasn't sure he trusted the woman, but he didn't distrust her either. She certainly wasn't like any witch he'd heard stories about. Esslla carried an air of timelessness about her that made her words and movements slow and methodical, not harried or grasping as he'd imagined a witch would be. He also couldn't label her *good* or *bad*, as the stories had suggested. She felt like neither and both at the same time, and it frustrated him.

What if this potion revealed a hidden truth or the quest before him? That would be worth the risk, wouldn't it? Then again, it might show him something he didn't want to see. Still hesitating, he asked, "Do I have to take it?"

"It is your choice and your choice alone. I do not insist or even offer it to you. I simply show you that it is here, in my hand. What you do with it is up to you. That is the way of the Light."

Reinier moved closer, his paws moving silently against the floor. A low grumble emanated from his throat, and the wiry fur along his back bristled with caution.

"Peace, Reinier," Esslla said, and the wolfhound's growls subsided. "It is not our place to choose for him."

The woodcutter looked between the potion and his faithful companion and back again.

"Reinier is wise to be cautious, but this is no trick," Esslla explained. "The Light only shows the truth. It never deceives. That is the way of the darkness."

Landon lifted the vial from her hand, and it changed color. He was about to ask if it was supposed to do that, but instead said, "Will it hurt?" It was a childish question. He didn't even know why he'd asked it.

"Only if you fear the truth within you."

He might.

"If you give yourself to it freely and unhindered, the Light will shine upon you, Landon Quilson, and it will guide your steps to reclamation."

Landon didn't know what that meant, but if it helped him reclaim something—anything he'd lost—he wanted it with every fiber of his being. Grasping the vial between his calloused fingers, he popped the cork off the top. It had no scent, but the cool glass felt like a promise...or a threat. Either way, he needed to find out, so he placed it between his lips and tipped the glass container.

As if mimicking how he felt, the liquid hesitated at the brim of the vial, hovering between the known and unknown. Then, he leaned his head back, and the vial's contents slipped into his mouth. For a moment, he paused, and then, giving in to his desire to find the truth, he swallowed.

"Remember," Esslla's distant voice echoed in his mind, "Do not look to others for the answers you seek. Answers lie within."

As the potion took effect, Landon felt an icy chill race through his veins. He would have been terrified if he had time, but rivers of colors flowed from the candles he'd been looking at and turned into enormous water beetles swimming through the air around him.

Esslla's earthen hut dissolved into a surreal dreamscape where stars twinkled in the sky, and lush grasses stretched as far as the eye could see. Only, they weren't stars; they were blinking eyes, and the grass was actually hills covered with red poppies. Image after image assailed Landon's mind until they formed a spectral haze from which a woman glowing with an ethereal light appeared. At first, he thought it was Thea, but no. This luminous woman had brown hair and piercing yellow eyes.

"Child of Kahr'anis," she said. Or, at least, that was what Landon heard because her mouth didn't move. "Do you know who you are?"

"Landon Quilson, son of Jardon Quilson of Brownwater," he said reflexively.

"No."

"What do you mean, no? That's who I am."

"Do you know who you are?" she asked again, her voice both comforting and insistent at the same time.

"I don't understand what you want from me."

"Then Kahr'anis is lost."

"Wait!" Landon yelled. "Tell me who I am!"

"I cannot. You must discover that for yourself."

"Then tell me how I can find out."

"Seek the Light, for it seeks you, Landon Quilson."

"Where can I find it?"

"Where the mists part. Where the ground is not the ground. And where the land meets the sky. It is there that you will meet your true self."

"But I know of no such place."

"The Light will guide you."

"Do I have to go alone?"

The woman floated closer and placed a hand on the wood-cutter's head. "Those who walk in the Light are never alone." Then she faded into the swirling dreamscape.

Landon felt a tug at the center of his body as he was dragged back to the waking world. "Wait! I have more questions!"

Landon's eyes snapped open, and he realized he was screaming at the top of his lungs. Sorin and Thea were by his side, holding him down, and Reinier was howling at the top of his lungs.

"He's back," Sorin said, letting go of Landon's arm. "What a nightmare."

"That was no dream," Thea said, leaning closer. "Tell us what you saw."

Landon tried to answer her, but he was too disoriented to make sense of his surroundings. He yelled again, scratching at his arms as if to brush off the beetles that had swarmed around him.

Reinier nuzzled his hand, and he snapped back.

"Something really must have gotten under your skin," Sorin said, jiggling his arms as if he could shake off his nervous energy. "I thought you were being torn apart or something."

"That's what it felt like," Landon explained, finally calming down. "I had a vision."

"And?" Thea asked. The note of concern in her voice didn't escape Landon's or Sorin's notice.

"I think there's something I need to do."

• • •

Over the next few days, Sorin and Thea made Landon recount the experience over and over again as they tried to parse out its meaning. Sorin focused on the part about Kahr'anis being lost, believing that Landon was some kind of chosen one, which he found to be exceedingly cool.

Thea kept repeating, "Seek the Light, for it seeks you," insisting Landon should join her in her prayers, but the woodcutter politely declined.

He had no experience with clerical ways and hoped there was a more earthly answer.

"But it might be a prophecy. A sign from the Light itself," she insisted.

Landon wasn't sure about that. No light other than flickering candles had ever shone on him, and he didn't expect it to start now. He was, and would always be, a lowly woodcutter from the wrong side of the river, no matter where he went.

"Or, it could just be a dream brought on by a strange potion," Sorin suggested. "Mushrooms that grow along the edge of the forest have that effect. Maybe Esslla gave you an extract."

Landon rubbed his temples. "Possibly, but it felt pretty real."

"Either way, I'm in," Sorin said resolutely. "Prophecy. Quest. Thingamajigger. Any of that beats hanging around this forest."

Thea shot Sorin a glance, which he took to mean he was being irreverent, but the archer laughed it off.

The one thing they all agreed on was that the woodcutter wouldn't find any answers hanging around Esslla's hut. They needed to go out into the world, and that was precisely what they intended to do.

• • •

Early one morning, Esslla appeared, and Landon understood that the time had arrived for him to continue his journey. He'd come to like the mystic's home. It felt safe and distanced from the troubles of the plains, but Esslla insisted the refuge he sought only existed in the Light, not in a hole in the ground.

When they'd collected their things, the High Priestess handed each of them a small bag filled with rations and a waterskin. "It may not look like much, but it's been blessed with the Light and will serve you well."

"Thank you, Esslla," Thea said, bowing her head.

"But this is empty?" Sorin said, inspecting the waterskin.

Thea tucked hers into her robes. "I will supply water when we can't find any. The spell is simple enough, but draining, so I must not use it often."

Sorin glanced at Landon. "She can make water appear out of thin air?"

The woodcutter didn't respond, too worried about venturing back into the forest.

Esslla tapped him on the chest, bringing him back to the moment. "You can't go about the world looking like you have your pajamas on."

"What's wrong with my jerkin?" he asked, aghast by her insinuation that his clothing was insufficient in some way. It had always served him well.

"The world is a cold place in more ways than one. Take this. It will protect you from the elements."

Esslla handed Landon an oiled cloak and a burlap sack closed with hemp rope. It wasn't much, but to him, it looked like it cost a fortune. Truthfully, he'd always wanted a cloak, and a sack was the perfect traveling companion as far as he was concerned. How had she known?

However, as much as he liked the gifts, he said, "I couldn't possibly," pushing them back toward the priestess, but the look in her eyes told him she wouldn't accept no for an answer. Feeling somewhat awkward but also thankful, he put the garment on.

"Nice threads," Sorin said, making Landon even more uncomfortable.

As they prepared to leave, the mystic raised her hands, palms up, and intoned, "As tall as the ash grows, it began as a sapling. Learn from your mistakes. Listen to your heart. And most importantly, believe in each other, for that is where you will find strength when all seems lost."

Reinier howled.

"That didn't make me feel better," Sorin mumbled as they stepped into the forest.

This time, Thea didn't restrain herself and slapped him in the back of the head. "Where's your respect?"

"Right here, where I can keep an eye on it. It's just that I could've done without the whole *all seems lost* bit."

Landon didn't speak. He was trying to come to terms with the future of Kahr'anis being laid at his feet. If only the Leering Ones hadn't attacked his village, he wouldn't have been thrust into whatever this was. Any way he looked at it, things sucked, but at least he had a cool cloak and a sack.

7 ALDERBEASTS

Shrouded by the never-ending darkness of Bleeding Tree Forest, Landon, Sorin, Thea, and Reinier struggled to find a path through the undergrowth—all the while being careful not to trip on the sinewy black roots covering the woodland floor.

"Is it me, or are these vines trying to trip us?" Sorin asked, doing his best not to brush against anything.

Thea shook her head. "If they were trying to trip or grab us, we'd already be worm fodder."

Sorin stopped short. "You really have a way of making things sound worse than they are. For once, could you—"

Reinier growled.

"Shh!" Landon said, interrupting the archer. "What is it, boy?"

The wolfhound barked, and they turned around.

The vines *were* trying to grab them!

"Alderbeasts!" Sorin yelled, spinning around and readying his bow.

Landon whistled for Reinier as more of the creatures emerged from between the trees, but the dog wouldn't move from in front of him. "Together then," the woodcutter said, not knowing what use he'd be considering he'd left his axe in Brownwater.

The monsters weren't particularly fast-moving, being an amalgamation of sinewy tendrils coiled into humanoid forms, but the way their moss and fungus-covered appendages blended into the forest made them nearly impossible to spot before they attacked.

"I thought Alderbeasts only existed in fairy tales," Landon said, trying to get a handle on the situation.

"No such luck," Sorin hissed as his bow twanged with the sound of an arrow taking flight.

It didn't take long for the archer to find the Alderbeast's drop spot. It was an area that appeared slightly more solid than the rest of their writhing form. The trick was hitting it because it moved around like every other part of their bodies!

"Esslla!" Thea called out. "What should we do?"

In response, the mystic woman's melodic voice spoke in their ears. "The Light will guide you."

Sorin wasn't impressed. "What is it with mystics, always talking in riddles?"

"Don't I know it," Thea agreed, exhaling in exasperation.

"Well, the Light better do something fast, or we're done for," Landon said. "There are too many of them!"

Arrow after arrow found its mark, but where one Alderbeast crumpled to the ground, two additional creatures slithered out of the vine-covered canopy.

Thea instinctively lit a candle and prayed for protection. Instantly, a radiant shield formed around the group.

Sorin forced himself not to fire his next shot, unsure if his arrow would pass through the magical barrier or be reflected back onto them. "Is it safe?"

"No! It isn't safe!" Landon snapped, feeling useless.

"I mean, can I still shoot them?" the archer asked Thea.

The cleric's blue-gray eyes grew sharp and cold. "Send these beasts back to the foul magic that spawned them!" she bellowed, and Sorin let his arrows fly.

At first, the Alderbeasts recoiled from Thea's spell, but the insatiable hunger that drove them was too powerful to be vanquished, and they smashed themselves against the magical barrier until it faltered.

"They're coming through!" Landon said, pointing to several vines penetrating the shield.

Thea grimaced. "I can't hold them back much longer."

Forgetting where he was, the woodcutter reached for a broken branch to beat back the vines and screamed.

"What is it?" Sorin asked.

"Nothing. Look out!" But it wasn't *nothing*. The evil acid had burned Landon's hand so severely that he wasn't able to make a fist. Distracted by the pain, he didn't see an Alderbeast lunge for him.

Reinier leapt into action, barking fiercely. The wolfhound tore through the monster, sinking his teeth into its foul flesh and ripping off bits of its vine-like arms.

"Reinier!" Landon shouted, fearing for his companion's safety, but the wolfhound succeeded in incapacitating the creature before returning to his side.

With one last flicker, the cleric's shield failed, and she collapsed to the ground.

"Thea's fallen," Sorin yelled, reaching for another arrow, but his quiver was empty. "Perfect timing!" he said sarcastically, using his bow to fend off another Alderbeast. Then, he threw the bow over his shoulder and grabbed the cleric, pulling her toward Landon and Reinier. "I don't know what you're doing over there, but do it quicker!"

Landon spotted a stone structure poking out of the trees. "I see something. Hurry!"

"That might be difficult," Sorin said, still supporting Thea.

"I'm all right," she said, clambering after Landon.

Before Sorin could follow, an Alderbeast lunged at the archer. He pulled one of his arrows out of the monster's side and used it to stab the creature in the chest before tossing it into his quiver. "At least I've got one left." But while he was focused on that one, tendrils from another slithered toward him from behind a tree.

"Look out!" Landon yelled.

Sorin was trapped. "Damn."

"By the Light, return to where you came from, foul beast!" Thea bellowed.

There was a bright flash, and the Alderbeast recoiled. It was all Sorin needed to escape.

"Whew, that was close," he said, letting Landon pull him the rest of the way up a short slope. "Thanks, Thea."

"We aren't out of danger yet."

"You're always a bundle of joy, aren't you?"

Reinier ran ahead, making it to what looked like the dilapidated castle's entrance first, but didn't go in. He just stood there growling.

"There's no time for that," Landon said, smacking the wolfhound's rump to get the dog moving, but Reinier held his ground.

The woodcutter stopped. "Something's wrong."

"You think?" Sorin asked dryly.

"First things first," Thea said. "Help me with the gate."

Not willing to leave his master by staying outside, Reinier slipped in as they closed the heavy door. It slammed with a resounding thud, and Landon sighed in relief. Then, they barred it with a wooden beam and any other materials they found lying around.

"Thank you for helping me back there," Thea said.

Landon was about to say, *You're welcome*, but realized she was speaking to Sorin.

"It was nothing," the archer said, blushing.

"And thank you, Landon," she added, addressing the woodcutter, "for having the presence of mind to find us sanctuary. Though I'm afraid it may not prove to be much safer."

Landon wasn't sure that was a compliment, but he said nothing. They had more pressing matters to attend to, like figuring out where they were, determining if they'd escaped the Alderbeasts, and seeing if anything in here planned to have a go at them.

Reinier growled again, and the woodcutter stroked the wolfhound's wiry fur. "Easy, boy. Easy."

Thea looked into the dark corridor that gaped before them.

"What is it?" Sorin asked.

"We may have escaped one danger, only to find ourselves ensnared by another."

"That doesn't sound good."

"It isn't. I sense something unnatural about this place."

"Could you be more specific?" the archer asked, trying to peer into the gloom.

She looked at him with her sharp blue-gray eyes and said, "Evil."

"Sorry I asked."

"I think the Light will keep it at bay for now, but I sense a presence watching. No, *searching* would be more accurate."

"For what?" Landon asked.

Sorin put his finger to his mouth. "Don't ask. She might answer you."

"I suggest we move as quickly as possible to see if this unholy place can tell us anything of value," Thea suggested. "Then, we leave."

Sorin looked shocked. "What? And go out there with them?" he asked, using his bow to point toward the Alderbeasts.

"Trust me. *Them*," she said, motioning to the forest, "might be better than *them*," turning toward the corridor.

"When am I going to learn to keep my mouth shut?"

"Probably never," Landon said, patting Sorin on the back much like he did with Reinier.

"Thanks for the vote of confidence." The archer stooped to pick up the remnants of a torch, which he lit with a flint he carried in his pocket. "Yuck. I almost wish I couldn't see."

The moist stone walls were covered in inky black mold, no better than the oozing trees they'd left behind.

Thea looked at him. "I don't suggest spending any time in the shadows with the Shadehaunter lurking."

"I was being facetious."

"And I was being truthful."

"The curse of being a cleric, I suppose."

"There are worse things," Thea said, taking the torch from the archer.

"Hey, wait a second. I thought you just told me to stay in the light."

Picking up a second half-spent torch and lighting it from the first, she handed Sorin's back to him.

"Oh, I see," he said, taking it from her.

"Isn't anything in this forest not covered in ick?" Landon asked, cradling his injured hand.

"Let me take a look at that," Thea said, but the woodcutter pulled away.

"There's time for that later. Let's find a safe place to regroup."

"Hold on," Sorin said, stuffing what was left of a few more torches into his quiver. "You can't be too careful."

Thea nodded toward him. "On that, we can agree."

"Did you hear that, Landon? She agreed with me."

"Don't let it go to your head," the woodcutter said. "I have a feeling it won't happen very often."

The woodcutter's footsteps echoed between the stone walls as they pressed deeper into the fortress. Not far ahead, they discovered a heavy iron door inscribed with intricate symbols. The markings looked like they'd been hurriedly scratched into its patinaed surface with a sharp object as opposed to the work of a craftsman or incantation. Landon suggested the tip of a dagger, and the others agreed that it was likely the case.

"Are those symbols intended to keep things out or lock something in?" the woodcutter asked, turning to Thea.

She studied them closely and said, "It's a containment sigil, possibly? They aren't of my faith, so I can't be sure, but I don't sense malice."

"Well, we only have two options," Sorin said. "We can go back outside and play with the Alderbeasts or open this door." Then, without waiting for an answer, he grabbed the handle to see if it was locked.

"Stop!" Thea yelled, but it was too late.

The handle moved, and a gasp of air escaped when Sorin pulled on it. He looked around, smirking. "Anybody dead? Did anyone get burned by acid? Hit by a poison dart. No? Then, in we go."

"That didn't take long," Landon said, holding Reinier's collar in case the dog got it into his head to run ahead.

Thea shook her head in disbelief. "You don't get this whole *rune-covered, possibly trapped door* thing, do you?"

"I got us in, didn't I?"

Landon gave the archer a sideways glance. "Next time, listen to the cleric, okay?"

"What? I got us in."

Putting a hand on the door handle, Thea said, "We might as well see what lies beyond."

The rusted hinges protested loudly, and all three winced as they worked together to open the door the rest of the way. Beyond it lay another passage, only this one was illuminated by an undulating silvery light that flowed along the ceiling.

"Lunar Glow," the cleric whispered.

Sorin looked perplexed. "What's that?"

"A rather unique spell that is self-perpetuating."

"Which means?"

"It doesn't wane with the caster's strength or when its components are spent. Once it is successfully cast, it glows basically forever."

"Excellent. Can you cast it over our heads or something so that we don't have to worry about torches anymore?"

"I'm afraid not. It's an ancient spell, and the skill to invoke it has been lost to time. Some insist it's not a spell at all but the remnants of the ancient mystics' magic that refuses to stop glowing. Others believe sorcerers were working on a universal incantation to dispel Volgreth's darkness altogether. Either way, it's beyond my power to recreate."

"Darn. At least it will keep the Shadehaunter away."

"Will it? What if I'm wrong and it's not Lunar Glow at all, but an illusion to trick us into the darkness?"

Sorin stopped tamping out his torch. "She's playing with me, right?"

Landon stared blankly back at him without saying anything.

"Great. Just great," the archer complained, sticking the rest of the torch into his quiver. "Is there anything that's just normal? How about that rock over there? Is it going to try to kill us, too? Wait! No. Don't answer that. Forget I said anything. I don't want to know."

"If you're done," Thea said. "Let's keep moving."

8 WOODLAND FORTRESS

As disgusting as the forest was, shuffling through a magically lit corridor with no doors or openings was infinitely worse.

"Are you okay?" Landon asked, seeing Thea stumble and catch herself before falling into the wall.

"I'll be fine. The darkness pushes on me."

"At least the lunar thing makes it easier to see," Sorin said, nocking the last of his arrows. It had a slight bend, having been wrenched from the Alderbeast's side.

"Not that kind of darkness," Landon corrected.

"Oh, yeah. Right."

After rounding the next corner, they stumbled upon an ancient kitchen, long since abandoned and left to rot. Dust covered every surface, and cobwebs stretched between everything that stuck up from the refuse. The scent of decay hung thickly in the air, wrinkling their noses.

Sorin coughed. "It's a good thing Esslla gave us something to eat. We aren't going to find anything sustaining here, that's for sure."

"Agreed," Landon said, moving a broken clay pot. A giant millipede more than a foot long scurried away, and he stepped back.

Thea noticed that Landon was still pressing his hand to his body, and she asked to see it. At first, the woodcutter refused, embarrassed that he'd made the mistake of touching one of the forest's evil trees, but in the end, he gave in.

"This needs attention," she said, inspecting the burn.

"It'll be fine."

The wolfhound whined.

"Reinier understands. This is an evil wound that will fester if left untreated."

"I don't like the sound of that," Sorin said, skirting a large pile of garbage. It looked too deliberate to be detritus, and he had no intention of finding out what might have made it, or disturbing whatever lived inside it.

Preparing to cast a spell, Thea removed a candle from her robes. The Lunar Glow provided plenty of light, but she always liked to have a pure source nearby when she was casting, if possible.

Noticing what she was doing, Sorin asked, "Do you need my flint?"

The cleric smiled politely as she passed her hand over the wick. When she pulled her hand back, it was lit.

The archer whistled. "That's some trick."

"No trick. The Light burns within me. Come Landon. Sit by me."

The woodcutter did as she asked, and Thea prayed over his wounds.

As the spell took effect, his hand glowed with a light so pure it hurt his eyes, and he turned away. But curiosity got the better of him, and he peeked, watching as the cleric drew a symbol with her finger over the burns. At first, he reflexively pulled away, but her touch made him feel better, and he relaxed. Soon, the flesh returned to a more wholesome color, and his wounds closed.

Landon flexed his hand in amazement. It wasn't completely healed, but the pain had all but vanished. "Thank you," he said earnestly. "Am I mistaken, or are your powers getting stronger?"

Reinier sniffed the woodcutter's hand and licked it, showing his approval.

"The Light within me grows," Thea said, smoothing her robes. "Praise be to the Light."

"That was impressive, but I think we should search for answers elsewhere," Sorin suggested. "I don't like it here."

Helping Landon to his feet, he ushered the woodcutter and cleric out the door.

As the hours passed, they found nothing of import, only long hallways that led nowhere. Making the search even more frustrating was that each hallway ended with a tall mirror, taunting them by displaying where they had come from, which added to the feeling of being trapped.

"Hold on a second," Sorin said, turning around.

Landon tried to see what he was looking at. "What is it?"

"Stay here."

Before the woodcutter could stop him, the archer ran back the way they'd come and turned a corner. Afraid they'd be separated, Landon, Thea, and Reinier followed, but they didn't get far before Sorin appeared behind them. "Just as I thought!"

"Wait. How did you get behind us?" Landon asked, trying to figure out what had happened.

"We're going in circles."

"No, we're not," the woodcutter insisted. "I've been making sure we don't turn the same direction at each intersection."

"Nevertheless, it's obvious that he's correct," Thea said, peering around the corner. "We're stuck in a maze, of sorts."

Landon suddenly felt even more claustrophobic. "Can you get us out?"

"I'm no sorcerer."

Sorin sighed. "More riddles."

"It's no riddle. It's the truth. The Light does not deceive people, so I am unable to create or dispel magic made with that intent. I can only pray for guidance. The rest is up to us. Have you seen anything that might suggest a way out—a key to the illusion?"

"A key? No, I haven't seen any keys." Sorin said, checking his pockets.

Landon stopped him. "She doesn't mean that kind of key. She means a clue or a crux, right? I've read about them in my father's parchments. Old ways of hiding things you don't want found."

"Precisely," Thea said, closing her eyes and thinking. After a few uncomfortable minutes, she said, "There's no point in retracing our steps. All we can do is continue on and hope we find a way to see past the spell."

Sorin produced a grease pencil from his messenger bag. "I'm not leaving anything to chance." Walking up to the mirror, he wrote the number one in the lower right-hand corner. Then he took a step back and admired it, his reflection looking very pleased with himself.

"I have to hand it to you. That's a great idea," Landon said.

"Why, thank you. Let's find the next mirror."

That was precisely what they did, but still, they found no way out of the maze.

"Thirteen! Thirteen mirrors and we're no closer to getting out of here," Sorin said, breaking his grease pencil on the number three. "Would you look at that?"

"Think of it this way: now you have two pencils," Landon said, leaning against the wall. "I'm beat. Can we take a break?"

"Not yet." Thea had been quiet as they walked through the fortress's spell-lit hallways, and her voice sounded strange to them.

Sorin put his pencils away. "Huh?"

"Let's check one more hallway. If we don't find anything, we'll rest."

"If you don't mind my saying, which I'm sure you do, you look like you could use a rest now."

"One more hallway," Thea insisted, starting without them.

Reinier padded after her, as did Landon and Sorin.

Ten minutes later, they were standing in front of a mirror with the number one written on it.

Sorin was beside himself. "So, we've been walking around the same thirteen hallways all this time?"

"Looks that way," Landon said, inspecting the mirror. "Unless someone else has a grease pencil."

"Nah. That's my handwriting. Hey, why do you look so smug?"

Thea was standing in the middle of the hallway, stroking Reinier's back and staring past them at the mirror.

Landon and Sorin looked too, but they didn't see anything unusual. There they were, staring at themselves with Thea between them, a few feet back. Behind her was the hallway lit by the Lunar Glow spell.

"Don't you see it?" she asked.

Sorin scratched his head. "See what?"

"The opening to the other corridor."

"Yeah, I see it. So what? Every hallway has been connected to another passageway."

"Look again."

Landon leaned in, but he couldn't see anything unusual.

Sorin looked at the reflection and then the hallway, but he also didn't see anything out of the ordinary.

"It's on the wrong side," Thea said, pointing at the mirror.

"By the gods, she's right!" Sorin yelled, getting excited. "It should be on the right, but it's on the left. How is the mirror doing that?"

"It's not a mirror."

"Of course it is. I wrote on it."

"Did you? Where's the mark?"

Sure enough, Sorin's number one had disappeared.

"The illusion has been broken. Follow me."

To Landon and Sorin's surprise, the cleric stepped through the mirror into the hallway beyond. Reinier followed, thinking this was a fun game, as did the others. Once on the other side, they could see the hallway they'd just left as if they were looking through a one-way mirror.

"Neat trick," the archer said. "Unbelievably annoying but neat."

Tired and frustrated, they located an easily defensible room with only one door and made camp for the night. Sorin surprised the others by producing a host of candles he'd collected along the way. The silvery light of the Lunar Glow spell shimmering overhead chased away the shadows, but its light wasn't as wholesome as the candlelight, and they were thankful for Sorin's resourcefulness.

Since they'd only seen one broken handpump in the kitchen and no running water, Thea was forced to cast a spell to fill their waterskins. It worked surprisingly well, but as expected, it drained her of her energy, and she soon fell asleep.

Landon and Sorin stayed up and chatted over the nuts and berries Esslla had given them until Sorin also fell asleep, and Landon was left to keep the first watch.

Reinier, however, never slept, keeping a watchful eye on the door the entire night.

9 A WAY OUT

In the morning, they continued their search of the fortress with even less luck than the previous day. After hours of searching, Sorin became so frustrated with their lack of success that he opened the next door without taking any precautions.

"I thought we discussed this," Thea hissed. "Doors can be booby-trapped."

"How many more doors do we have to check to prove there are no boobies in this place, present company excluded, of course, and there are no traps. This place is totally dead. There isn't even—" He stopped short.

"You were saying?" Thea asked, looking past the archer with the unmistakable expression of *I told you so* on her face. "That looks like something to me."

Beyond the door lay a broken contraption that had clearly once been a trap of some kind. It had a counterweight and a guillotine-like blade that was rusted and bent.

Doing his best to ignore it, Sorin said, "Hey, look at that!"

The room appeared to be an expansive library, or it had been at one time. Now, the book repository lay in utter ruin.

"This wasn't done by time," Landon mumbled, carefully moving the collapsed trap out of the way so they could get by.

"No. Something terrible happened here," Thea agreed.

Ancient tomes lay scattered across the floor, and the scent of mildew and rotting parchment made them sneeze and clear their throats.

"This is a travesty," Thea said, lifting one of the damaged books. "So much knowledge lost to the darkness."

Landon touched her arm. "Be careful. There still could be hidden dangers amongst the wreckage."

Showing more emotion than usual, Thea blushed, having been called out for the same reason she'd admonished Sorin.

"Or maybe something useful," Sorin said. "Look over there."

A skeleton was lying on the floor next to an overturned library desk. Its bony fingers clutched a dusty, leather-bound tome. Thea lit several candles, knelt, and prayed over the body. Then, she gently removed the book to examine it. Opening the cover, she read words written in a flowing script. "*Rise Shadow Rise: A Chronicle of Ascension.*" She gasped and almost dropped it.

"Is it cursed?" the archer asked.

"No. It's not a grimoire. It's a history of Kahr'anis. Or, I should say, the early days of Volgreth's reign." Thea turned one of the book's ancient pages, careful not to damage it.

"It looks like this guy paid for his efforts with his life."

"It would seem so."

"Hey, Landon. You're always talking about being the son of a scribe. Why don't you read it?"

"I've had enough of death," the woodcutter said with a slight edge to his voice. "I'll leave tending to the dead to Thea, if you don't mind."

"Suits me fine," Sorin said, taking the hint.

While Thea delved into the unholy depths of the journal, Landon and Sorin sifted through the mountains of books and shattered bookshelves.

Under different circumstances, Landon would have been delighted to be surrounded by so many books, but something told him to keep his guard up. "See anything that could help us?" he asked, glancing at his companion.

Sorin was knee-deep in a pile of moldy scrolls. "Nope. Not unless you're interested in who paid their taxes on time."

Thea slammed the skeleton's book shut, accidentally blowing out the candles she'd lit, and Reinier growled.

Landon put the book he was looking at down and moved toward the cleric. "Looks like Thea's had more luck than us."

Deep worry lines etched into her forehead.

"What did you learn?"

"Nothing good," she said, gathering her candles. "If this book is accurate, and I have no reason to believe it isn't, Volgreth was hired by the last true Anisen potentate, *King Horacentine the Third*, to help convert the plains to farmland. But Volgreth's magic wound up poisoning the Brownwater River, making the situation in the valley much worse. Furious at Volgreth's mistake, the king threw the sorcerer in the dungeon, but that didn't keep him from casting spells. Soon, everyone in the castle fell ill and eventually died. Volgreth assumed the throne and continued his efforts to restore fortune to Kahr'anis. You can probably guess what happened next. Failure after failure led to anger and uprising. Believing Anisens didn't appreciate his efforts, instead of helping people, he cursed them instead."

"And?" Sorin asked.

"That's it. Whoever the storyteller was, he died before finishing his tale. At least Volgreth hasn't succeeded yet."

"What makes you think he hasn't succeeded already?"

"The Light still shines even if we can't see it."

Thea and Sorin's discussion stirred painful thoughts in Landon of his father and the Leering Ones. "He needs stopping before darkness is all that's left of the valley."

"And who's going to do that?" the archer asked.

"We are, of course. I've lost my family and my home. Volgreth is responsible for both."

Sorin laughed self-consciously. "Okay then."

"You mustn't let your hatred consume you, Landon Quilson. That is not the path of the Light."

Thea's words stung, but Landon held his ground. "Well, someone has to stop him."

"His power is immense, and he has many creatures to do his bidding. If you truly believe this to be the quest Esslla spoke about, I will follow you to the Unwrought Tower, but we'll need help. The three of us can't do it alone."

"The three of us?" Sorin asked. "I haven't said anything about helping."

"So you would turn your back on us now?" the cleric asked.

"No, of course not. I was just saying I hadn't said I'd help yet. Now I'm saying it. I'll help."

Thea shook her head.

"I agree our odds would be a lot better if there were more of us, but how will we expand our numbers?" the archer asked earnestly.

When Thea moved the book, something caught Landon's eye. "What's that?"

The cleric gently lifted the skeleton's other hand. On it was a shiny gold ring.

"Ooh!" Sorin said, reaching for it.

"Wait, Sorin! It might be cursed." But, once again, she was too late.

The archer snatched it from the skeleton's finger. Immediately, his body shivered uncontrollably. Then, with foam spewing from his mouth, Sorin flopped onto the floor.

"Light help us!"

Sorin burst out laughing. "I got you! You totally thought the ring was cursed. Did you see that, Landon? I played her like a vielle!"

"That wasn't funny," Landon grumbled under his breath before calling Reinier to his side.

"No, it wasn't," Thea agreed, slapping the archer on the arm. "Don't ever do that again. Do you hear me?"

"Yeah, I hear you, but everything's been so serious lately, I thought it would be good to lighten the mood a little."

"Sometimes it's better to let the mood be what it is and not mess with it. And that thing could still be cursed. Put it back."

"Are you serious?"

"It is pretty," Landon said, peering over the archer's shoulder.

"Listen to the two of you!" Thea huffed. "You have no idea what you are dealing with. Put it back before something bad happens."

"Maybe it's just a ring, plain and simple?" Sorin asked a little defensively. "Not everything we find in this forsaken place has to be tied to evil deeds."

"I won't deny it," Thea conceded reluctantly. "But it would behoove us to be cautious or, at the very least, not take any unnecessary risks."

Sorin cocked an eyebrow. "There's something else that worries you, isn't there?"

"Well, I…"

"Yes?"

Huffing, she said, "I don't have the skill to find out what it does."

"If anything."

"Yes, if anything, but I'd rather not take the risk."

The archer rolled his eyes. "Fine. I see your point," he said, placing the ring on the table.

Thea's lips pressed into a thin line, and she stared at him as if to say, *Good, but don't pick it up again.*

"Are we done here?" he asked.

While Sorin and Thea sparred over the ring, Landon continued searching the room to see if the library held any other secrets. After a lifetime of studying the subtle differences between wood grains, he'd developed a keen eye for noticing things, and he detected an irregularity in the floor. It was barely visible amongst the scattered books and dust, but it was there, nevertheless.

Crouching down, he ran his calloused fingers over the worn stone, tracing the outline of a hidden trap door. "If you two are finished," he said, pushing a pile of fallen books to the side. "You need to see this."

Sorin perked up. "Ooh, a secret door."

"Indeed," Thea agreed. "Let's see what it hides."

Landon located a handhold, but before he pulled, Sorin said, "Don't forget to inspect it first. You never know. It might have traps or, better yet…" He cupped both of his hands.

Thea kept a straight face, though she did think what he'd said was funny. Even so, she had no intention of revealing that to Sorin. The last thing she wanted to do was encourage him.

Taking hold of the stone, Landon lifted. A puff of air blew dust into his face, and he coughed. He lost his grip, and it fell back down, splitting in two. Before he could grab it, the smaller of the two pieces dropped into the empty void below with a loud crash, and they all cringed. Thankfully, nothing jumped out at them.

Once Landon recovered from his coughing fit and Reinier stopped sneezing, all four peered into the hole.

Like everywhere else they'd explored, it was lit by the eerie Lunar Glow spell. The shimmering light revealed a ladder leading to a subterranean corridor.

"What do you think? Treasure? Rats? More skeletons?" Sorin asked.

Landon shrugged. "Whatever's down there must be better than what we've found up here."

"Are you sure about that?" Thea asked, leaning closer to the hole. "We're still alive, so I doubt we've seen *worse* yet."

"Oh, we've seen *worse*, all right," Sorin corrected. "It's *worser* that I'm worried about."

"Is that even a word?" the woodcutter asked.

"Oh yeah. And when it happens, you'll be like, *I'm so glad Sorin taught me the right word to describe this situation because this is definitely worser!*"

"Do I have to help you get focused again?" Thea asked, holding her slapping hand at the ready.

Sorin stepped back. When Thea turned away, he pointed at her and mouthed, *worser.*

Landon couldn't help but chuckle. "Do you sense anything?" he asked the cleric.

"I sense the presence of evil is waning," she whispered, concentrating on the space below. "You may have found a passage not entirely corrupted by Volgreth's dark sorcery."

"That's good enough for me," Sorin said, "Ladies first…"

Thea gritted her teeth.

"How about I go first?" Landon asked, moving the stone and climbing into the hole with Reinier across his shoulders.

Sorin stood with his arm out, gesturing for Thea to go before him, which she did.

"Let's go!" she called when Sorin didn't immediately climb down behind her.

"I'm coming. Is everyone out of the way?"

"Yes, now get down here."

"Watch this!" Sorin deftly leapt onto the ladder and slid to the ground. "Ta da!"

Thea turned and started walking. "Show off."

Sorin smiled broadly and nudged Landon. "She totally liked it."

The woodcutter looked doubtful. "If you say so."

10 TRUST

Deep beneath the Woodland Fortress's aging stone walls, a tunnel hewn by forgotten hands stretched into the distance. Though Landon had learned to carry a healthy dose of skepticism about anything they encountered, he relaxed. This air smelled cool and damp, carrying with it the scent of earth and moss, not the mold and decay that pervaded the fortress above. Even better, there were no mirrors.

Overhead, the shimmering Lunar Glow spell continued to light the way, but he sensed its strength was waning. He wondered if the incantation hadn't been cast down here at all and they were simply benefiting from magical overflow from the corridors above, though he didn't know if that were possible. What he did know was this: if it gave out before they reached the end, they'd be easy pickings for Volgreth because the meager pieces of nearly spent torch they carried were no match for underground dark spaces.

"I'm hungry," Sorin announced, interrupting Landon's thoughts.

"Sounds good to me," the woodcutter said, wiping his brow.

Reinier made a low, muted woof and flopped onto the ground.

"If we are to rest, it would be wise for us to do it here in case the tunnel branches or opens into caverns," Thea suggested. "At least here, we only have two fronts to defend, and the light above us still shines."

The others agreed.

It didn't take long to set up camp, mainly because they didn't have much, and none of them wanted to start a fire in the tunnel. Perhaps if they found a larger space or one with a natural chimney, they'd risk it, but not here, where the space was tight and the air didn't move.

Landon was so exhausted, he nodded off.

"Wakey-wakey," Sorin said, nudging the woodcutter.

"What? Did I fall asleep?"

"Yeah. You and your wolf took a nap. You've both been snoring for the last hour. I couldn't take it anymore."

"Wolf*hound*. And I don't snore."

Reinier yawned and shook. Snoring was a way of life for him.

Sorin offered Landon a hand. "Like you're sawing logs!"

"If you two are finished, I'd like to get moving," Thea said, heading down the tunnel.

"What's gotten into her?" the archer asked.

Landon patted Reinier's back. "Let's find out. Come on, boy."

Just as Thea had predicted, it wasn't long before the tunnel opened into a vast arched chamber with smooth stone walls.

"Wow," Sorin said, leaning back.

The walls were covered with paintings to such an extent that many scenes were painted right over older images.

"How did they get up there?" Landon asked, pointing to the ceiling high above them.

Thea stepped closer to the wall. "I have no idea, but this is familiar to me."

"Really?" Sorin asked, joining her.

"These are stories from the skeleton's book, *Rise Shadow Rise*. Here is the king. And here is Volgreth taking his vow to serve Kahr'anis.

"And here is an angry mob," Landon said, looking at a painting on the other side of the cavern.

"I guess we know what happened to Volgreth, now," the archer said, walking over and tracing the image with his hand. "He doesn't look terribly happy."

Thea scoffed at the remark. "Would you be happy if a bunch of people with pitchforks and torches chased you into a dungeon?"

"It's a fair point. Hey, Landon, can you read any of this?"

"No. I've never seen this script before."

"Nor have I," Thea said, trying to follow the story as it wound around the room.

Sorin blinked his eyes. "I've been meaning to ask, is it me, or is it getting harder to see?"

Landon pulled one of the torch pieces out of the archer's quiver. "It's not you. I think it's time we lit some of these."

Using his flint, Sorin lit one of the torches and touched two others. "They won't last long, and I only have a couple more."

"With any luck," Landon said, holding his torch high, "they'll be enough to get us out of here."

Thea wanted to stay and learn more from the paintings, but with the torch situation being what it was, she agreed to keep moving.

They hadn't made it a hundred yards down the tunnel when Sorin whispered, "Wait," and drew his bow. "There's something down there."

Now that he was paying attention, Landon saw it too. There was a shimmering light emanating from around the corner, but it wasn't like the Lunar Glow. "Is it firelight?"

"I don't think so. The color's not right."

"Fire comes in many colors and forms. We'd do well to remain on our guard." Thea said, inching forward.

When they rounded the corner, the archer screamed. He'd almost been run over by a translucent horse galloping right at him. After jumping out of the way, he watched it disappear into the stone on the other side. "Is that a ghost?"

"I don't think so," Thea said. "I don't feel any presence. It's a projection of some kind. Look out!"

The horse came again, running between the stalagmites rising from the ground, and disappearing into the stone again.

"Help me!" Landon yelled. He'd taken a step back, away from the galloping horse, only to lose his footing at the edge of a deep hole in the ground.

Reinier's powerful jaws were clamped onto his belt, but they were both slipping toward certain death.

Sorin and Thea rushed to his aid, pulling him back from the precipice.

"Thank you," Landon said, falling to one knee. "That was close. Are you okay?"

Reinier barked.

Sorin peered into the hole. "Everyone, be very still. I think there's something down there."

"Back away slowly, Sorin," Thea instructed, already moving.

"No, really. I see something moving."

"Back away from the hole."

"Oh, crap! There's something down there!" he yelled, leaping back.

An enormous brown and orange centipede at least ten feet long scrambled into the tunnel, rearing up before them.

"Run!" Landon yelled, and they scattered.

At first, the centipede wound its way through the cavern, but when it didn't find its prey, it started smashing stalagmites with its heavy body and powerful mandibles. The combination of crashing, sharp legs on stone, and clicking sounds threatened to drive them crazy.

"It's got me!" Sorin yelled.

When Landon rounded the pillar-like stone, he saw the archer had one of the animal's fangs in each hand, struggling to keep it from biting him in two. The woodcutter lifted a heavy stone off the floor and smashed the centipede on the head. It let go of its quarry and scurried away, but it wasn't defeated. They heard it scraping and scratching, waiting to launch another attack.

"Looks like we're even," Sorin said, thanking the woodcutter.

Thea didn't sound as relieved. "We aren't out of danger yet."

They were back at the edge of the hole with no way to escape. The galloping horse sped by, and the centipede attacked.

"Do you trust me?" Thea asked.

Landon, Sorin, and Reinier all looked confused.

"Do you trust me?" she asked again.

"Of course," Landon answered for them.

"Then, jump!"

Reinier yelped as Thea pulled them into the hole.

"AAH!" Sorin screamed. "AAH! AAH!"

"Would you stop that?" Thea asked calmly.

"Huh?"

"Open your eyes."

Sorin looked around. He was lying on the ground with Landon and Thea standing over him. "What happened?"

"It was an illusion, like the horse or the mirror," Thea explained. "Once we challenged it, it was dispelled."

"It felt pretty damn real to me!" Sorin said, getting to his feet.

"Illusions *are* real, if you believe in them. But they are easily dispelled if you stop believing in them."

"But I did believe. Why didn't I fall into the hole?"

"It's a common misconception about illusions that everyone perceives them separately. It can't be that way, you see. Even believing in it, as you did, you still would have been lying on the floor because you only fell in your mind. That is the nature of an illusion. It isn't real. But if I'm standing here talking to you, you can't be falling, right? So the spell broke."

"Just to be clear, you're saying there was no centipede?" Sorin asked, expecting the monster to scurry out from behind a stalagmite, which he noticed was no longer broken.

"No."

The archer got to his feet. "That is frickin' weird!"

Landon looked perplexed. "How did you know?"

"The horse tipped me off. Illusionists can't help themselves. Deep down, they're showmen like circus performers. It's funny to them to show you that you're being tricked. Then again, it's not unreasonable to assume a centipede would live down here, so I couldn't be sure at first. It was the sound that gave it away. It wasn't coming from the centipede. It was everywhere. No matter which direction I faced, it sounded like the centipede was right in front of me."

"Wait, are you saying that you told us to jump into that hole solely on what you heard?"

"Precisely."

Sorin shook his head.

"Real or not, I want to get out of here," Landon said, listening at several openings in the chamber. "I think we should try this one. I hear water."

"Better let Thea listen to make sure it isn't another illusion," Sorin said, rolling his eyes.

Thea sighed. "Next time, I'm letting the centipede eat you." After checking, she agreed that the tunnel Landon had chosen was as good a place as any to continue their journey, and they headed on their way, far more cautiously than before.

The path turned sharply down, making it harder to navigate, and they slipped and slid as they descended further into the earth. Pools of water appeared, and the sound of movement overhead made them quicken their pace, not wanting to get trapped underground if there was a cave-in.

Thankfully, the water they'd heard wasn't from overhead but underneath their feet. The tunnel crossed a subterranean river flowing with cool, clear water, nothing like the sludgy Brownwater River, and before them, a wooden bridge connected the two sides of the passage.

"Finally, something that isn't trying to kill us," Sorin said, testing the bridge with his foot. "Seems sturdy to me."

"I wonder who built this," Landon asked, always interested in fine woodwork. "This is teak. Very sturdy and doesn't rot."

Sorin laughed. "Does it matter if it gets us safely back onto the plains?"

"That might be the first time I've ever heard someone use the words *safe* and *plains* in the same sentence," Thea remarked, and Sorin stopped laughing.

When the tunnel began moving up, they all sighed with relief, but they weren't out yet. An ancient iron padlock stood between the trio of adventurers and freedom from the cursed fortress in Bleeding Tree Forest. It was a substantial piece of craftsmanship, bold in its construction but elegant in design. Rusted with age, the patterns etched into its face were barely visible. A message, perhaps? A warning? It was impossible to tell. The one thing easy to make out was the keyhole at its heart—a portal to another realm—taunting them because they didn't have the key.

"Keys again," Sorin said. "You know, I have a cousin who is a master at picking any lock. They say he—"

There was a crash, and the sound of metal shattering filled the air. Landon had slammed a rock into the old lock, which had obligingly exploded into dozens of misshapen pieces.

The woodcutter threw the piece of granite he'd used to unbar the way to the ground. It landed with a thud and rolled a few feet before coming to rest where it would sit for generations undisturbed.

"Whew. Remind me never to get on his bad side," Sorin said, picking up one of the metal shards and tossing it aside.

Reinier made a low sound that might have been a bark if he'd opened his mouth.

"What in the world?" Landon asked, sliding open a metal door. They were in a depression, concealed by wooden planks and bits of scrubgrass.

After pushing out, they found themselves standing on the murky plains of Kahr'anis! The tunnel under the fortress had led them on a long journey, true enough, but guiding them out of the forest and under the river was much farther than they'd expected.

"Will you look at that," Sorin said, stepping beside Landon. "Seems luck *is* on our side."

"For the moment," Thea added.

Sorin kicked a pebble. "Such a downer. Can't we just take the win for once?"

"Yes, you're right. My apologies. Sometimes, I miss the forest for the trees."

At the mention of the forest, Landon turned around. "I'm glad we're out of there, but the plains are no place to wander at night. Best we keep moving."

"This is the Westrin Road," Thea observed. "It's the road I followed south to the village. If we take it in the other direction, it stays on this side of the river and passes the border town of Endog. But watch your back. Endog isn't the kind of place to let your guard down."

"I think she's seen more of the world than both of us combined," Sorin whispered to Landon. "I bet she's got great stories she could tell us."

The woodcutter sighed. "You've both got me beat. I've seen more of the world since meeting you than I have in my entire life. And no, I don't see Thea as the type to sit around a campfire recounting adventures over skewered rat and a beer."

"You might be surprised," Thea said with a smirk.

Sorin and Landon locked eyes for a second as if to say, *I didn't think she was listening.*

"Besides, woodcutter," she continued, "it's the journey, not the destination, that counts."

Sorin turned around and walked backwards so he could look at her. "You know you're sounding more like Esslla every day."

Thea stopped. "What's that in your hand?"

Sorin immediately stuck his hands in his pockets. "Oh, nothing."

"You took the ring, didn't you?" she asked, turning red in the face. "Even after I told you it might be dangerous!"

"I couldn't leave it there. It has an arrow on it. See?"

The three companions gathered around to look at it.

"Isn't that cool?" the archer asked. "It's like it was made for me."

"Not the word I would have used," Thea said, taking it from him, "but it *is* interesting."

Sorin fidgeted, worried Thea would keep the ring or toss it away, but that wasn't the cleric's way. The ring was Sorin's now, as far as she was concerned, and she said as much, for good or ill.

The tone of her voice and the mention of being ill took the edge off the archer's elation at getting to keep the ring. He wound up walking in silence for the first time since they'd left Esslla's.

PART II

NEW FRIENDS
AND DANGEROUS ENEMIES

11 ENDOG

Mile after mile, Landon, Sorin, Thea, and Reinier trudged along the winding dirt path known as the Westrin Road, accompanied by the relentless murmur of the Brownwater River to their left and the bleak plains to their right. Fatigue had long since settled into their bones, and the wave of energy that had accompanied their desire to see the Shadehaunter vanquished had long since ebbed.

In areas where the river oozed over its banks, they plodded through ankle-deep mud, but most of the time, dust hung around them like a persistent memory, clogging their lungs and minds. Too exhausted from being chased by Alderbeasts and searching the fortress, they walked in silence, secretly hoping to find lodging and, if they were lucky, help in Endog.

With each passing day, Landon had grown more and more withdrawn. Any time Sorin or Thea mentioned it, he shrugged it off because he was too tired to get into another discussion like they'd had before they left Esslla's, though he sensed the cleric might have an idea what he'd been dealing with. Ever since leaving the mystic, his dreams had been plagued by visions. The trouble was, they were too indistinct to make out—mostly foggy shapes and strange sounds. They were obviously connected to the potion, but until he figured out a way to see through the mist, they were meaningless to him, so there was no point in talking about it.

Reinier's ears perked up, and he gave a sharp, warning bark.

Thea lifted her eyes to see if they'd reached the westernmost outpost of Kahr'anis, but the increasingly dense fog reflected the light from the torches they carried. "It seems your dog can hear what we cannot see. Endog must not be far."

"I still can't believe you've been there," Sorin said. "It's no place for maidens."

The cleric rounded on him. "Maidens?" she asked sharply.

Sorin immediately backtracked. "I mean, you know, for travelers to go there alone. That's all I meant. Slip of the tongue."

"I have done many things and been to many places."

"But Endog? That town's a cesspool."

"What better place to share the Light?"

"Speaking of light," the archer said. "They don't lower the drawbridge for people after dark, but I know another way in."

Landon shushed them.

"Mummm…mmmumah…"

"What is that?" Sorin said, nocking his one and only arrow.

"Look! Over there!" Thea said, running toward the river.

"Don't go near it. You can't tell where the edge is," Landon said, grabbing her arm. "It's too dangerous!"

"We have to help him. He's dying!"

The horror of the situation struck Landon hard. His entire life, he'd heard stories of someone being subsumed by the Brownwater River, and now it was happening right in front of him. All he could see was a contorted hand and forearm sticking up from the surface, slowly…so slowly…moving downstream.

"Quick, grab a branch or something," Sorin said, scrabbling around on the ground, but there were no trees on the plains.

Landon looked at Thea. "Can't you cast a spell?"

"What kind?"

"Any kind!"

"I'll do my best."

Kneeling on the ground, she lit a candle and prayed while Landon and Sorin attempted to get close enough to grab the man's hand.

Not accurately judging where the ground gave way to the river, Landon's foot slipped on the embankment and was immediately pulled in. "Help!"

Reinier barked furiously.

"Crap. My other foot is stuck, too."

"Fall back," Sorin suggested, being careful to keep behind the woodcutter.

"Are you kidding?"

"Do it. I've got you. Then, slowly move your legs until they are free. Hey!"

Reinier had clamped his powerful jaws onto Sorin's belt and was pulling, too.

There was a terrible sucking sound, and Landon despaired. "It's not working!"

"Calm yourself and do as I said. See, you're breaking free."

With one final yank, Sorin and Reinier helped Landon extricate himself just in time to see the drowning man's fingers slip under the surface.

The archer stared in disbelief. "That's awful."

"That would've been me if it weren't for you. Thank you, my friend," Landon said, grasping Sorin's hand.

"You'd do the same for me."

"Without hesitation."

Not far off, Thea sat with her face covered by her hands. "His Light went out before I could save him."

The three huddled together for some time before a loud *gloop* made them decide to move farther away.

That night, the protective candles they used to surround their camp took on a particularly somber glow.

• • •

Ultimately, it wasn't hard to locate Endog because it had literally been built on the road that ran through the front gate and exited on the other side of the city. Travelers were all but forced to enter because the river blocked the western route, and the eastern route took them far out of the way and onto the plains.

The town was surrounded by a wooden fence that resembled a series of tree-sized pikes planted side by side, more than a wall. Outside of the fence, part of the Brownwater River had been diverted as a kind of makeshift moat—a formidable barrier, to be sure. Drawbridges were maintained to the north and south, with no visible entry from the east. To the west, a tall bridge crossed the Brownwater with heavily guarded gates that were barred after dark.

If they had arrived earlier, they would have been joined by other travelers waiting for the drawbridge to be lowered. But since they'd come after dark, they had to rely on Sorin's assurances that he could get them inside, which turned out to be true, but no one was happy about it.

The archer led his friends along the eastern side of the town to a place where trash had been dumped in great heaps outside the city's walls. Hidden within the refuse, they encountered what Landon thought was a dirty boulder but turned out to be an extremely broad, bald man named Nurf. He had a flat nose and skin so tough it looked like worn leather.

"Haven't seen you here in a while," Nurf said after Sorin produced a coin.

"I've been traveling The Long Road."

At this, the boulder's eyes widened. "Then I'm surprised to see you at all. How's your Mum?"

"Passed a couple of years back."

"Sorry to hear that. She made a fine bacon tart."

The archer got a wistful look in his eyes. "That she did."

The exchange struck Landon. He'd been so consumed by his own grief that he hadn't asked his companions if they'd lost people, too.

"Off you go," Nurf said, pointing to three ropes hanging over the moat—one to walk on and one on either side to hold.

"You have got to be kidding me," Thea said.

Nurf gave a stony chuckle. "The only other option is to take your chances out here and wait for the day. And I can promise you, little Missy, things get pretty rough in the wee hours of the morning."

Left with no other choice, one by one, they crossed the moat. Landon had the most difficult time with Reinier across his shoulders, but he made it in the end, only to see Nurf waiting on the other side. "But—"

The boulder-like man burst into a raucous landslide of a laugh. "Gets them every time!"

"That's Thurf, Nurf's twin brother," Sorin explained as he gave the gatekeeper a coin. "See, all you have to do is cross the right palm and you can get inside any time of the day or night."

"Or left," Thurf said, laughing again and holding up his left arm. "Lost the other one in a cage match with a bear."

Thea pushed her way through. "Thank you, Mr. Thurf, but I think we should be going. This is payback, isn't it?" she said to Sorin, hitching her robes higher than her knees so they wouldn't get sullied by the rank and rotting trash around them.

"Why, Thea, I don't know what you could possibly mean?" the archer asked, looking as innocent as possible (which wasn't terribly innocent at all). "In you go."

The door was a space about three feet by three feet that had been cut into the tree trunk fence.

Thea wasn't thrilled and let Sorin know about it.

Once inside, the sooty air burned their eyes as they moved along Endog's cobbled streets. They passed weathered timber and stone buildings with facades adorned with creeping vines and faded painted signs that hinted at illicit trade and certain treachery. It was no surprise that torches lined every pathway, and candles were piled on every windowsill. People in Kahr'anis did everything they could to keep the shadows at bay, not to mention whatever other dangers lurked around the corner.

More than once, Landon thought they'd stumbled into trouble when a merchant chased after them for not stopping at their booth. Though anyone foolish enough to drink the disgusting elixirs being offered at discount rates deserved what they got, as far as he was concerned.

"What's the trouble here?" a deep voice growled.

The woodcutter turned to see a man even taller than himself wearing a brown uniform and carrying a pikestaff.

"No trouble, officer," Sorin squeaked.

"There most certainly is!" a hunched merchant yelled, holding up two of his elixir jars. "These ruffians were insulting my wears. It's bad for business!"

"Is this true?" a second guard asked. He was equally large, only more side to side, and had a face that looked like it had seen the other side of a fist on numerous occasions.

"Pardon me," Thea said, radiating the soft glow of kindness. "We are passing through and want to make no trouble. If you'd be so kind as to tell us where we could find a hot meal after a long journey, we would be much obliged and on our way."

The tall guard grumbled and sputtered, trying to find what words to say. The stout guard bowed and pointed down the street. Take your first right, ma'am—"

"Thea, friend. Thea Starheart."

"Oh, um, my apologies. As I was saying. Take the first right, and it will be two blocks down on the corner. Can't miss it. It's called *The Last Stop Watering Hole*."

Thea ushered Landon, Sorin, and Reinier down the street with the vendor yelling behind them. "You're not going to just let them go, are you? Throw them in the dungeon!"

"We don't have a dungeon and you know it, Gunnar," the tall guard said. "Now stop harassing the tourists, or you'll find yourself behind bars."

"Well, I never!"

"Why did you ask for directions?" Sorin asked once they turned the corner. "I know where the *Watering Hole* is."

"So do I," Thea whispered. "The longer you speak to people like that, the more likely you are to find yourself in a situation you can't get out of. By asking for directions, I put them off their guard, so to speak."

"That and, well, you're you," Landon said. "Sorin and I were both overwhelmed that day back at Esslla's."

The archer got a faraway look in his eyes. "That's so true. I think I called you stunning. I can't imagine what I was thinking."

Thea shot him a glance before marching them directly to the center of town, where a towering stone statue of a long-forgotten hero held a silent vigil. The man might have been wearing a helmet and armor, but it was hard to tell because someone had draped laundry over his head and outstretched arm. Around the statue's base, a dried-up pool of dead weeds encircled the monument, where the sword it had once held lay in ruins.

"We need to split up," Thea said, sitting on the low wall.

Sorin remained standing, intrigued by the statue.

"But it's so late," Landon said.

"Endog never sleeps, and Sorin's quiver is limp," she added, looking at the archer.

"Hey, now! No need for that." Sorin tried to look nonplussed but snuck a glance at his quiver to make sure it hadn't gone limp.

"We need to be properly prepared for the journey ahead. I doubt we'll find much to help us on the road from this point forward, only desolation and the dangers of the Cragfall Mountains."

The archer whistled. "You really know how to bring a guy back down to earth."

Thea ignored him. "I'll see to rations, though you'll have to carry everything in your sack, Landon."

"No problem," the woodcutter said, patting his trusty sack. "Plenty of room."

Sorin straightened the straps that crossed his chest. "Limp or not, you're right, I need to track down some arrows and candles."

"Can't you make light for us?" Landon asked Thea. "I've noticed you practicing."

"Indeed, though I should conserve my energy as much as possible for when we need it most."

"Like I said," Sorin mumbled, "lots of candles, and maybe a lantern or two."

"For the candles or the oil kind?" Landon asked.

"Anything I can get my hands on."

"Let's meet back here in an hour," Thea suggested. "Stay out of the way of those guards. Then, we can head to the tavern. And don't say a word about what we're doing to anyone. Understood?" the cleric called after Sorin.

"Are you talking to me?" the archer asked, turning around. "I'm as good at keeping a secret as the next man."

"That's what I'm afraid of. Just keep your mouth shut and meet back here in an hour."

"Okay, I've got it. Sheesh."

Thea headed in a different direction.

The distant howls of wolves hovered in the air, and Landon paused to listen.

Reinier whined.

"Agreed. Something doesn't feel right. I don't like this place, but after what happened on the river, I'm never going anywhere without a rope again. Let's track some down and find a decent torch or two. Then we'll regroup with the others as quickly as we can."

The wolfhound woofed in apparent agreement.

• • •

Unsurprisingly, Landon and Reinier were the first to return to the statue.

"Out of the way, outlander!" a shriveled, dark-skinned woman said, attempting to push Landon to the side.

Not wanting to get into an argument, he stepped back. Landon was amazed at how deftly the woman climbed up the statue to retrieve her laundry. At one point, she actually climbed onto the statue's head and sat on its shoulders.

A faint melody reached the woodcutter's ears, and he looked around. No one was there. Shaking off the sensation, he turned back toward the statue. "What's that in its mouth?"

"I don't see nothin'," the old lady said with a dry cough.

"It's right there."

"Have you been drinkin'? Makin' fun of old Winsill like that. You should be ashamed of yourself."

Winsill climbed down with her laundry in her hands and placed everything in a wheeled basket.

"Honestly, I wasn't making fun of you."

Winsill turned, spat on Landon's foot, and rolled her laundry away, mumbling to herself.

"Ew."

Unable to let it go, Landon stepped into the dry pool surrounding the statue's feet. How Winsill had gotten up there, he didn't know, but he had to try. At first, he used brute force to haul himself up. That didn't work. Then, he tried bracing himself between the enormous legs, but that didn't work either.

"I guess I have no choice," he told Reinier, making a loop in his newly acquired rope and tossing it in the air.

He missed.

He missed again.

The more Landon tried to lasso the statue's head, the more people gathered to see what he was doing, and to offer all manner of advice.

"Throw it harder!"

"That loop's too small."

"Look at that. He doesn't even know how to tie a lariat knot."

When Landon finally got it around the statue's head, a cheer went up from the crowd, and then everyone got very quiet. Now the real excitement began.

A small child tugged on Landon's cloak.

"Yes?"

"The last guy who tried to do that broke his back."

Landon tried to look confident. "Thanks, kid. That's very helpful."

Being from Brownwater, the woodcutter had never had the opportunity, let alone the need, to scale anything before, and he had no idea what to do. After repeatedly slipping only a few feet off the ground, the crowd lost interest and dispersed.

"Lame," the little kid said, also leaving.

"Hey, Landon, what are you up to?" Sorin asked, returning just as the kid was walking away.

"Making a fool of himself," the kid said.

Sorin laughed. "No, really. What gives?"

"There's something in the statue's mouth."

"I don't see anything."

"I don't either," Thea added, also returning. "Now that we're all back, let's get indoors."

"After I see what it has in its mouth."

"Does it even have a mouth?" Sorin asked.

"Help me and we'll find out."

Shrugging, the archer stepped into the basin and onto the platform where the statue stood to help Landon get started. This time it worked, and the woodcutter made it to the top, but there was nothing there.

"I swear I saw something right here, in its mouth."

"I don't know how," Thea said. "It's so worn, it barely has a face at all."

When Landon looked again, he saw what Thea saw and sighed. All that for nothing. "I must have—"

"Landon!" Sorin and Thea yelled at the same time.

The woodcutter's foot slipped, and he fell, but not before accidentally thrusting his hand into the statue's face. His fingers went straight into where the mouth should have been. There he hung from one hand.

"Would you look at that," Sorin said. "You'd better hope that thing's jaw doesn't give way."

Landon didn't need to be reminded. As quickly as possible, he twisted the rope around his waist and carefully slid to the ground.

When he stepped out of the basin, Sorin punched his arm. "I never took you for an acrobat."

The woodcutter didn't say anything.

"What's wrong?" Thea asked.

Landon uncurled his fingers, and there on his palm was a smooth stone, and it was glowing.

"How did you see that when no one else could?" Sorin asked, touching it with the tip of his finger. "It's warm."

"I don't know. I sort of knew it would be there."

Thea smiled. "The Light guides you. Let this be the first of many pleasant surprises."

"Hey, what's the deal? Why is his rock okay but my ring dangerous?" the archer asked.

"Landon's glows with the Light. Can't you feel it? Yours doesn't."

"Whatever."

"But what do I do with it?" the woodcutter asked.

Thea winked and whispered, "Time will tell. Maybe those dreams you've been having will make more sense now."

Landon started to say, "How do you know about..." but he let it go. She was Thea. He knew that was all the explanation he'd ever get.

Sorin leaned over to get a better look at the statue. "I still can't see where you got it from."

"We're attracting attention," Thea said, trying to get Landon to leave.

"Wait, I need my rope." But no matter how hard he tried, he couldn't get it off.

"Just leave it," Thea hissed.

"No way! I just got it."

"Here, let me help," Sorin said, raising his bow. Before Landon could stop him, he deftly shot an arrow that split the rope, and it fell to the ground.

"Hey! You broke my rope!"

"Uh, that's what knots are for. Let's go. And, you're welcome."

With Landon's rope, torches, and now stone, complemented by the rations Thea had procured—mostly dried fruit, hardtack, and nuts, but there was a little jerky and cheese, too—and Sorin's bag of candles and arrows, the party felt ready for their next adventure.

"Hey, you got an axe, too, if you can call it that," Sorin said, snickering.

It wasn't much more than an old metal head strapped to a broken handle, but it was something.

"It was the best I could find," Landon said, self-consciously covering it with his hand.

Thea didn't care one wit about Landon's axe. She was more concerned with the archer's rosy appearance. "Did you go to the pub already?"

"Who me? Nah. I only had a nip to keep me going."

"I get the impression it was more than a nip. You're cut off until we get out of Endog. We need to keep our heads."

"But we're going to a pub!"

"You should have thought of that before you had a drink."

Sorin stumbled over one of the street's cobblestones. "I swear, it was only a little bit."

12 LAST STOP WATERING HOLE

After speaking with the innkeeper, Landon and Thea had to direct Sorin away from the bar. They'd been lucky enough to secure the last room available on the *Last Stop Watering Hole's* second floor, and neither of them had any intention of letting anyone sneak it out from under them while the archer drank himself into oblivion.

The tavern and inn was the last place to get a drink before leaving the plains, but that wasn't how it got its name. It was because the roads that crisscrossed the plains were so dangerous that the barkeep never expected to see out-of-towners pass through a second time. That's why he'd placed a large sign out front that stated: *If a peddler returns to the bar after journeying across the plains, their first drink is on the house.* To date, no one had earned the privilege.

That night, Reinier dutifully watched over his pack, but he didn't hear much more than the scurrying of mice and the faint rustling of bat wings in the attic. The rest of the party was out like a light, feeling safer and more comfortable than they had in weeks.

Thea took the straw bed on the western wall, Landon slept with his head on the wolfhound's back in the center of the room, and Sorin curled in a corner near the fireplace, not caring that the floor was hard and smelled of piss and rot.

After locking and barring the door, they'd set up the prerequisite candles, but it wasn't strictly necessary. Bright streetlamps directly outside their windows filled the room with light, but old habits die hard, and it was always good to be cautious where the Shadehaunter was concerned.

In the morning, Reinier barked, and everyone jerked awake.

"What is it, boy?" Landon asked, rubbing his eyes.

The wolfhound whined and scratched at the door.

"Ah. Sorry about that. We must have slept in. Reinier needs a walk. Anyone want to come?"

"Sounds good to me," Sorin said, gathering his things.

"Thea?"

The cleric sat up. "Yes?" Her golden locks resembled a rat's nest.

Sorin snickered, and she shot him a one-eyed look from under the mass of hair. He immediately shut his mouth and went back to tending to his things.

"I'll meet you downstairs," she said.

"Shouldn't we stay together?" Landon asked.

"Downstairs."

"Got it. Come on, Reinier. You too, Sorin. Let's find some breakfast."

Outside their room, they stepped over several travelers who hadn't managed to rent a room. Half-price got you a space in the hall, and even that had sold out.

"Pardon me," Landon said, when a tiny girl wearing rags with bits of straw in her hair scootched by carrying a rickety stool in one hand and a jug of oil in the other to refill the lamps that lined the hallway's dingy walls.

"I can help with that," Landon said, not needing a stool to reach the nearest lamp, but his offer frightened the girl.

She put her finger to her lips.

A round-faced lady (if *lady* wasn't too polite a term) wearing what looked to be a tablecloth with a hole in the middle, poked her head out of a room farther down the hallway. "She ain't botherin' you none, is she?"

"Not at all, m'lady," Landon said, bowing. "We were just heading to breakfast."

"Best be off with ya then. And you, get back ta work!"

Landon went over to the girl, who was currently standing on the stool and straining to reach one of the lamps. He surreptitiously slipped a coin into her pocket.

Not used to having such things in her possession, she tried to give it back. "She checks my pockets and I'll get in trouble," the frightened girl explained.

"Does she check your shoes?" Landon looked down and winced. The girl was wearing bits of burlap tied around her ankles with a length of hemp rope.

She shook her head.

"Then stick it in there and get a warm meal tonight," he said, patting her on the head.

For the first time, the worry lines on the girl's face faded, and she stuck the coin under her foot before getting back to work.

The sound of the stairs creaking caught the woodcutter's attention, and he realized Reinier and Sorin had continued on without him. Hurrying after them, he passed the tablecloth lady as she backed out of a room, dragging a drunken man by his feet.

Up ahead, Reinier led the way, his tail happily wagging at the promise of relief.

"By the sound of it," Landon said, catching up to Sorin, "everyone's already awake."

Sorin pushed ahead. "Fine by me as long as there's food left. That smells delicious!"

Landon had to agree. The stench of stale ale, woodsmoke, and body odor that usually pervaded taverns in the evenings had been replaced with the smell of frying eggs and sizzling bacon.

When they reached the bottom floor, Reinier trotted out the open door to do his business, and Landon searched for a place to sit amongst the random mismatched wooden tables that dotted the room. Sorin headed for the cook to place their order, giving a table of guards a wide berth on his way across the room.

At right angles to the bar, a massive stone fireplace dominated the far wall. In front of it was a sturdy workspace with a man studiously cooking. Beneath him, a young boy played with bits of broken wooden toys: a headless horse, a cart with three wheels, and a straw doll. The boy didn't seem to care that his toys were broken. He was having a grand time making the doll ride the horse up his father's leg.

Landon smiled. He used to play under his father's desk while he copied manuscripts. But those days were gone, and so was his father, thanks to Volgreth. The woodcutter's face darkened, but before he sank into a sullen mood, Thea sat down next to him.

"What could they possibly be hunting around here to have so many trophies?" she asked, looking at a burdened shelf covered with ribbons and cups.

"Rats?" Sorin suggested, plopping three tankards on the table.

Landon nodded toward the fireplace. "That doesn't smell like rat."

"No, it doesn't," the archer said with a devious grin on his face.

Feeling better than they had in ages after a good night's sleep, they chatted happily as they waited for their food. During that time, Reinier returned and lay down at Landon's feet.

At one point, the boy came over with his toys, and Sorin made the doll do acrobatic tricks. The boy asked him to do it again, but he was interrupted when the cook yelled, "Urine! Order up!"

Sorin looked perplexed. "Did he just say what I think he said?"

"I believe he called your name," Thea said, stifling a giggle.

"No. Couldn't be."

"Hurry up, Urine, or I'll give your food to someone else."

This time, Thea didn't bother trying not to laugh, and neither did Landon.

"You heard him, Urine," she said. "Get our food."

The archer pushed back his chair and stamped over to the fireplace. "Sorin. My name's Sorin."

While the archer was off collecting their breakfast, Thea excused herself.

Landon watched as she made her way to the right side of the fireplace, where, against the wall, a small table was tucked into a corner.

"Pardon me," the cleric said politely, approaching the man seated at the table.

"Oh, excuse me. I didn't see you there." The man fumbled with the book he was reading and stood. After removing his worn hat, he made a slight bow. "I always have my head buried in a book. Eyes aren't what they used to be. Must have read too many spellbooks in the dark. Do you need this seat? It's quite nice by the fire." The wizard held his damaged hands self-consciously in front of his equally distressed reddish-brown robes.

"No, thank you, but I would join if you'll have me."

"By all means. My name is Loric. How may I be of service?"

Sorin returned with three hand-hammered tin plates heaping with fried eggs, strips of thick-cut bacon, and a pile of breakfast potatoes and onions.

"Where'd she go?" the archer asked, placing the plates on the table.

Landon pointed to the corner.

"Who's he?"

"Don't know, but I bet we're about to find out."

Reinier whined.

"Have no fear," Sorin said. "I didn't forget about you."

Reaching around his back, the archer pulled a large bone out of his belt, where he'd put it because he didn't have enough hands to carry it along with the plates.

The wolfhound sat with his tail wagging, making a grand show of what a good boy he was.

Sorin held it out to Reinier's drooling jowls, but the dog didn't move until Landon gave him the command.

"That made your wolf's day," Sorin said with a twinkle in his eye.

"Not as much as this will," Landon said, grabbing the bacon off of Thea's plate and tossing it to Reinier. "She doesn't eat bacon, remember?"

Sorin practically leapt out of his seat. "Hey!"

"You've got plenty."

"I always have room for more bacon."

The sound of Reinier scarfing up the meat and contentedly chewing his bone filtered up from the floor.

"I'm not standing on ceremony. If she wants cold eggs, that's her problem. I'm eating." Sorin said, digging in.

Landon did the same.

It wasn't long before Thea reappeared at the table. Landon stood and moved her chair for her.

"Thank you." After she sat down, she said, "Loric will make a fine addition to our group."

"Who?" Sorin said through a mouthful of potatoes.

"That wizard over there. His name is Loric, and he's offered to help us with our quest."

"Don't we get a say?"

Thea wrinkled her nose at the food and pushed it away, instead pulling out a pouch of nuts and berries. Before Sorin could grab it, Landon snatched some eggs for Reinier.

"You don't trust my judgment?" she asked, raising an eyebrow.

Sorin scooped the extra potatoes onto his plate. "I didn't say that. I just think we should have a say."

"If you must know," she said, sighing, "he seeks redemption for past mistakes."

Landon glanced at the wizard. "That doesn't sound good."

"Don't let it worry you, friend Landon. Most wizards his age seek to make amends for the insatiable appetite for knowledge that inevitably leads them to the forbidden in their youth. And since Volgreth represents the furthest extreme of that kind of pursuit, he is eager to join our party to try and do some good for Kahr'anis. When it comes down to it, the most important part is that he's a scholar, knowledgeable in lore and magic—the kind of magic that is beyond my skills. That will make him an invaluable asset to our quest."

"Where's he going?" Sorin asked, watching the Wizard leave the tavern. "Don't we get to meet him?"

"Later. I've asked him to join us after dinner. For now, he's off to collect some spell components that might aid us in our travels."

The archer swallowed hard, having bitten off more than he could chew. "Why don't you need that stuff?"

Thea looked indignant. "Because I'm a cleric. The Light is my guide."

"Oh, sorry, I didn't mean to offend you, *Your Brightness*."

Stepping in before things got out of hand, Landon asked, "What are these components for?"

"A wizard gets his power from the world around us. He uses certain plants or minerals—even animals can have magical properties. For example, Loric might use bat guano to create a fireball to defend us from Volgreth."

"Wait, did you just say he carries around bat poop so he can make fire?" the archer asked.

"It was just an example."

"That is so weird."

Thea shook her head. "You have no idea."

13 THE JOURNEYMAN

After breakfast, Thea suggested they explore Endog more during the day, not that the murky sky was much different from the night. Sorin liked the idea, but Landon was hesitant. Reinier, for his part, didn't care either way. He still had a piece of bone, which he brought with them.

The woodcutter had thought the city was busy the previous night, never having been to a city before, but it was nothing compared to the waking hours. Vendors haggled with passersby, struggling to be heard over the thrum of daily life. Textiles hung from stands leaning against buildings, vegetables lounged in wooden crates, and chickens hung in rows in front of butchers' shops. It was nothing short of overwhelming.

A creepy person who looked surprisingly like a shriveled apple carved on the shortest day of the year stared at Landon from behind a small table covered with an assortment of trinkets that one would be wise to avoid. Landon kept moving.

The only thing that reminded the woodcutter of home was the stench of sewage running in the gutters, its fetid aroma mingling with the scent of overripe fruit and freshly slaughtered meat. There were fire-roasted rats on sticks, bowls of jellied eel, and fried beetles. Sorin even spotted deep-fried spiders. There were also a surprising number of noodle stands —only the noodles didn't look like they were made from flour. Landon was confident he saw them moving in the large glass jars next to open-faced griddles.

As before, the party decided to split up to see what they could find.

"And no ale for you," Thea said, pointing at Sorin. "Return to the fountain before the sun meets the horizon."

"Got it," the archer said, wringing his hands. "Now let's see what Endog has to offer."

Landon didn't move.

"I know you don't like us separating, but we cover more ground that way," the cleric explained.

"I won't deny it, but I don't trust this place."

"As well you shouldn't, but this is probably the safest we'll be compared to where we are going. I recommend enjoying the freedom while you still have it."

Reinier put down his bone and barked.

"It seems I'm the odd man out," the woodcutter said, picking up the bone and putting it in his sack. "Alright, boy, let's check out the western side of the city.

For several hours, Landon and Reinier walked through the narrow streets, leaving the busy town center and entering a more residential district. There were still vendors and shops, but far fewer than near the tavern where they were staying. After a while, the woodcutter got tired of wandering and found a small café with a couple of outdoor tables, called *Miss Sherry's*. According to the sign, their specialty was cream cheese sandwiched between two custard-like pieces of bread, topped with fresh strawberries. It was so different from everything else they'd seen, Landon insisted on giving it a try.

Reinier didn't look impressed, so Landon handed the dog his bone. "You don't know what you're missing."

The woodcutter had never had anything like the *Gallian Toast*, as it was called. Brownwater didn't have treats of any kind, let alone fresh fruit, which refused to grow that close to Bleeding Tree Forest.

When he was finished, Landon woke Reinier, who was snoring gently at his feet, with the intention of heading to the fountain before the sun went down. They only made it a few blocks before the woodcutter whispered, "We're being followed."

Reinier sensed his master's concern and growled.

"Easy, boy."

As nonchalantly as possible, he turned down the next road and waited. The cloaked figure that had been keeping its distance never passed the intersection. Landon turned to keep moving, and a person was standing inches away, staring at him and puffing on a pipe.

"Who are you?" the woodcutter said, without thinking.

Reinier barked and bared his ferocious teeth, looking much more like a wolf than a dog.

"Easy, friends," the man said, lowering his hood.

"Why have you been following us? Do you want something?"

"Possibly," the man said, taking a long drag on his pipe and blowing a heavily scented smoke ring into the air. "Though it's more likely that I can help you."

"How's that?"

"Let's say, I have information and skills that might be invaluable to your," the man paused for effect, "undertaking."

Landon looked around nervously. "Who said anything about an undertaking?" the woodcutter asked, his voice sounding a little higher in pitch than usual.

"Let's see," the man said, removing the pipe from his mouth. "You wear the clothes of a traveler, are staying at the inn with an archer and a cleric, and you spoke to a wizard about helping you with a—how shall I say—quest that will take you to Cragfall Mountains. How am I doing so far?"

"What is this? Are you a thief come to rob me? Spying on me and waiting to get me alone. Well, I just spent my last centime, so you'll get nothing from me except my sack and a broken axe."

"You carry more than that."

As the man spoke, Landon became aware of an uncomfortable feeling in his leg. He reached into his pocket, and the stone he'd found at the statue was blazing hot. He reflexively pulled his hand back. "Ow!"

The man chuckled and took another drag on his pipe. "You wear the burden of your troubles as a sheep wears heavy wool waiting to be shorn. Call off your dog, and we'll speak."

Landon didn't trust the man, but he also wanted to hear what he had to say. Placing a hand on Reinier's head, he said, "Easy," and the dog quieted.

"Will you join me?" the man asked, motioning to a space between two buildings.

Landon couldn't tell if a structure had once stood there, but all that remained were piles of rocks and scrubgrass. It was a sufficiently open area so as not to be ambushed; therefore, the woodcutter agreed, though he was keenly aware that the sun was fading and he'd promised Sorin and Thea that he'd meet them at the statue.

The strange man talked about nothing of import for a while until Landon got tired of waiting. "Enough of this. You've been spying on me and my friends. It's time you explained yourself. Start by telling me your name."

The man gave him a sideways glance. "You first."

"I'd be a fool to think you don't already know that."

"True. Your name is Landon Quilson."

Landon tried to see behind the man's eyes, but he couldn't tell if he was being cautious or if he was dangerous. There was no way to tell, so he settled on assessing the man's outward appearance instead.

He was lean, and his skin was pale from lack of sunlight— neither of which was unusual in these parts. Unruly dark hair fell in strands around his face, which could either be an attempt to hide his identity or he hadn't had time to get a haircut. Maybe because he'd been traveling? The condition of his boots supported that possibility. As for the man's clothing, he wore a brown vest over a loose-fitting tan shirt and heavy workman's pants, which told Landon nothing since lots of people were dressed in a similar fashion. The only conclusion that made sense was that he was a journeyman, but to what profession, Landon couldn't tell.

Realizing he wasn't skilled enough in the art of whatever this was, Landon went with the direct approach. "Yes, my name is Landon Quilson."

"And where do you hail from?"

"Brownwater."

"You have my condolences."

"You've heard."

"Who hasn't?"

"I wouldn't know. And now you."

Taking another puff on his pipe, the man said, "You can call me Anslim."

Landon noted that he didn't offer a surname. "Are you from around here?"

"Yes and no. I move around."

"That isn't an answer."

"And yet, it's the truth."

"What are these skills you have that would benefit me and my friends?"

"Patience, Landon Quilson, patience. All in good time."

"That is a luxury I don't have. I must return—"

"To the statue to meet your friends," Anslim finished for him.

Unsettled by how much the journeymen knew, Landon said, "You aren't making a good case for yourself."

"How do you mean?"

"I don't trust someone who spies on me but reveals little."

"Then you are wise. How about this? I will come to *The Last Stop Watering Hole*. I believe that's where you're meeting the old man, correct? We'll speak there, and then we'll deal. Does that sound acceptable?"

"Indeed."

"Then I will see you and your friends later."

A sound caught Landon's attention. It was a lamplighter, tending to the oil lamps that lined Endog's winding roads. When Landon turned back, Anslim was gone.

"I'm not sure we can trust him," he said to Reinier. "And why did the stone grow hot? Was it a warning? It isn't hot now."

The dog cocked an eyebrow.

"Exactly," Landon said, taking it out and looking at it. "It's late. Let's get back to the statue."

Reinier woofed, and off they went.

14 A Meeting of Minds

"Where have you been?" Sorin asked when Landon and Reinier appeared in the lamplight.

Even though the streets were well-lit, the woodcutter carried a small torch over his head for good measure. "Sorry, we got delayed."

"I should say so! Let's get going. We're supposed to be meeting Loric, remember?"

"Wait," Thea said, standing in Landon's way. She was much smaller than the woodcutter but formidable in her own way.

Sorin stopped talking.

"Landon has something to tell us," she said.

"This is true, but not here. Let's go to the tavern, and we can speak until Loric arrives."

"And if he's already there?" Sorin asked.

"I'm sure he'll understand if we ask him to wait a moment."

Thea gave Landon a strange look but agreed.

It turned out, Loric hadn't arrived yet, so Landon and Thea found an out-of-the-way table while Sorin procured three pints of ale—two for himself and one for Landon—and a glass of wine for Thea. Once they were settled, the woodcutter recounted his experience of being followed and eventually speaking with the journeyman who called himself Anslim.

"I don't like the sound of that," Sorin said, starting on his second pint. "He's obviously been following us around."

Landon didn't know what to think. "He didn't give me the impression of malice or evil intent."

"He could have been faking."

"True, but I think if he were trying to hurt us, he would have ingratiated himself more with me, which he didn't. Either way, I invited him to meet with us tonight. If he shows, we may get some answers.

"Or not. Hey, wait a second. Is that who I think it is?" the archer asked, pushing back from the table.

Even Reinier raised his head at the tone of Sorin's voice.

"Do you know that man?" Thea asked.

"Everybody does."

Landon finished his pint and plunked it on the table. "I don't."

"No offense, buddy, but you don't know anyone outside of Brownwater besides us and Esslla."

The woodcutter shrugged. It was the truth.

"I'll be right back."

Landon and Thea watched as the archer wound through the tables toward a man wearing a dark green cloak sitting at the bar.

"Barkeep, another round for my new friend," Sorin said, gesturing to the hunched man. "Mind if I join you?"

"Anyone willing to buy me a drink is welcome," the drinker replied, blowing the head off the top of his freshly poured tankard of ale.

He had a swarthy look about him, but his hair was cut neat and short, and his leather clothing was well cared for. Beneath it all, he had a sharp-eyed look that belied his easygoing manner.

Sorin sat on a stool. "You're known to me, friend."

"Then you have me at a disadvantage, for I do not know you."

The archer laughed. "Nonsense. No one has Braydn Hornswall at a disadvantage if the stories are true. My name is Sorin."

"Ah," Braydn said, leaning back to get a better look. "I'm not at a disadvantage after all. Your name precedes you, friend. That is, if you are the same Sorin who split the baronet's arrow in two from the viewing stand."

Sorin was taken aback. He hadn't expected to be recognized. "Why yes. That was me."

"They say, if you'd been allowed to compete, you would have swept the tournament the past three years running—not that being part of the nobility means anything these days. People *do* hold onto the past."

A woman approached Braydn from the other side, but he waved her away. "It's the eyes. Something about blue eyes drives women crazy in these parts. Can't keep them off of me," he said with a chuckle.

Sorin thought people's interest in Braydn was more based on the outlandish stories told about him than his eyes, but the archer said nothing.

"So what brings you to my side, Sorin? It isn't for a good yarn, I guess."

"My friends and I seek allies to help us face what lies before us." Sorin pointed at their table across the room.

Bradyn glanced at Landon, who was patting Reinier on the head, and Thea, who was staring directly at him.

"And why would I be so inclined?" Braydn asked. "Your friends don't look like the kind of people who are cut out for the challenges that lie beyond these walls."

"We've made it this far. There's more to them than meets the eye."

"If you say so."

"Listen, where we're going, I'm sure you'll find plenty to make it worth your while."

Sorin knew he'd overplayed his hand, and he waited to see if Bradyn would bite, which he did.

"North or South?"

"North."

"Good. The South is nothing but ruin and poverty. Strongholds, castles, or villages?"

"Castles."

"Hmm. Is—"

"Uh-uh-uh. If you want to know more about it, you need to talk to all of us. We'll be right over there."

Sorin slapped a couple of coins on the bar and left.

Upon returning to the table, Sorin eagerly shared what he'd learned.

"He sounds like a bit of a rogue," Thea said as they ate dinner.

"That's exactly what he is, but members of the guild are required to see their contracts through, as long as they get paid, so I doubt we have anything to worry about. Hmm. I wonder if Loric thought better of joining us. And where is this Anslim fellow you told us about, Landon? I'm beginning to think you were pulling our leg."

An unfamiliar voice said, "No legs were pulled."

"Ho! Where did you come from?" Sorin said, almost choking at the journeyman's sudden appearance.

"I've been over there since before you arrived."

"But I looked for you," Landon said, confused.

"Look harder next time."

The woodcutter got the sense that no matter how hard he looked, he wouldn't see Ansilm unless he wanted to be seen.

The journeyman threw his oversized bag under the table and grabbed a chair, but before he got himself situated, Thea started in with a list of questions. "She gets right to the point, doesn't she?" he said with a laugh.

"Well?" Thea pressed.

"I'm confident that you'll find me most useful."

"I think we'll need something a little more concrete," Landon said, losing patience. He was but a simple woodcutter and not fond of doublespeak.

"Patience, my friend," Anslim replied with the easy manner of a negotiator. "They wouldn't be secrets if I told what I know to everyone I meet. But should you let me travel with you a while, I'll reveal what I know when the time is right."

"We're looking for companions, not hangers on," Sorin said, leaning forward.

"I'll pull my weight, that's all that matters."

Before Landon had the chance to add his two cents, Braydn appeared.

"Forgive my forwardness, but ever since Sorin came to speak to me, I've been listening to your conversation," the rogue said, sitting on the table's edge.

"From over there?" the archer asked.

Braydn got a twinkle in his eye. "I have good ears."

"Apparently."

"I believe you may be of service to me."

Sorin was taken aback. "What? We're looking for people to join our party, not the other way around."

"I guess it's all in how you look at it. I have some business at the keep—a certain trinket some say doesn't exist, but I'm confident that it does—but I can't go there alone. And since you're the first and only people I've ever heard of embarking on such an audacious undertaking, I'd be a fool not to take advantage of the situation."

"Take advantage of the situation, or us?" Landon said, looking even less convinced than he was about Anslim's lack of commitment to their quest.

"You have nothing to fear from me, as long as I get paid."

Landon leaned back. "Charming."

"And what skills do you possess besides being able to hear people across a crowded room that would make us accept such an uninspired offer?" Thea asked, staring at him with her piercing blue-gray eyes.

Braydn was unfazed. "People talk to me."

"About what?"

"Everything."

"I see how that could be helpful, but a warrior might be more what our party needs."

Braydn brushed off another woman who was trying to get his attention. "I didn't say that was my only skill. Besides, I am tenacious when it comes to getting what I want, and Volgreth has something I want."

"Who said anything about Volgreth?" Sorin asked.

"To me, no one but you've been all over town talking about evil sorcerers and oppression and things like that. Honestly, my best advice to you, friend Sorin, is: Don't play poker. You'll lose your shirt."

The archer sputtered. "But people love to play poker with me."

"I bet they do."

People at the next table laughed, and Sorin sat a little lower in his seat.

Braydn chuckled, too. "Look. The three of you—"

"Four," Landon corrected.

"Forgive me," he said, looking at Reinier. "Ever since the four of you sauntered into town, you've been filling your quiver full of arrows and stuffing your bags with rations and candles. What else would you be doing than going on a quest? That and Sorin blabbed everything to Jimmy-the-Mouth. Now, everyone in Endog knows what you're up to, but they mostly think you're a bunch of drunken fools. You'd have to be, right, talking about taking on Volgreth? But I know you're serious, which, I must admit, is more than a little intriguing."

Sorin was still focused on being accused of revealing their plans. "I didn't! Honest. I wouldn't have said anything to a guy with a name like that."

Thea stared at him until he started to sweat.

"Look," he continued, producing a tiny flask. "I did chat with this nice old guy who gave me this, but his name was James Montague, not Jimmy—"

Even Reinier groaned at his admission.

"We told you to keep your mouth shut," Thea said sternly.

"But he asked me why I needed so many arrows. I mean, an archer of my skill only needs one arrow to fell a hart."

Landon put his head in his hands. "So that's it. Pride. You didn't want to look like an amateur."

Braydn laughed. "I can relate."

"There's nothing we can do about it now. You," Thea said, pointing a sharp finger at Sorin, "need to keep your mouth shut."

"Are you saying I should have lied? 'Cause my mom and her switch were pretty clear on the subject."

"Yes!" the cleric snapped, cutting him off. "Where our safety is concerned, yes."

"A cleric telling me to lie. Now, I've heard everything."

"Ah, and here's Thea's contribution to your party," Braydn said, shutting the argument down. "Fallen as he is, Loric may be of some use to us."

Thea bristled at the rogue's impolite language. "Welcome, Loric."

"I see you've invited others to help you fulfill your task," the wizard said, surveying the party with his hazel eyes. His gray hair and beard had been carefully brushed, and several holes in his robes were freshly darned.

"We haven't made any decisions yet," Landon mumbled, trying to make sense of the strange situation they found themselves in and even stranger company.

"As I'm sure fair Thea has already told you," Loric continued. "I wish to put things right if I can. By joining your party, I hope to protect others from the darkness I once foolishly embraced."

"Don't worry, Loric. You're already in," Sorin said. "Thea made that abundantly clear. As for the other two, the jury's still out."

"Name your terms," Landon said to Anslim and Braydn.

"What are the chances we come across items we can...let's say...liberate?" Anslim asked.

Sorin slipped his hands under the table, but the journeyman had already noticed the ring he was fiddling with. "Treasure, you mean?"

"You say potato..."

Thea placed a small pouch on the table. "We can offer you a few gold coins now, and you can keep anything you find."

Braydn looked curious. "No questions asked?"

"What's yours is yours," Sorin answered.

"That's enough for me," Anslim said, shaking Landon, Sorin, and Thea's hands.

Landon coughed expectantly.

Understanding what the woodcutter was insinuating, Anslim leaned over and let Reinier sniff his hand. "It'll be good to have companions on the road for a while."

"And you?" Thea asked.

Braydn looked thoughtful. "I've got a good feeling about your band of merry folk. I believe you might actually succeed, or at the very least, help me get to the keep, which is more than I've managed to do on my own. Count me in."

After Braydn shook everyone's hand, Landon stood. "Now that we've settled that, we should rest the night and set out on our journey in the morning. It's time to free Kahr'anis from Volgreth's reign of terror."

Sorin's eyes widened. "That got real in a hurry."

15 The Revenants

The bell tolled one, and Landon rolled over. Falling asleep had been easy, aided by the soothing murmur of Thea's nightly entreaties to the Light. Staying asleep, however, had been impossible. The mysterious shapes in his dreams had become more distinct but remained far enough out of reach to provide little meaning or purpose to their nightly visits. Now, as the city's clock tower chimed the hour, he lost any hope of going back to sleep. Opening his eyes, he stared at the ceiling.

Here, as in most of the city, the room was made of wood. Old wood. The kind of wood that wasn't found in the safe parts of the forest north of Bleeding Tree anymore, having been harvested generations ago. Now, only young pine trees grew along the western bank of the Brownwater River, and although it was nice-smelling and easy to work with, pine didn't resist rot well and wasn't terribly strong. This meant the wood he'd spent his days cutting—oak, ash, maple, and hickory—hadn't come from this or any forest he knew about.

Where the bossman got it was a mystery, but here it was again —oak, to be precise—hanging over his head in hand-hewn beams. It was weathered by time but no less beautiful than the day it was felled.

All of the buildings he'd seen were built in a similar style, with stone first stories and wooden upper levels finished with flowing thatch or terracotta roof tiles. Here and there, plaster found its way between the timbers, but most buildings were clothed in simple clapboards. Landon liked it. They didn't sag like the shacks back in Brownwater, and being on the second floor meant the air was easier to breathe. Shifting his focus to the candles he and Sorin had placed on the window sills, around the door, and above the fireplace, he checked to see if they were still burning.

Several were disturbed by some unseen draft, and he sat up. Someone was moving about the room.

Thea was still in the straw bed. Sorin was in his corner near the fireplace, and both Braydn and Anslim were fast asleep on the floor. That left Loric.

Landon was shocked. If anyone had asked him who would be most likely to sneak away, it would have been Anslim or Braydn, not the kind old wizard.

Reinier lifted his head questioningly.

"Did Loric cast a spell? How else could he have left without you alerting me?" he asked the wolfhound.

Reinier whined softly.

Moving to a window, Landon noticed a dark shape exit the first-floor tavern below and cross the street. Getting up to follow the wizard, the woodcutter moved to the door. Reinier came with him.

"Stay," he commanded the wolfhound.

Reinier moved closer.

"Not this time. Watch over the others."

The dog reluctantly lay back down but didn't look happy about it.

• • •

Taking care not to be seen, Landon followed Loric through Endog's winding streets to the same clock tower that had rung the hour. Strangely, he didn't see anyone along the way, not even the city's guards, which unsettled him. Ever since they'd arrived, Endog had been a hive of activity, but not this night. Tonight, silence reigned, and that made the hairs on the back of the woodcutter's neck stand on end.

When Loric reached the clock tower's doors, he glanced furtively around before entering. Landon ducked into a doorway to keep from being seen. While he stayed there, pressing himself into the opening, he tried to see the clock-face. It was shrouded in fog, but he could still hear every tick of its giant mechanism.

"What could Loric possibly want with the clock?" he asked himself.

When the coast was clear, he crossed the street and entered the tower, too, but he saw no sign of the wizard.

"Strange."

With no other direction to go but up, he climbed toward the source of the ticking.

Click. Click, click. Clunk!
Click. Click, click. Clunk!

He was worried the ancient wood creaking beneath his feet would give him away, but he saw no sign of the wizard. Higher and higher he climbed the tower's spiraling steps until he could go no further.

"This must be it." He was about to enter the clock-room itself when he heard a sound.

Beneath him in an adjoining room, Landon saw a circular gathering of wizards surrounded by tools, ropes, and gears, which were probably replacement parts for the clock mechanism. A sigil had been drawn on the worn floorboards, and at least a hundred candles had been placed around its circumference.

None of the wizards reacted when Loric joined them, sitting down at the only empty point on the diagram. Removing a candle from his robes, he lit it, completing the circle. Then he removed several items from his robes.

The other wizards weren't idle either. Each held a leather pouch on their lap with carefully sorted items placed around them. One woman used a mortar and pestle to grind a glittering powder. Another delicately stitched a small silver charm onto a plain woolen shawl.

That's when Landon noticed the wizards were adding various objects to their collection from a pile in the center of the sigil.

"What is this unholy gathering?" he asked himself, shifting to see better. But there was so much bat guano on everything, he didn't want to put his hands down.

Didn't Thea say something about guano and fire? And there was an entire group of wizards beneath him.

Suddenly, Landon felt like he'd made a terrible mistake coming here. He abruptly stood to go, forgetting where he was, struck his head on a metal beam, and collapsed to the floor.

• • •

"Landon Quilson."

"Yes?"

"Why do you hide yourself from me?"

"I'm not. I'm right here."

"Then open your eyes."

Landon did as he was told. In front of him was the same luminous woman he'd seen at Esslla's hut, only this time, her piercing yellow eyes glowed so brightly that they were painful to look at.

"Child of Kahr'anis," she spoke in his mind. "Have you come to tell me who you are?"

"I still don't understand what you want from me. I am who I am. Nothing more."

"Then Kahr'anis is lost."

"No," he insisted.

Unlike the last time, the woman paused. "How so?"

"It's not lost, yet, at least. My friends and I seek to banish the evil that inhabits Nachturm Keep."

The woman's eyes burned brighter. "Light is the bane of the darkness. Which do you have in you, Landon Quilson?"

"I am trying to figure that out."

The woman stepped closer and placed a hand on the woodcutter's head. "If that is what you seek, the Light will guide you." Then she faded into the swirling dreamscape.

• • •

"Landon, wake up."

When the woodcutter's eyes opened, he saw Loric standing over him with six other wizards peering over the wizard's shoulder.

Suffering from hitting his head, the vision, the paranoia that had overtaken him, and a searingly hot pain in his pocket originating from the stone he'd found, Landon panicked.

"How could you betray us?" he asked, leaping to his feet. "We trusted you."

"Please, Landon, you must listen to me."

But there was nothing Loric could do to prevent Landon from pushing through the wizards and bounding down the steps toward the street.

The woodcutter's voice echoed up the tower. "I must tell the others."

Loric frowned. "Oh, dear."

16 BATS IN THE BELFRY

By the time Loric returned to the room, Landon had woken everyone up with tales of dark magic in the clock tower. When pressed on specifics, a mixture of what he saw and the vision he had after hitting his head morphed into a display of magical incantations, terrifying beasts, and fire.

"But the clock tower didn't burn down," Thea said. "I can hear it chiming."

"No, it didn't burn down," the wizard said, sitting on the edge of the straw bed, "but Landon is right. I have betrayed your trust."

"See! He admits it!" the woodcutter yelled.

"Maybe you should sit, too," Sorin suggested. "That's a nasty bump on your head, and you don't seem to be steady on your pins."

"Not until Loric explains how he betrayed us."

"No, no. I didn't betray you, Landon. I betrayed your trust," the wizard explained. "I was referring to sneaking out.

I knew you'd follow, since you don't sleep soundly, and I thought it would be a way to show you the good that magic can do."

"Then why didn't you invite me in the first place?"

"Because I couldn't. That's forbidden. I had to let you follow me. I know it's really the same thing, but that's how the spell works. If I'd invited you or told you about it, you wouldn't have been able to see us."

"Wizards," Braydn said. "Always mucking around with stuff like that. Why do you have to make everything difficult?"

Anslim, who appeared interested in the conversation, didn't appreciate the interruption. "Let Loric speak."

Braydn shrugged his shoulders and said nothing else.

The woodcutter also quieted, and Thea tended to his head.

Loric moved over to the small fireplace and, using the poker, moved the logs. The fire danced in the hearth, casting flickering light across the wizard's face. Much to everyone's shock, the years melted away, leaving a young man in his twenties, clad in bright red garments with shoulder-length black hair. Although his appearance had changed, his eyes remained the same. Sad. Lonely. Weary.

"Magic in its purest form is neither good nor evil. It simply is. But, like water taking the path of least resistance, it flows into a wizard according to their personalities. That's why every wizard is different. We cannot change who we are, and we must either accept that or forsake the power that is offered to us." Loric paused, poking at the fire again. "Have you ever wished to have curly hair, Landon?"

The question caught the woodcutter off guard.

"I...uh...as a matter of fact, yes. When I was a boy, I wished I had curly hair like my mother's."

"No, you don't," Sorin said. "Stick with what you've got. Curly hair is a nightmare to comb."

"As if you ever comb it," Thea said.

Everyone laughed, but it wasn't a jovial laugh. Even the smile on Braydn's face looked strained.

"You see," Loric continued. "People always want what we can't have. Wizards are no different. A wizard who has a special talent for growing plants might wish to change the weather, or one who has an affinity for fire might want to work with water instead."

"But I thought spells were spells. All wizards have to do is learn them, and they can cast them, right?" Sorin asked.

"That's true to some extent, but if you were to see two wizards cast the same spell, where one of them has a particular skill in that area, you would understand what I mean. That, young Sorin, was what consumed me. Hungry to be the first wizard to master incantations from all branches of magic, I learned every spell I could find. I read reams of ancient scrolls and spent years perfecting potions."

"And did you succeed?" the archer asked, leaning forward expectantly.

This time, when Loric looked at the others, he looked older. Now, he was in his thirties. His robes weren't as vibrant, and his hair was unkempt. "Alas, in so much as it was possible, I did."

"Wow. That's amazing. Shouldn't you be excited about that?"

"No, because I wanted more."

Landon didn't follow the wizard's logic. "How can you have more than everything?"

"Precisely. I began to search for a way to go beyond what was possible, and when the Light could no longer quench my thirst for knowledge, I looked to the Dark."

"I know Thea always talks about stuff like that," Landon said, "but you told me magic wasn't inherently good or bad."

"Magic isn't, but people can be. I sought out wizards who did things I couldn't dream of and fell into despair."

The wizard grew older but stronger, too. This made Thea nervous, and he reassured her.

"Do not fear, Thea. I will not bring darkness into this place. It is only a story. One I have longed to tell for it is my penance: to never forget."

Even so, Thea moved away and prayed over one of the candles.

"I had a partner back then—a companion whom I loved dearly. Do not ask his name, for I dare not speak it, or he might return. You see, the power of the heart is strong, and I long to see him again." Loric sighed before continuing. "Together, we learned how to access the darker parts of our beings, the parts that were not meant to channel magic. There came a day when I saw the error of our ways and tried to stop him, but it was too late. He'd been consumed."

The wizard once again looked like the Loric they knew, and he ran a scarred hand through his long gray hair.

"After that, I sought out others who'd also lost their way. There are seven of us, masters of arcane power. We have dedicated the rest of our lives to a singular purpose: atonement. Together, we seek redemption by channeling our magic into ordinary objects and imbuing them with gifts for those who need them most. I convinced them to help make gifts for all of you. That is what we were doing when Landon found us. We were enchanting *Pouches of Belonging*."

Sorin sat closer. "That sounds interesting."

"It is. We gathered basic necessities—a warm scarf, dried fruit, herbs, even notes of encouragement—and placed them in the bags. Then, when the bearer found themselves in dire need, all they had to do was put their hand into the bag, and it provided them with a remedy."

"Can I see one?" the archer asked.

"Alas, I'm sorry, my friend, but no. Landon startled us, and the spell was broken before we finished. I'm afraid the components for that particular incantation are rare, and it will be some time before we can gather again."

Amid many angry stares and mumbled curses, a distraught Landon moved to the other side of the room. "I'm sorry. I didn't know."

"You acted rashly," Thea said, startling him.

"I see that now. I, too, would have liked to have one of those pouch things, though I realize I do not deserve it."

Anslim lit his pipe. "Landon was looking out for our best interests, too, but if we are to succeed, we'll have to learn to trust one another."

"I'm afraid that will be easier said than done," Braydn said, getting up and moving to the window.

After a pensive pause, Thea addressed the wizard. "Thank you for sharing your story with us, Loric. We will all learn from your experience. And as for you, Landon, caution can be appropriate at times, but survival is often afforded to those who think quickly and act on instinct. I would like to trust your instincts. Yes, that is something I'd like very much." She took a few steps away before turning back and fixing the woodcutter with her sharp blue-gray eyes. "But if you ever jump to conclusions again like you did tonight, I'll turn you into a frog."

Landon didn't know if Thea was joking or not, so he nodded, rolled over, and tried not to dream of spending the rest of his life eating flies.

17 THE LAST WARM MEAL

It had been three days since the party left Endog, traveling north along the Westrin Road, and it had been more of the same: damp, misty, and miserable. However, that wasn't strictly true. Some things had changed.

The Brownwater River still inched its way south, but the pine barrens had given way to small foothills, the southernmost edge of the Cragfall Mountains. That certainly brought home how close they were getting to the end of their journey—Nacturm Keep and the Shadehaunter's dreaded Unwrought Tower growing out of it.

Along their route, they'd encountered one of the wells that dotted the plains. Most were barren or broken, but this one worked, and they were able to fill their waterskins without Thea's aid, but even fresh water did little to comfort them.

Not wanting to find out what a functioning well on the plains might attract in the middle of the night, they set up camp farther up the road. By now, the routine was so deeply

ingrained that no one asked what to do. Reinier kept watch
while Anslim and Sorin built a fire with the aid of the archer's
flint. Landon prepared the candles for Thea to set out, and
Loric lit them with a wave of his hand. Braydn made a big
showing of preparing dinner, but he never seemed to get very
far, so as usual, Anslim took over.

While the journeyman worked, the others occupied themselves by making reasonably comfortable spaces to pass the
night, though that meant little more than kicking small
stones out of the way and laying down a thin blanket.

It wasn't long before Ansilm announced, "Dinner's ready."

"Very funny," Sorin said, removing his quiver and messenger bag. "What did you do, slice the dried berries?" He
longed for a succulent rabbit stew, instead of choking down
nuts and dehydrated mystery meat twice a day, especially
when they were accompanied by a piece of hardtack that reminded him of poorly made mud bricks.

"No, really. Dinner is served. But don't get used to it. I
only brought enough for one meal."

Thea was as unimpressed by the joke as Sorin until she
caught sight of the makeshift spit turning over the fire. How
had she not smelled it before? Wait, she *had* smelled it cooking, but her brain had told her it was a mirage, and she'd ignored it. "Is that mutton?"

"I figured we could use a pick-me-up. That and the meat
wouldn't have lasted another day. I made potatoes, too."

Sorin sat as close to the fire as possible, inhaling deeply.
"You're a magician!"

"Thank the Light," Thea said, blessing the food. "This will
do us all a world of good."

Braydn pulled a silver flask from under his short green
cloak. Sorin wondered where he kept everything, considering
he wore such tight-fitting leather clothing, but the rogue always seemed to have what he needed at hand.

"I'll drink to that!" the rogue said.

After taking a swig, he offered it to Loric.

"Don't mind if I do. Oh, that's awful. I can help you with that." The wizard whispered a few unintelligible words and sprinkled something over the open container.

"Hey! Give me that. That's all I've got," Braydn said, snatching the flask back and sniffing it cautiously. "What did you do to it?

"Made it palatable."

Braydn ventured a sip and smiled. "Brandy! My favorite! How did you do that? Here you've got to try this," he said, offering the flask to Anslim. "If you can turn water into wine, you're going to be my new best friend!"

"Alas, no. Water does not contain alcohol. But I can, how shall we say, refine alcoholic beverages."

"That's good enough for me!"

Everyone laughed and tried Braydn's brandy.

"I can't take it anymore!" Sorin said, leaning closer to the spit. "The aroma of seasoned meat and salty potatoes is making my mouth water more than Reinier's!"

The wolfhound made a funny sound.

"Don't worry, boy. You're not that slobbery," Landon said, patting him on the head. "If you'll excuse us for a moment."

"But you'll miss the first cut," Anslim said.

"I won't be far. Come, boy."

Reinier hopped to his feet and followed Landon.

"Your loss," the journeyman said, slicing into the meat.

A stream of juices dripped onto the fire, sizzling contentedly, and everyone clapped.

"Now that is music to my ears!" Sorin said, snatching a potato from the fire, but it was so hot that he dropped it onto his lap.

The usually stoic cleric laughed. "Use your knife."

Despite the short time they'd spent together, the challenges of traveling across the plains, and the looming threat that lay ahead of them, everyone's spirit was lifted by the simple pleasure of sharing a meal.

"We have food," Anslim said.

"Here, here! Compliments to the chef!" Sorin said, raising the potato stuck on the end of his knife.

"And drink," Braydn added. "Can't forget that."

The journeyman smiled. "Wouldn't think of it."

"But where's the entertainment?" Sorin asked. "You can't have a meal like this without entertainment."

"Yes, that would be nice," Thea said, her golden hair shimmering in the firelight. "A game, perhaps?"

"I've got dice," Braydn said, reaching into his cloak. "How about a few rounds of *Lucky Pig?*

"Hold on a minute," Sorin said, holding up his hands. "Do you honestly think we're going to fall for that?"

"Fall for what?" the rogue asked with a gleam in his eye.

"I don't trust those dice as far as I can throw them."

"Are you saying my dice are loaded?"

"Are you seriously asking me that? A rogue just offered to play a game of chance with his own set of dice. Of course, that's what I think!"

"Rest easy, my friend. You have nothing to worry about. *These* are my loaded pair," Braydn said, producing another set of dice, and everyone burst out laughing. "The real question is, what are we playing for?"

"Uh-uh-uh," Loric said, wagging his finger. "Tonight is just for fun. I will provide money for the kitty."

Everyone watched as the wizard pulled out a bag filled with tiny pebbles from his robes. One by one, he dropped them into his hand. As soon as they landed, they turned into gold coins with Braydn's face on them.

Again, everyone clapped.

"Now that's a great trick!" Sorin said, biting one of the coins. It instantly turned back into a pebble, and he spit it out.

"Sorin's lost his money already, and we haven't even started playing yet!" Anslim said, clapping the archer on the back.

The archer reached for the dice. "Not for long!" But after many rounds, Sorin proved that he had absolutely no luck at all until he absently slipped the arrow ring onto his finger.

The next time he rolled the dice, it looked like he was going to lose again, but wishing with all of his might for it to turn once more, it did.

Anslim, who didn't miss a trick, leapt up. "Hold on. No magic!"

"What do you mean?" Sorin said, not knowing what the journeyman was talking about.

"You used that ring of yours to move the left die."

"No way! I was… It just… Did I?"

"Take that thing off and roll again," Anslim insisted.

Sorin did as he was told and, to no one's surprise, he lost.

"Told you," Anslim said, gathering the coins.

The archer looked at the ring. "Did you do that?"

"May I see it?" Loric asked.

The camp grew so quiet that the only thing making any sound was the crackling fire.

Sorin reluctantly handed the ring to the wizard. "It's got an arrow on it."

"I see that. And you thought that meant it was made for you because you're an archer?"

"Well, not made for me, but yeah, that it might have been made for archers in general, I guess."

"A common mistake."

"Huh?"

Braydn leaned over to look at it. "Speak plainly, old man."

Thea frowned. "Show a little respect."

The rogue smirked. "Speak plainly, old man, please. How's that?"

"Would you two let him finish?" Sorin asked, eager to hear about his ring.

"Arrows can mean a great many things," Loric explained. "Obviously, your thoughts are likely the most common."

"He just called you common, if you missed that," Braydn whispered, nudging Sorin, but the archer was too focused to be offended.

"But there are lots of other things it might represent, such as guidance—"

"Like a compass!" Sorin blurted.

"Correct. Or secret messages, divination, and even masculinity. The list goes on."

"Masculinity? You mean it might make my, ah-hem, bigger?"

"It's not out of the realm of possibility."

Sorin grabbed the ring, slipped it onto his finger, and peeked into his pants. "No luck."

Everyone chuckled.

"So if it doesn't mean that masculinity thing, what does it mean?" he asked, taking the ring off again.

The wizard stared blankly at him. "You're asking me? I don't know."

"What? I thought you... Can't you cast a spell on it or something to tell me what it does?"

"I could, but that would be unwise. Contrary to popular belief, asking magic to reveal itself is a tricky business. I'd rather not risk something so dangerous. What if it's cursed? Meddling with it could release its malice on everyone."

Not liking the way things were going, Thea tried to distract Sorin by saying, "You think he's bad at dice. You should hear one of his jokes. They're terrible."

For a second, it looked like her ploy wouldn't work, but then Sorin's face broke into a smile and he put the ring into his pocket. "Now, wait a minute. I have great jokes. In fact, I'll tell one now, and everyone can judge for themselves."

"Oh no, here we go," Thea said, making a show of it.

Loric winked at her, and she nodded.

Sorin stood near the fire. "Why did the skeleton run and hide?"

"Why?" Braydn asked, tipping back the last of his flask.

"It didn't have any guts!"

Groans erupted from the group.

Thea looked vindicated. "See? I told you. Terrible. Now, sit down and let someone with talent go," but her smile never reached the corners of her eyes. The ring was enchanted, just as she'd thought. The question was, would it help them or be their downfall?

"What do you mean?" the archer asked, breaking Thea out of her thoughts. "That was pretty good."

"In your dreams."

Anslim stood next, clinking two of Loric's coins together. When he displayed his palm, there were three. Now one. Now none. "Where did they go?" he asked, reaching behind Braydn's ear and pulling one, two, three coins out of thin air.

Sorin was impressed. "He really is a magician!"

"It seems friend Anslim has been holding out on us," Loric said, smoothing his long whiskers.

"Speaking of holding out," Braydn said, getting everyone's attention. "Have I told you about the time I liberated the Duke's crown while he was still wearing it?"

"No way. You're full of it," Sorin said, moving closer so as not to miss a single word.

"Maybe, but this story is true. Gather 'round and I'll tell you how I did it."

As Braydn recounted his tale, Loric excused himself.

• • •

A gentle rustle drew Landon's attention. He looked up to see the wizard standing before him.

"I see you haven't participated in our frivolity this evening," Loric said, handing the woodcutter a plate of food leftover from the meal.

Burdened by his misstep in Endog, the woodcutter placed the plate on the ground where Reinier eagerly lapped it up.

"May I sit down?" the wizard asked. "I understand feeling alone, even amongst friends.

Landon's gaze remained fixed on the candles he'd helped set up. "I'm not sure I deserve such good friends."

Loric put a hand on the woodcutter's shoulder, and their gazes met. The wizard's hazel eyes held a burden much greater than his own, which only made Landon feel worse. Why had he not given Loric the chance to explain himself? Or even just asked what he was doing before jumping to conclusions?

What Loric said next shocked the woodcutter. "I owe you an apology."

"No, it is I who owes you an apology! I baselessly accused you of betraying us, and that is not what companions should do. Plus, it's my fault that we lost the gift you and your friends meant to give us."

"Yes, the *Pouches of Belonging* may have served a purpose, but nothing is more valuable than trust, and for that, we must have honesty. I shouldn't have snuck out the way I did. At the time, I thought it was the best course of action, but I see now there was folly in my actions. We did not know each other yet, and suspicion was all that could have been gained from my behavior. I promise, from this day forward, to be honest with you."

Landon's heart lifted at the wizard's words. He didn't believe the wizard was at fault, but he appreciated Loric giving him a way to make amends. "Thank you, Loric, but I still insist that I should be the one promising that to you. I spoke out of turn, and it cost us. I won't do that again."

"Ah, well, you might."

"But…I…"

"And I might too. Everyone makes mistakes."

"Then let me try to right the wrong I have done to you. I promise to be honest and to earn your trust."

Loric nodded. "Ooh, look here. Blackthorn. I've been searching for a bit of that." The wizard selected a short piece of stem and hid it in his robes.

"What is it used for?" Landon asked.

"A rather nasty spell, but one that might come in handy if we need a barrier of some kind."

This didn't mean anything to Landon, but wizards were supposed to be circumspect. It came with the profession.

"Shall we rejoin our friends?" Loric asked.

Reinier whined.

"Yes, I'd like that, and Reinier would, too. I have a story or two about Sorin that will get everyone laughing, I'm sure."

"I imagine you do," the wizard said, helping the woodcutter to his feet. "I imagine you do."

18 TA DA!

The crunch of gravel accompanied Landon's footsteps as he and his companions continued along the Westrin Road. Only a couple of nights had passed, but any relief or goodwill that had been fostered during their last warm meal was entirely long gone, leaving only the unwavering desolation of the plains.

That's what it was like to cross Kahr'anis. Travelers rarely met anyone, and they saw even less. It wasn't that no one lived on the plains, as many towns had been built along its crisscrossing cart paths, but few people ventured far from their homes, and even fewer returned if they did. And given its vastness, the number of villages didn't make a difference to their isolation. Every single one was a lonely sentinel, watching and waiting for the next time the Shadehaunter chose to appear out of the shadows.

"Color has abandoned us," Sorin muttered, kicking a stone.

It tried to roll down the road but, seeing no real point to the endeavor, only traveled a few feet before flopping down in disgust.

"Even the wind shuns this place," Thea added, the air being so still it took effort to breathe.

Braydn coughed. "The promise of a quest was made."

"What's that supposed to mean?" the archer asked, not needing anyone else to point out how miserable the situation was.

"He has a point," Anslim chimed in. "Not only is this boring, but we haven't seen anything for days, let alone the treasure we were promised."

"No one promised any treasure, only that you could keep what you found," Thea corrected.

Braydn laughed. "And how do you propose we find anything out here?"

The wolfhound let out a sharp bark, and everyone stopped quibbling.

"Reinier senses something," Landon said, trying to see what had disturbed the dog, but the fog was too thick.

"No kidding. We heard him," Sorin said, standing at the ready. "It's a good thing Volgreth isn't the *Foghaunter*."

"Enough of that!" Thea hissed. "This is no time for jokes."

"Who's joking? I'm just saying that I'm glad fog isn't the same thing as shadows or we'd be goners."

"It's probably a hare or something," Braydn suggested offhandedly, but Landon noticed the rogue's hand move his cloak out of the way so he had access to his dagger.

"Shh," Thea said, putting her finger to her mouth.

"Oh no! Is someone else caught in the river?" Landon asked.

"No. Listen."

Landon became aware of a woman's voice, singing a gentle melody. "Wait, I heard a voice like that in Endog. Is that Esslla?"

Reinier howled

"Yup. Esslla." Sorin said.

"But why is it coming from your pocket?" Thea asked.

Landon produced the stone.

"It seems you have a singing stone," Loric said, knowingly.

"Really? That's what it's called?" Sorin asked. "Are you sure it isn't one of those magical words that has more syllables than I have fingers and toes?"

Loric shrugged. "Simple spell, simple name."

"But why is it singing?" Landon asked. "And why does it sound like Esslla?"

"Are you referring to the Forest Mystic?" Loric asked, raising a bushy eyebrow.

Landon, Thea, and Sorin stared at the wizard questioningly.

Braydn hooked his fingers into his belt. "I feel like we're missing something, don't you, Anslim?"

"Indeed," the journeyman replied.

Thea approached the wizard. "Do you know what it means?"

"Typically, these kinds of things are a warning or an alarm of some kind, though they can also be reassuring, as in revealing good intentions instead of bad. Has it sung before?"

"No. Well, I don't know. Like I said, I heard someone singing in Endog just before I found it. Maybe it was the stone," Landon said, turning it over in his hand, "But it has definitely gotten very hot more than once."

"When?"

"When I first met Anslim. I thought it was a warning. And then again in the clock tower."

"Hmm," the wizard mused, stroking his long gray beard.

"That's good, isn't it?" Sorin asked. "Anslim joined our party, and the wizards weren't doing anything bad."

"Could be. I need to check something."

Landon watched the wizard closely as he collected several spell components from various pockets, but when he spoke the incantation, nothing happened.

"Isn't that strange?" Loric said, looking rather puzzled. "I know I got the words right. Oh, yes. That's it!" Reaching behind his neck, he pulled out a tiny shard of glass. With it, he cut a small hole right in the air! Leaning close enough to peer through with one eye, he said, "Yes, yes. That's very interesting."

"What is?" Sorin asked, trying to see, too.

"I just need to…" Loric expanded the hole by pulling on it and stuck his head through.

"Loric!" Thea yelled because his head had disappeared, though his body remained.

The wizard pulled his head back through and said, "Yes? What? Oh, not to worry. I'll only be a minute. That stone of yours is very helpful indeed." Then, he widened the hole further and stepped through.

Landon tried to grab him, but the hole closed, and the wizard disappeared entirely.

"What do we do now?" Sorin asked.

Many minutes passed, and Thea suggested they look around, but no one moved because a dark shape had emerged from the dense, gray fog.

"Look out!" Landon yelled, knowing full well that nothing taller than a spear of dry grass existed on the plains.

Everyone readied their weapons, though the woodcutter wasn't convinced he'd be much help in a fight with only a broken axe to defend himself.

To their surprise, Loric appeared, standing in front of a cavernous opening in the side of a stony hill.

"Ta da!" he said with a bow, sounding a bit like Sorin.

Thea slapped him on the arm. "Don't do that again. We were worried something had happened to you."

"Oh, no. I did it again. My apologies. It was a simple reverse spell. See?"

"I do now."

"Are you saying it was here all along, but we couldn't see it?" Anslim asked.

Loric nodded. "No one could. For some reason, it chose to reveal itself to us."

"With your help."

"Why yes. I helped a little. But I believe Landon's stone played a large part."

"You might be right. Ow! It's hot again. And it's glowing!" the woodcutter said, nearly dropping it on the ground.

Sorin moved to catch it. "Don't lose it! It's magical."

"I'm trying not to, but it's doing a good job of making me want to chuck it in the Brownwater."

"Shush, you two! For good or ill, finding this place was no accident." The cleric's sobering words commanded everyone's attention. "This shouldn't be here," she said, under her breath.

Loric agreed. "Arcane magic."

"Is it me," Landon asked, "or are those markings moving?"

"Someone used an indecipherable spell on them," the wizard explained.

"Then why can you and Thea read them?"

Thea didn't bother turning around to answer. "Because it isn't a *good* spell."

Loric stepped closer to see them better. "It feels like the kind of spell one casts to conserve energy or because they weren't actually trying to hide anything."

Braydn sidled up beside the mage. "You mean, it might have been designed to make people curious about what was inside, not warn them off."

"Precisely."

"Then it's likely a trap," Thea said, backing away.

Apparently, Reinier agreed. The dog's hackles were raised, and a low grumble emanated from his throat.

"Easy, boy," Landon said, soothing the wolfhound.

Sorin nocked an arrow. "So, what do we do?"

"Let's see. Not long ago, the two of you were complaining about the lack of treasure," Thea said, looking at Braydn and Anslim. "Here you go: a mysterious cave covered in magical markings. I say put your feet where your mouth is and tell us if it's safe."

Braydn took a step back. "Let's not be hasty."

"I agree," Loric said in an even tone. "The Shadehaunter lurks in shadows such as these. If that is who we are looking for, this might be an excellent place to find him."

No one responded because the wizard had said the quiet part out loud. Yes, they intended to confront Volgreth, but not in such a scary place and certainly not this soon!

"Why don't we draw lots?" Anslim suggested, but his eyes never left the cave.

"Sounds reasonable," Braydn agreed, tearing a handful of dry straw from the ground. He held them out, but nobody moved to take one.

Then, Landon did the unthinkable. "Enough of this!" he said, reaching into Sorin's pocket and pulling out his flint.

"Hey!"

But before the archer could grab it back, Landon struck a spark, lit one of the torches he'd procured back in Endog, and walked straight into the cave.

Sorin looked at Thea and said, "Why aren't you yelling at him?

"Someone had to do it," she said, and followed Landon with Reinier by her side.

A sharp bark echoed out of the cave.

"The dog's right, we need to stick together," Loric said, "but I'd rather have more than torchlight if no one minds."

"Not at all. By all means, work some of that fancy magic of yours," Sorin said, sticking close to the wizard.

Loric pulled a leatherbound spellbook from his tattered robes. He studied one of its worn pages and returned it to his pocket. Then, he reached into one of his many pockets and pulled out a tiny pouch, from which he removed some kind of herb or ground mineral. Sorin couldn't tell. It looked like dust to him.

When the wizard was ready, he raised his hands and mumbled. Gradually, light gathered in shimmering streams along the cave's walls.

Sorin whistled. "Is that the Lunar Glow thing?"

"No. This spell is called *Mirror Mirror On The Wall.*"

"Impressive. I wish I could do that."

"I could show you how, but it would take seven years of practice before your first spell took effect."

The archer coughed. "Thanks, but no thanks. I'm more of an instant gratification kind of guy, myself."

"I hadn't noticed," Anslim said, stepping into the cave.

"So why this spell and not another?" Sorin asked, obviously trying to delay going in.

"It uses less energy because instead of creating light, it reflects and amplifies what light already exists in a space."

"That means if Landon's torch goes out, the light does, too?"

"Yes."

The archer paused for a second, then ran after the woodcutter. "Hey, Landon, don't let that thing go out!"

"After you," Braydn told the wizard.

19 THE GLYPHBLADE

Landon slid to a halt. Somehow, the air felt even more still than on the plains in the cavernous space, and he paused to catch his breath.

"...OUT...Out...out..." Sorin's voice echoed into the distance. "How big is this thing?" he whispered, stopping alongside the woodcutter.

"Big."

By that time, the rest of the party had caught up, but no one moved, mesmerized by the vastness of the cave. The ceiling had to be a hundred feet above them, and the tunnel ahead seemed to have no end.

"We'd better stick together or we might never find each other again," Thea suggested.

"I have a thought," Loric said, taking out the same bag of pebbles he'd used to make coins for their game.

"What's he doing?" Sorin asked Landon.

The woodcutter shook his head.

When the wizard finished, he held up his hand. "Bread-crumbs. In a manner of speaking."

Sorin picked one up. "They look like glowing stones to me."

"Very clever, old man," Braydn said.

"Why, thank you."

"Am I missing something?" the archer asked. But then he saw Loric drop one on the ground and realized what he'd meant.

An hour later, they found themselves in the same place with Loric's little glowing stones leading in every direction.

Sorin stopped the party from continuing. "This feels a lot like the mirror maze in the fortress, but with no mirrors."

Anslim lit his pipe. "I don't know what you are referring to, but I can guess. Someone is keeping us walking in circles."

"That seems to be a thing with magic, doesn't it?" Sorin asked, but no one acknowledged the question.

"Landon," Loric said. "Why don't you try your stone. It led us here in the first place. Maybe it will show us the way."

"It's worth a shot. Reaching into his pocket, the woodcutter removed the magic stone.

Sorin peered around the wizard. "How do you turn it on?"

"I don't know. It seems to turn on and off on its own."

"Or maybe," Thea suggested, "You don't realize you are triggering it. Ask it something."

"What?"

Loric whispered in Landon's ear.

"Oh, that's a good idea," the woodcutter said. "Stone, tell us why you brought us here."

Nothing happened.

"It was worth a try." But when Landon turned to speak to Loric, the stone glowed briefly. "Did anyone see that?"

Sorin got excited. "Sure did, but what did it mean?"

"Ask it again," Thea insisted, staring at it.

Landon did as she suggested, but again, nothing happened until he turned toward her.

"That's it," she said.

"What's it?"

"Hold the stone out in front of you and turn around. Slowly."

The woodcutter spun in a circle.

"Stop!" Thea yelled.

Landon froze. There on his palm, the stone was glowing. "It *is* telling us where to go."

"That's a nifty trick, to be sure," Braydn said, adjusting his cloak. Thea gave him a sideways glance, which he pretended not to notice.

"Follow the leader, it is," Sorin said, slapping Landon's bottom. "Tag, you're it."

This time, when they set out to search the cave, the stone led them to something special indeed.

At the heart of the enchanted space was a black, gabbro casket with a meticulously crafted statue of a warrior, preserved in a state of eternal repose, on top. His hands were clasped around the hilt of a metal sword, and its blade was etched with runes shimmering with a faint luminescence.

Thea knelt before the fallen warrior, lit a candle, and offered a prayer.

"Who's that?" Sorin asked, leaning in to take a look.

Reinier woofed quietly, and the archer took the hint not to bother Thea.

Landon noticed Loric looking pensive and asked, "Do you know who this is?"

"I believe I do."

"Does it have to do with this?" Landon displayed the singing stone, which was humming and glowing more than it had since he found it.

"It would seem so."

"Well, out with it, old man," Braydn said.

The wizard cocked his head. "No."

"Huh?"

"I'll show you, instead." Loric searched through his robe's pockets until he found what he was looking for: a crystal, a purple candle, and a pouch of sparkling dust.

"Should we stand back?" Landon asked.

"This is the Glyphblade," the wizard said, pointing at the sword. "It's said that long ago, a great hero wielded it against celestial gods who took pleasure in torturing their worshipers."

He lit the candle with a wave of his hand and placed it on the ground next to the crystal, making a faint rainbow appear.

"Do you see these runes? These were etched into the sword every time the hero struck down one of the evil gods of old," he said, sprinkling a tiny amount of dust over the first crescent-shaped marking.

The rune floated up from the sword and turned into a ghostly image of the moon. The wizard directed it over the crystal, and a warrior appeared.

"Many considered this first trial to be our hero's most dangerous, for self-doubt is a most insidious malady that infects all people's brains."

Braydn and Anslim moved to see better as Thea continued to pray in the background.

"Back then," the wizard continued, "in places where the sky could be seen, people believed the moon god protected them from evil by illuminating the night. But the moon was capricious and once a month it tired of protecting the earth and shuttered its light, delighting in watching the people far below be devoured by the evil things that lurked in the shadows."

The image of the hero grew small, and the moon grew large, moving through its phases until it turned black.

"Some god," Sorin said.

Landon put his fingers to his lips.

"At first, the hero lashed out at the moon god, but his efforts were in vain. All the moon had to do was disappear, and our hero was left flailing in the darkness. Having failed in his task, he needed to find another way to challenge the moon god. For years, he traveled across the world, searching for a weapon strong enough to defeat his foe. In the end, he found it in the most unlikely of places."

The image of the hero, weary from his travels and battles with the moon each night, collapsed at the edge of a clearing only to be found by a little girl. Because word of the hero trying to liberate the world from the moon's tyranny had reached the poor farming family, they brought him inside and nursed him back to health.

"When the hero regained his strength, he lamented, 'Will I ever be able to conquer such a formidable foe?'

"In an effort to prove to the hero that he was up to the task, the little girl raced to her mother's bedroom table and retrieved a mirror. She used it to show the hero how strong he looked, but he did not see himself in the mirror. Instead, he saw a way to defeat the moon god. With renewed vigor, the hero scoured the land for as many mirrors as he could carry and sought out mages to enchant them. When he was ready, he climbed the highest peak in the world and challenged the moon.

"For many days and nights, our hero wouldn't let the moon hide. Sometimes it almost slipped below the horizon, but our hero never lost sight of it until a day finally came when the moon disappeared.

"The world despaired. Our hero had lost! But that wasn't the case. He waited for night to fall, and just as the last ray of day shot out from the horizon, he used his mirrors to direct it into the heavens, revealing the moon was there all along. People simply couldn't see it. Her trick revealed, the moon god gave up, and our hero prevailed."

"Wow," Sorin said, breathlessly.

"However," Loric explained as the image of the great warrior vanished, "his victory, like all victories, came with a price. Before he vanquished the moon god, she took sleep from him, and for the rest of his life, when others rested peacefully, he was forced to stay awake, watching the moon as it glared at him from the heavens. Only on the twenty-ninth day, when the moon grew dark, could he rest."

The archer shivered. "That's a spooky story. You know, he looks a lot like that statue we saw where Landon got his stone. Was his name Albr'en Dog?"

"How do you know the statue's name?" Landon asked. I didn't see a plaque.

"I'd rather not say. Thea might get mad at me."

"No," Loric answered the archer, "but it wouldn't surprise me if Albr'en made his statue look like our hero. Many leaders like to do that kind of thing."

"Yeah, he was probably some scrawny dude with a pockmarked complexion. So what was his name?"

Loric doused the candle and picked up his crystal. "I don't know. No one does. Our hero lost his name in a battle with Mangala, the god of people's inner fire." The wizard sat on the ground to rest.

"You can't leave me hanging like that!" Sorin said, throwing up his hands. "Tell us about Mangala!"

The soft sound of Loric snoring told everyone that storytime was over.

Resigned to not hearing what the rest of the runes stood for, Sorin told Anslim and Braydn, "I imagine Thea will pray a while longer. Now's your chance to do a little treasure hunting."

"No thanks," Braydn said. "I have no desire to get lost in this place."

Anslim agreed, so they waited for Loric to wake and Thea to finish.

"Praise be to the Light," the cleric said, standing up.

Loric awakened with a start. "Oh, yes. Is it time?" he asked the cleric.

She nodded.

Landon looked perplexed. "Time for what?"

"For you to take The Glyphblade, of course," the wizard said, groaning as Thea helped him off the ground. "It awaits the bearer."

"Maybe this would be a good time to remind everyone that we were promised treasure, and that definitely fits the bill," Braydn said, sounding put out.

"You didn't find this," Thea corrected. "Landon did. And, in point of fact, he's the rightful person to carry it."

"Why me?" Landon asked, looking at his calloused hands. "I'm no warrior. I'm a woodcutter."

Sorin clapped him on the back. "I see where she's going with this. You have the strength. No one doubts that. But you also have skill with an axe. Not to mention, you're straight as an arrow if you take my meaning. No offense."

Landon glanced at the others, but no one offered any additional guidance.

"Sorin's words are crude but true," Thea said, sounding less than pleased. Wielding such a noble weapon should be a solemn affair. This was *not* a time for jokes.

Sorin smiled. "Thank you."

"It wasn't a compliment."

"Oh."

Landon decided the only opinion that mattered was that of Reinier, so he knelt on one knee and looked the wolfhound in his golden eyes. "What do you think, boy? Should I take it?"

Reinier licked Landon's nose, which the woodcutter took to mean, *Yes*.

"Okay, then," he said, handing his torch to Anslim and limbering up the way an athlete prepares for a contest.

However, before he did anything, Braydn stepped between him and the casket and reached for the sword. When the rogue's skin touched the hilt, a spark of electricity jolted his fingers, and he yelped.

Sorin snorted. "Tsk, tsk. Thea's always warning me about traps and stuff. You should heed her advice."

"That was no trap," the cleric said, inspecting Braydn's hand to see if the burn needed tending. "You aren't worthy."

Braydn pulled his hand back. "Exactly what does that mean?"

Thea looked into the rogue's eyes and repeated, "You aren't worthy."

Braydn laughed it off, but it was apparent to everyone that he was shaken. "Yeah, I should've checked for traps. It's the first rule of the trade." Turning to Landon, he added, "Your turn, if you dare."

The woodcutter didn't like the idea of trying, but maybe this was connected to the vision he'd seen at Esslla's, or the stone, or something else he didn't understand. It was worth a shot. That, and Braydn didn't die when he touched it, so it must not be too dangerous.

The tension in the cave could be cut with a knife as Landon stood there wringing his hands. Finally, he reached for the sword, and Thea touched his arm. Anticipating a shock, Landon jumped. "Don't do that! You scared the life out of me."

"Are you sure we want someone so high-strung flailing that thing about?" Anslim asked under his breath.

"It's always wise to be cautious with wondrous magical items, especially weapons," Loric said in a thoughtful tone.

Thea stepped back. "Be pure of heart, Landon Quilson, and the sword will accept you."

When the woodcutter reached for the hilt this time, the stone carving's hands moved out of the way.

Sorin gasped. "Is stone supposed to do that?"

"Enchanted stone does whatever it wants," Loric explained.

"I'm never going to look at sculptures the same way again. Is it possible for one of those things to come to life and attack us?"

"It's been known to happen."

The archer gulped.

Screwing up his courage, Landon gripped the hilt. Magic surged through his body, and he sucked in air. He could feel the sword's energy, almost like the low rumble of an earthquake. Lifting the Glyphblade, he noticed that even though it was a full-sized weapon made of steel, it had no weight, and he swung it around.

Sorin jumped out of the way. "Hey, watch it!"

Landon smiled. He liked holding the Glyphblade. It made him feel confident in a way he'd never experienced in his life. Then a burning sensation told him the stone was singing again. Pulling it out of his pocket and tossing it around like a hot potato, he noticed that it glowed brighter every time it neared the sword.

Sorin's keen eyes saw why. "There's a place for it in the crossguard. See?"

Landon did indeed see, and when he brought the stone close to the sword, it leapt from his hand and embedded itself in the space from which it had undoubtedly been taken in the first place. Instantly, the runes glowed brightly and then faded.

"You *are* worthy," Thea said, bowing her head.

The light around them flickered, and Loric said, "I believe it's time to go."

"Why?" Sorin asked. "Maybe there's other stuff in here."

"Because the reveal spell is fading."

"What will happen when it ends?"

Loric thought about this for a second or two and said, "I guess we'd be trapped in the cave until someone else revealed it."

"Would that be a long time?"

"If the stories about the Glyphblade are true, a thousand years or so."

The archer's eyes grew wide, and he pushed to the front of the party. "Pardon me. Person who doesn't want to be trapped in a magical cave for a thousand years coming through."

20 BETRAYAL

As the days passed, the oppressive fog enveloping the Westrin Road thickened around Landon and his companions. Somehow, obtaining the Glyphblade had elevated his status in their group, whether he wanted it or not, and the misty isolation gave him plenty of time to contemplate his new role as a leader of sorts. However, no matter how hard he tried, he couldn't think of a reason why anyone should look to him for guidance. What's more, ever since he'd started carrying the Glyphblade, his dreams had come clearly into view—horrible visions of him battling great foes, gods even, and every morning he woke up exhausted as if he'd actually been wielding the sword. The worst part of the dreams was the fire. Lots and lots of fire, which only served to make him think of the Leering Ones and the loss of his father. The more he considered this, the more he began to worry that it wasn't Sorin's ring that was cursed, but the sword hanging by his side.

Still, a small part of Landon liked it. He'd never known anything other than the life of a peasant, and it was nice to have people look up to him for a change. The question was, would he be up for the challenge when the going got tough? He didn't know, and that was what concerned him the most.

As if on cue, the party stopped moving because the fog became so impenetrable that the road vanished at their feet.

"I can't see anything," Sorin said. "And that's saying something."

Thea cleared her throat. "Modest as always."

"Hey, it's true."

"No one doubts it," Landon agreed, "but reminding us of how good your vision is doesn't help, either."

Sorin rolled his eyes, not that anyone could see him, as everyone had been reduced to semi-vacuous shapes. "Does anyone else feel strange?"

"What do you mean?" Anslim asked.

"Like we're being watched."

Landon turned toward the shape he assumed was Sorin. "In this?"

"There are many ways to watch people that don't require eyes," Loric said, sending a shiver down everyone's spine.

Sorin laughed out loud. "Now we've got two people who like to make things sound worse than they are."

"I'm not sure that would be possible," Thea added, ending Sorin's nervous banter.

Anslim took a more pragmatic approach. "If we continue, we risk losing our way or worse, falling into the Brownwater. I say we make camp until we can see where we're going."

"I don't mean to contradict you, young man," Loric said politely, "but it would be my suggestion to keep moving. I fear this weather may not be natural."

"Wait. Look over there," Landon said, pointing into the mist.

A series of faint lights shimmered in the distance, and Thea's face lit with joy. "The Light is showing us the way!

Praise be the Light!" she exclaimed, hiking up her robes and running toward the glowing orbs.

"Thea, wait!" Sorin yelled, racing after her. "We don't know what's out there."

"Will-o'-the-wisps," Loric muttered knowingly. "Tricksy things, they are. We must retrieve our friends before we're separated."

But the damage was done.

"Reinier!" Landon commanded. "Lead us to Thea."

Barking loudly, the wolfhound shot into the fog.

"Okay, everyone. Follow Reinier."

When they caught up to Sorin and Thea, he was holding onto her robes, but he couldn't keep her from chasing after the lights.

Loric wore a worried expression. "She's mesmerized."

"By will-o'-the-wisps?" Landon asked.

"No. It's a spell. In combination with the lights, it can be very powerful."

"But Thea wouldn't fall for a trick like that," Sorin insisted.

"Spells such as *Mesmerize* are insidious. If someone knows what you fear or desire, they can trick almost anyone."

"Like someone who worships the Light in a dark place?" Landon asked.

"Precisely."

"Can you help her?"

"Yes. I'm embarrassed to say this kind of thing used to be my specialty." Taking a small pouch out of his pocket, he pulled on the string and reached inside with his first two fingers and thumb.

Sorin noted that this time, the pouch was made of silk, not leather. "What's that?"

"Think of it like magical smelling salts. Hold her still."

Landon took one of her arms. "She's pretty strong!"

"You're telling me," Sorin agreed. "She's been dragging me all over the place."

"One more second, and…" After placing the dust on the palm of his outstretched hand, Loric blew.

A shimmering cloud enveloped Thea's eyes, nose, and mouth, and she snapped out of the trance. "What happened? Why are you holding me?"

Landon and Sorin immediately let go.

"Someone mesmerized you, my dear. Do you remember the lights?" the wizard asked.

Landon pointed into the distance. "Hey, where did they go?"

"The spell is broken."

"Yes, I think so," the cleric said. "Everything's a little fuzzy."

Loric took her hand. "It will take some time for the effects to wear off. Let's get back to the road."

"Over there!" Sorin yelled, reaching for his bow as several Leering Ones lumbered jerkily out of the fog with their horrifying sunken faces and eyeless holes.

"Just as I feared," the wizard said, stepping in front of Thea to protect her in her weakened state. "It was a trap."

Sorin nimbly dodged the nearest creature's attack and let an arrow take flight. It struck its mark, and the Leering One fell, but the black ooze that seeped out where the arrow had pierced the creature's body congealed into a shadowy wraith.

"Look out!" Anslim warned. "The shadows don't perish with the body."

Landon knew what was happening. "There's no sunlight to dispel them!"

The journeyman threw a dagger, striking one of the monsters in the heart. As with Sorin's kill, a shadow oozed out of its body, too. "Then how do we kill them?"

Sorin raised his bow but faltered. He felt a malevolent force hovering near him, but his eyes wouldn't focus on it. Shaking his head, he looked again, but his eyes failed him a second time. The amorphous black haze was about to envelop him when a glowing spherical enclosure sprang up, and the shadow was repelled.

"I think Volgreth is here. Or maybe inside one of those things," the archer said, breathing heavily. "Is that possible?"

"How clever," Loric said, thoughtfully. "He has created a vessel that makes it possible for creatures of the darkness to walk in the light."

"Clever wasn't the word I was thinking!" Sorin said, loosing another arrow because although Thea's spell kept the shadows at bay, the Leering Ones continued to advance. "Landon, use the Glyphblade!"

"Right!" The woodcutter reached for the sword, but his hand went straight through the hilt. "I don't understand. It's right there, but I can't grab it!"

"A simple cantrip," Loric explained as if they weren't in the midst of being attacked. "They're quite popular with mountebanks. If the caster is skilled enough, they might use a rudimentary substitution spell to take an object without touching it. Then, they replace it with an image that looks like the original item. I'm afraid what you see is no more than a projection. If you find a coin in the scabbard, that would prove the use of such a spell. That is what is usually used for the swap. It's rather impertinent if you ask me."

"Who would do such a thing?" Landon asked. "Sound off!"

"Here!" yelled Sorin, his bow twanging time and time again.

"Here!" said Thea, Anslim, and Loric.

Even Reinier barked.

"Braydn!" Landon hissed.

Sorin spat on the ground. "That traitorous rogue! He's lucky I'm almost out of arrows again!"

"Focus," Anslim said. "Ten o'clock!"

Sorin let an arrow soar, releasing another shadow from a Leering One, only this time, the specter almost made it through the shield before evaporating in its light. "How did that happen?"

"Thea hasn't recovered her strength. The shield is failing," Loric said, adding radiance to the incantation.

Landon hurled his broken axe. It embedded itself in the Leering One's shoulder, but the monster didn't seem to notice. "We have to get out of here."

A sound so indescribable that he never forgot it the rest of his life emanated from nearby, and he forced himself to turn. *Don't make me look!* his mind screamed, rebelling against his body, but he had to see what was happening.

There, near the other side of the glowing dome, Loric was being consumed by a Leering one.

"Oh, no! Loric!

The wizard was still protecting Thea, but one of the creatures had him by the shoulders. Its mouth was open unnaturally wide, and it was vomiting a cloud of shadowy tendrils into the wizard. Landon tried to help, but Reinier latched onto his belt and pulled him in the other direction.

As the shadow seeped into their friend with chilling fluidity, it drained his life force. The wizard's eyes rolled back into his head, leaving vacant darkness, and the skin on his gaunt face tightened the way a wet cloth clings to the shape of one's naked body, revealing the shape of his skull.

Before the woodcutter's eyes, Loric was transformed into a Leering One. No longer did he wonder how Volgreth created his evil army. He knew.

Reinier barked, and Landon came to his senses.

Like a moth to a flame, the released shadows and Leering Ones converged on Loric, drawn to Volgreth's power.

As he watched the horror unfolding in front of them, Landon caught sight of Loric's contorted hand. It was...was... casting a spell! "Duck!"

A bright streak jutted from the wizard's finger, blossoming with a roar into an explosion of flame, and several Leering Ones were engulfed before Loric succumbed to the Shadehaunter's magic.

The burst of fire jolted Thea out of her daze. Finally comprehending what was happening, she screamed, releasing a wave of Light that knocked the monsters off their feet and dispelling the shadows feeding on their friend.

"Now!" Landon yelled. "Run!"

With no shelter in sight, what was left of their party—Landon, Sorin, Thea, Anslim, and Reinier—plunged deeper into the murk.

Lighting torches, they ran the rest of the day and night until the morning sun burned off the worst of the billowing fog, leaving them breathless and lost in the desolate void of the Kahr'anis plains.

21 REINIER

By the time day bothered to lift its weary head, the Leering Ones' shrieks had faded into the mist, leaving only gray, eerie silence.

Clutching at her chest, Thea stumbled. "Wait. Please. I must rest."

But Landon had no intention of stopping. "Not yet. The more distance we put between us and those things, the better."

"Hold on," Anslim said, taking one of Thea's arms and helping her sit on the ground. "I haven't heard them for at least an hour."

"None of us heard them before they attacked, either," Landon insisted, still in the throes of fight-or-flight mode.

Anslim flopped beside the cleric. "I don't deny it, but Thea's not the only one who needs rest."

As the minutes passed, the fog continued to lift, as much as it ever did in Kahr'anis, yet Landon couldn't see a single defining feature in any direction. The desolation of the plains was absolute, and aptly reflected how he felt inside.

Unable to keep his emotions in check a second longer, he leaned his head back and screamed at the sky. Sensing his master's pain, Reinier howled along with him, but no one but their companions heard their wailing. No sound traveled across Kahr'anis' stagnant air, and the gutwrenching melody dissipated nearly as soon as it left their throats.

When they stopped, it was like they'd never begun in the first place. The plains didn't care. It had heard generations of death knells uttered by wayward travelers. Sometimes they came as shouts or curses, but just as often they were nothing more than whimpers, the last utterances of inconsequential ends.

"Is our quest over before it began?" Landon asked, getting his breath back. "Shall we lay down our bodies and let them rot away, leaving our bones to lie undisturbed forever?"

"My, you're morbid," Anslim said, lighting his pipe. "And, in point of fact, have you ever seen a rotting body on the plains?"

The journeyman's question gave Landon pause. "No, I guess not."

"And bones? Have you seen any of those? Has Reinier sniffed any out to pass the time by gnawing on one?"

Landon stared blankly ahead. Considering all the stories of people dying on the plains, it was strange that they hadn't seen a hint of such things happening beyond the one unlucky soul taken by the Brownwater.

"He's got a point," Sorin said, patting the wolfhound on the back. "I've heard near-constant stories about people dying on the plains, but where are the bodies? Maybe it isn't as dangerous as they say after all."

Anslim chuckled. "Or the reason we haven't seen any is too horrible to imagine."

Sorin gulped.

"This is why we need to keep our energy up and our wits about us. None of us knows what we'll encounter out here, in the wilds."

Sorin moved a little closer to the journeyman. "He's right. I suggest we stick together."

Regardless of whether Anslim was trying to make a point or simply jolt him out of his doldrums, Landon wasn't ready to put aside his agony. "Fine, but that doesn't answer the question of why we let a rogue come with us in the first place. Of course, he was going to betray us! It's what he does!"

"We accepted his help because we felt we needed it," Thea said calmly.

"Maybe we should have chosen more wisely."

"Perhaps, but that might not have been possible under any circumstances. Might I remind you, we barely know each other as it is."

"How do you mean?" Landon asked, spinning around.

"If we had to take the time to get to know each other in any meaningful way, we may never have started in the first place. We must accept that trust, well-placed or misplaced, is a necessity of the situation we find ourselves in."

"What he's trying to say without actually speaking the words is that he blames me," Sorin mumbled. "I was the one who suggested inviting Braydn; therefore, what happened is my fault."

Thea grew indignant. "What happened was most certainly *not* your fault. It isn't anyone's fault."

"Not to contradict, but it was technically Braydn's fault," Anslim added.

The cleric gave him a withering look.

"Okay, if you're all so smart, tell me this," Landon asked. "What was the point of going to Endog? We've already lost two of the three people we found, and we haven't even made it to the mountains."

"I guess the odds don't look good for me," Anslim said, exhaling a smoke ring that floated into the air.

"Don't listen to him," Sorin said, nudging Anslim. "He's just ranting."

Landon was incensed. "What do you mean? That was a serious question!"

As his master and the others shouted about Braydn and Loric's loss, Reinier whimpered and padded away, tail between his legs. The woodcutter didn't even notice him leave.

"What exactly are you proposing that we do?" Sorin asked, trying to make sense of the discussion. "Give up?"

Landon, who was now pacing frantically back and forth, looked like he was about to explode. "I'm just saying that without the Glyphblade, we don't have the strength to face Volgreth. You saw what happened to Loric!"

"You speak as if we're out of danger," the journeyman said, also getting to his feet. "We don't need to search out the Shadehaunter to find peril. Stop wasting your energy yelling about what can't be changed. The dead are dead. It's time we focus on the living."

Sorin, who'd been pingponging between sides, clapped a hand to his forehead. "That's pretty callous."

"Not at all. It's practical. The cleric will pray for the wizard when we're off these gods-forsaken plains. And if we're lucky, he'll be the only member of our party in her prayers."

"Oh, I don't know. Braydn can join him for all I care!" Landon said with fury in his words.

"No!" Thea shouted, struggling to her feet. "If we think that way, we're no better than the evil we're trying to eliminate from the valley."

"But, he—"

"Absolutely not!"

"Can we get back on track?" Anslim asked. "If we are to recover the sword, we need information."

Landon scoffed at the suggestion. "There's nothing here. Are you suggesting we talk to the grass?"

"Answers are closer than you think, Mucklucker."

"I've had enough of this guy!" the woodcutter bellowed.

"Calm yourself, young Landon," an unfamiliar voice interjected.

"What? Huh? Who said that?" Landon looked to each of his companions. "Sorin, are you messing with me?"

The archer shook his head.

"Thea?"

Whirling around, he asked. "Okay, enough of this. Who spoke to me?"

"I did."

With the sensation of time slowing down, one by one, Landon, Sorin, Thea, and finally Anslim turned toward Reinier.

"Volgreth has possessed Reinier! Quick. Thea, pray to the Light!" the woodcutter screamed, lunging at the wolfhound.

"Wait, Landon!" Thea said, trying to block him.

Sorin and Anslim grabbed his arms, but even together, they were no match for his strength. Landon shook them off and squared his body.

Standing there, sweat pouring down his face and breathing like a bull about to charge, he snarled, "What is the trickery? What have you done with Reinier?"

The wolfhound sat, calmly staring back at him. "Do you not recognize your friend?"

"By the Gods if you've hurt him, I'll—"

"What? I'd like to know, because the Landon I watched grow up from a little boy is not the Landon who stands before me."

"That's not my fault! Volgreth took everything from me!"

"Everything?"

The question hung in the heavy Kahr'anis air.

Flustered and suffering, Landon stuttered, "But dogs can't speak!"

Reinier cocked an eyebrow. "I am no dog."

"What do you mean?"

"Exactly what I said."

The woodcutter fell to one knee. "Please. I can't take it anymore. No more riddles."

"No, my friend. No more riddles. No more secrets. No more silence."

Reinier got to his feet, and right before their eyes, he transformed. The dog's fur disappeared, revealing silky smooth skin. His limbs elongated, taking on the shape of arms and legs. And his long nose receded, leaving a comely woman with flowing brown hair. The only things that remained the same were her golden eyes.

"By the Light," Thea gasped, lighting a candle and kneeling to pray.

Sorin whistled. "Once I get a beer or two in me at the pub, I'm going to have one awesome story to tell. Heck, I won't even need a beer. This story's going to be great even without being drunk."

Thea hissed. "Behave!"

Landon's heart pounded so hard he heard it in his ears. "Where have you gone, my friend? Have you left me, too? Now, I have truly lost everyone."

"No, Landon. You haven't lost me," Reinier said, her human voice as gentle as a summer breeze. "You have found me."

"I don't understand."

"That makes two of us," Sorin whispered under his breath.

Reinier smoothed her silky hair, feeling it between her fingers for the first time since she'd transformed all those years ago. "I'm a shapeshifter."

"Then, I was right," Landon said, feeling the anger rise again. "You're a sorcerer like Volgreth."

"Shapeshifting isn't a spell. I was born this way, as are all of my people."

"Impossible! My father would have told me."

"Your father didn't know. It was your mother who sent me to protect you. Like Esslla, she was a mystic, and I was her apprentice before Volgreth stole her life."

Thea clenched her fists. "I knew it."

"You knew Volgreth killed my mother?" the woodcutter asked.

"No. That you have the Light in you. I've always sensed it, but wasn't sure until now."

Landon wobbled and then fell to all fours. "But none of this makes sense. A mystic? Father said she succumbed to illness."

Reinier looked kindly at the woodcutter. "How could he tell you? You were just a boy."

Landon's swaying grew erratic, and Sorin knelt beside him, placing a hand on the woodcutter's shoulder to keep him from collapsing. The wolfhound had been the pillar on which Landon had steadied his entire life. Now, after having lost his home and everyone he loved, he was losing his best friend, too.

When Landon lifted his gaze, he finally saw past the shock and horror of hearing about Volgreth's involvement in his mother's death and fully realized that, rather than his loyal wolfhound, a person stood before him.

"But you're a...a..."

Reinier surveyed her delicate female body. It was quite different than the muscular male wolfhound shape she'd adopted for so long, and she chuckled. "A woman. Yes. And I believe it is customary to cover one's body in these parts."

"Yes, of course!" Thea said, rummaging through her satchel. After a few seconds, she produced a spare set of robes. "Please, take these."

With a hand shielding his eyes, Sorin asked the journeyman, "Did you know?"

For the first time since their meeting in *The Last Stop Watering Hole*, the journeyman looked entirely out of his depth. "I had no idea."

As they talked, Thea draped the fabric over Reinier's thin frame.

The robes hung off the shapeshifter like a tent, but she looked grateful nevertheless. "Thank you, Thea. May the Light shine upon you."

"I have many questions," the cleric said. "About Landon's mother and your apprenticeship in my order."

"In time, all questions will be answered."

"Um?" Landon grunted.

Reinier turned toward him, and the woodcutter looked at the ground again.

"Is Reinier your real name?" he asked.

"It is."

"But how do we know you're telling the truth?"

The party had gotten used to Landon's near-constant state of being on edge, and the sincerity of his voice surprised them.

"I mean, maybe you took the place of my dog," he continued, "the way Braydn switched my sword with a coin? And how do I know my mother sent you? Maybe you're Volgreth in disguise. I don't see how you can expect me to take you at your word with everything that has happened."

Reinier's eyes glistened with sorrow. "I could tell you stories of your youth, but you would say I heard them from someone or read your mind. I could tell you of long, happy hours studying with your mother, but you would say I made it up. All I can offer is myself. Shapeshifters choose an animal and rarely reveal their birth form to others. This, I have done for you. My secret is yours. I offer it as a sign of my truthfulness and loyalty."

This was not the answer Landon longed to hear. "Truthfulness and loyalty? How can you say that after deceiving me my entire life?"

"It was not my intent to deceive you."

"But you did!"

"I suppose so."

"I'll never trust anyone ever again. The only thing that matters now is making Volgreth pay for what he's done!"

"Landon, please don't say things like that," Thea said. "Seeking to rid Kahr'anis of evil for the good of all people is one thing, but vowing personal vengeance is not the way of the Light. Do not stray from the path."

"He's shaking," Anslim said, regaining his composure. "He's in shock. We need to find shelter and make a plan. When he comes to his senses, if he still wants to seek vengeance on Volgreth, that's his business. I couldn't care less, as long as it doesn't get me killed, but that's for later. Right now, we're sitting ducks. We need to get off the plains and figure out how to get the Glyphblade back."

Sorin helped Landon to his feet. "That's all fine and good, but we don't know where we are."

"Speak for yourself."

That got everyone's attention.

The red glow of Anslim's pipe looked out of place against the grayness of the flatlands. "The plains hold many secrets. One of which, I imagine, will lead us right to our erstwhile friend."

Sorin wasn't impressed. "I thought we said we were done with riddles?"

"It's no riddle. Stay here if you want. I'm sure the Leering Ones will be back sooner or later and would be delighted to find you here alone. As for me, I'm going to find shelter.

Sorin thought about this for a moment and then said, "Ho, now! Let's not be hasty. I'm willing to give you a chance to prove yourself."

"Then help your friend and try to keep up."

Landon took only one step before finding himself face-to-face with Reinier. "I can't," he whispered. "I can't deal with this right now."

Without saying a word, the shapeshifter changed back into her dog form.

22 A Hole in the Ground

For the first time since leaving Brownwater, Landon found himself trailing the pack. It's not that he'd wanted to be in the lead before; it had just happened. He was handy with an axe, true enough, but he hadn't been much help when faced with Volgreth's evil minions, and never having left his village meant he had no idea how to get where they were going.

True, like Thea, Landon knew his letters, but that didn't make him half as knowledgeable as the cleric. And if a keen eye and deadly aim were the mark of a true leader, Sorin was the better choice, though, imagining the expert marksman bossing Thea around made the edges of Landon's lips curl into a smile.

"That would never happen," he whispered, chuckling to himself. "What about Anslim? Maybe. He seems to know his way around."

The journeyman had proved himself to be plains-savvy, which was undeniably more valuable than a cartload of centimes, but something in the back of Landon's mind made him cautious about putting too much faith in their pipe-smoking companion. So what had elevated Landon to the front of the pack?

"I'm large," he mumbled. "That's all. It was just a case of putting the big guy first."

However, that wasn't strictly true, and Landon knew it. When he'd acquired the fabled Glyphblade, he really had been anointed their leader. It didn't matter that he didn't know how to use it. One of the greatest mythological weapons of old had chosen him to be its bearer. How cool was that? It had felt good for as long as it lasted, but that was the problem. It hadn't lasted very long.

The woodcutter's initial shock at Braydn's betrayal had passed, but a sadness had settled over him as thick as the stagnant gloom that blanketed the Kahr'anis plains. Now, he was being led around like, say, a dog on a leash, and he didn't like it, not in the least.

Sensing his master's suffering, Reinier nuzzled his leg, and Landon instinctively patted the wolfhound's head. When he realized what he was doing, he jerked his hand back. He'd just patted a woman on the head! But had he? Reinier looked like the same old wolfhound he'd known and loved, but under that wiry coat, he knew a woman lurked inside, hidden from view. The more the woodcutter thought about it, the more confused he became. Reinier was a he-dog at the moment. Did that mean *he* wasn't a *she* anymore?

"I mean, he's a *he* on the outside. I can see that," Landon thought, "but is he a *she* inside?"

He stared at the wolfhound trotting along beside him. No answer presented itself, but that didn't put an end to the woodcutter's curiosity. What about the wolfhound's heightened senses? Did s/he retain those senses when s/he wasn't a dog?

Rocked by a sudden revelation, Landon stopped moving.

What if Reinier was still a human inside when s/he looked like a dog? And, because of him, s/he'd been stuck under a wolfhound's matted fur for years on end, forced to hide her true self for a lifetime!

Landon instinctively reached out to comfort his companion, but hesitated. He contemplated asking if it was okay to pet him...her...them...but he was so afraid Reinier might speak again that he let it lie. That's what you were supposed to do with dogs, right?

An odd sensation washed over him, and he noticed Reinier looking at him. "I—"

The wolfhound cocked an eyebrow, as if to ask, *Yes? I'm listening.*

But the words got stuck in the woodcutter's throat, and he said no more.

Reinier stared at him for a few seconds before padding off to walk alongside Thea. She had no reservations about scratching behind his ears.

• • •

Usually a keen observer, Sorin was oblivious to Landon's inner struggle. As far as he was concerned, Reinier had always been awesome. Learning that the wolfhound was also a shapeshifting mystic only served to elevate his cool factor past *super cool* to *ultra mega cool*. But no matter how great Reinier was, it didn't change the fact that the archer was damp, had been walking for days through soupy fog, and had a terrific hankering for steak and a beer. He didn't even care if it was some unknown mystery meat masquerading as a pig. He'd hold his nose to tamp down his gag reflex if it came to that. Anything but more fog!

"Are we there yet?" he asked, sounding like a small child in the back of a cart.

"Patience," Anslim responded, not turning round.

That, Sorin thought, was easier said than done because the archer's stomach wasn't the only thing gnawing at him. Ever since Braydn's betrayal, he'd found himself questioning if the sole remaining newcomer could be trusted. He wasn't the only member of their party who felt that way, either. Landon, Thea, and Reinier all appeared to be keeping a wary eye on the journeyman.

It wasn't that the rest of them had known each other much longer—except for Landon and Reinier, though that relationship had entered a new and unforeseen phase—but that the four of them shared an unspoken bond born of Alderbeasts, woodland fortresses, Leering Ones, and Esslla's earthen home. Consequently, a persistent question pushed uncomfortably on his midsection: Had Anslim proven himself worthy of the same level of trust? The journeyman had helped defend them from the Leering Ones, which was good, but that could have had as much to do with saving his own skin as protecting the group.

Shocked out of his thoughts when Anslim stopped for no apparent reason, Sorin instinctively reached for an arrow.

"There's no need for that," the journeyman said, not turning around. "It's not one of Thea's booby traps."

Landon and Sorin exchanged a glance. Together, they looked at Thea, who shrugged.

"There's no treachery here," he continued. "We've arrived at our destination. Or, should I say, the entrance to our destination."

The arrow's slender shaft remained clasped between Sorin's fingers. "What are you talking about? There's nothing but grass and dirt here."

"Are you telling me those keen archer's eyes have failed you? It must be better hidden than I thought."

"What is?"

Anslim stamped on the ground. To everyone's surprise, the ground thumped back.

"Welcome to Moors Hollow," he said, motioning for everyone to step back.

Sorin was about to ask what the journeyman was playing at when a large opening appeared in the plains. "I didn't expect that. No, I really didn't expect that."

"In you go," Anslim said, climbing onto the ladder, but the archer didn't follow.

Instead, Sorin took another step back, remembering the last hole they'd encountered contained a giant centipede. "Am I the only one who thinks going underground is the last place we should be with the Shadehaunter on the prowl?"

The journeyman stopped climbing. "Maybe that's why it exists in the first place. Did you ever think about that?"

"I'm just saying, I've had my fill of tunnels. The first one was fine because it got us out of that rotten fortress. But getting out of the second one, the one with the Glyphblade, wasn't much more than luck as far as I see it. So, why tempt fate a third time?"

"It's your choice," Anslim's voice echoed from below. "But if you don't get a move on, you're going to lose the chance to find out."

Sorin tried to muster support from his companions, but they were already heading for the ladder. "I'm telling you, I don't like it."

"He's had plenty of opportunities to stab us in the back," Thea said as she descended. "And without the Glyphblade, it's not like we have anything of value for anyone to steal from us."

"You're not wrong, I guess, but I'm lighting a torch."

The cleric pointed into the gloom. "It appears they've already thought of that."

The archer got down on his hands and knees and peered into the hole a second time. Sure enough, a tremulous glow emanated from the tunnel. "That doesn't look like the whatchamacallit spell."

"That's because it isn't an incantation. Whatever it is, it's bioluminescent," Thea explained, having seen similar plants and creatures before in her travels.

"What does that mean?"

"It's alive."

"You've got to be kidding me. Can this get any worse?"

The cleric shot him a sharp glance. "Shh! Don't say things like that."

"Right. Sorry. My bad."

After Thea and Sorin descended, Landon climbed into the hole. A soft whine came from above, and he looked up. A little dirt rained down as Reinier nervously paced along the edge. Every time he put a paw on the ladder, he pulled it back again and whined.

Landon almost said, *Why don't you transform and climb down yourself?* but he remembered that one: shapeshifters didn't like to reveal their true nature, and two, it meant s/he'd have to become a woman again, so he sucked it up and said, "Come."

Landon felt the dog's tail joyfully thump against his side as he carried Reinier down the ladder draped across his broad shoulders.

"Just like old times, eh?" the wolfhound said in his gravelly voice.

Landon almost slipped. "You aren't going to make this easy on me, are you?"

Reinier woofed, but it sounded a lot like, *Nope.*

23 CUSTOMS

"This place isn't so bad," Sorin said, kicking the sticky plains dirt off his shoes. "I was afraid we were going to—"

Someone tapped him on the shoulder with a finger so heavy he thought a lump of clay had broken loose from the ceiling and landed on him.

"Hey! What's the big idea?" he asked, spinning around and coming face to belly button with the largest man he'd ever seen in his life. "Ah! Troll!"

Anslim deftly clapped a hand over the archer's mouth. "Ignore him. He's excitable."

"Mum hum mum-a-mum hum," was all Sorin managed to say through the journeyman's fingers, but he continued to point animatedly at the hatch keeper.

The man grunted and held out a shovel-like hand. Anslim obliged by dropping a few coins onto it. One by one, the man used an elephantine finger to count them. Eventually satisfied they added up to whatever he'd expected, he grunted again and stepped out of the way.

Sorin finally stopped mumbling and flailing, but stood there looking puzzled by the man's appearance. His scruffy, bearded face and dirty clothing appeared to be out of a bygone age when swashbucklers sailed the high seas. Though they looked like they'd shrunk in the wash, leaving his belly hanging out. As far as the archer knew, there were no oceans nearby, so what was with the getup? In the end, he thought it best not to ask.

In addition to his strange clothing, the hatch keeper leaned a long pole with a peculiar brass hook on the end against his shoulder and wore a glowing necklace tied around the short stump that passed as his neck. "You go there!" he thundered, his voice booming in the cavernous tunnel.

Sorin didn't even have time to ask, "Huh?" Before he was shoved onto a platform that dangled precariously over a shaft. He saw timber beams holding the sides of the shaft at bay, and a thick hemp rope trailing off into the distance below them. "Are you sure this will hold all of us?"

The troll-ish man gave a dangerous-looking smile full of rotted teeth and pushed an iron lever. There was a jolt, and the platform descended into the earth. The only thing the archer saw beyond beams and dirt was a slimy, glowing ooze. He knew he should be thankful for the light it produced, but he wished Loric were here to do his mirror spell to make it brighter.

The shaft wasn't nearly as long as it had first appeared, and in a few seconds, the party was standing in a large, slimy cavern. Sorin shivered. He didn't like the way the glowing goo slurped and squished as it flowed over the rocks.

"Customs," Anslim said, pointing to rows of desks.

The archer's eyes went wide. He hadn't counted on being interrogated.

The journeyman took a seat at the closest desk. "You didn't think they'd let us saunter in here without checking us out first, did you?"

Sorin couldn't remember what had been going through his mind as he stood on the desolate plains, looking into the hole that had appeared at his feet at Anslim's stamp, but it wasn't this.

"This way," an irritable man said, guiding the archer to the back of the cavern.

Bizarrely, the man had a glowing jar strapped to the front of his chest. In fact, Sorin noticed everyone wore something that glowed, even the bundle of cloth piled on the chair beside him.

"Hoo!" he yelped, sounding like a surprised owl.

There was an ancient woman in the middle of the pile, snoring gently with a glass vial tied to her forehead with a bit of string. Doing his best not to stare, he focused on the soft murmur of agents talking to their clients, which, in this case, meant Landon and Reinier, Thea, and Anslim. That's when he realized no one was talking to him.

He almost got up to ask if anyone was coming when a rickety wooden door opened, and another so-called agent wearing a mishmash of clothing stumbled out, buttoning his trousers as he walked. The man was followed by a cloud of stench that made Sorin turn a putrid shade of greenish-yellow.

"That's better," the agent said, sighing as he sat down. "Nothing like the daily constitutional to cleanse the soul, eh?"

Sorin didn't respond because he was too busy holding his breath, not that Gerff (which was the man's name, according to the plaque on his desk) was looking for a response. Sorin got the impression the customs agent had this conversation with himself on a daily basis.

Gerff pulled out a pad and pencil from a drawer in the desk, sat back, and asked, "What's your business in Moors Hollow?"

The archers' blood ran cold. Thea hadn't told him what to say in situations like this. But being too nervous to hold his tongue, he blurted the first thing that came to mind. "Pith extraction and collection."

The agent stared at him for a second and burst out laughing. "If that weren't so ridiculous, I'd think you were pulling my leg. And your friends. Are they pith extractors, too?" he asked, pointing toward Anslim and the others.

"Oh, them? We just happened to arrive at the same time. We're not together."

"The archer over there?" Landon asked loudly. "That's Sorin. He's with us."

Sorin turned green a second time.

Gerff reached for a large stamp with the word *rejected* written backwards in large, bold letters, and the archer stuck out his hand. "Wait."

The agent paused.

"I promise. I'm not pulling your leg. I do know them, I just don't *know* them, if you know what I mean?"

Gerff put down the stamp. "This oughta be good."

"We met on the Westrin Road. Well, technically, at Endog, and before. You know how it is. You start walking, and you accumulate people."

"Go on."

Thinking he was getting somewhere, Sorin gained some confidence and continued. "And since we were all traveling north, our feet took us in the same direction. Besides, why wouldn't they want to travel with me? I'm on the leading edge of a burgeoning industry."

"Pith extraction?"

"Precisely. Now, I know what you're thinking. Pith is much maligned in culinary circles. Most recipes call for juice or zest."

"And?"

"It can be found in marmalade, of course, but that's only the tip of the iceberg." Sorin sat back. He was getting the hang of this lying thing. "Did you know, it can also be used to make homemade pectin for other jams and sauces. It can even be blended into drinks to add a subtle citrus flavor."

"I see. And that's why you carry a bow. This pith you're hunting is dangerous?"

Sorin did his best to laugh at the agent's joke, but it came out more like a squeak. "I…uh…ours is a highly competitive industry. You can't be too careful. It's a dangerous world out there."

That was something the agent understood, but the furrow on his brow told Sorin he wasn't entirely convinced.

Leaning forward, Gerff planted his index finger firmly on the desk. "That doesn't explain why you're here, in Moors Hollow."

"Oh, I would have thought that was obvious," Sorin said, straining against the urge to climb back up the shaft and out into the open. "I'm here to meet with growers and sellers to offer my services."

The man laughed heartily a second time, and the rest of the room turned to see what was funny. Sorin had no idea what to do, so he sat there motionless, turning his ring over and over again between his nervous fingers.

In a sweeping motion, Gerff grabbed a different stamp, used a roller to apply some ink, and slammed it down. "Here are your papers, but I don't think they'll do you much good. I haven't seen an orange down here in, well, never. Get your periapt on the way out." Still laughing, Gerff yelled, "Next!" and the old lady-bundle snorted.

Sorin sat there, stunned. On the paper was the word *Approved* in large red letters.

"What are you waiting for?" Landon hissed, grabbing the archer's shoulder. "Let's get out of here."

"He didn't even ask me if I had a sword or anything."

"Sorin, look around. Everyone's got a sword except me. So let's go find mine."

"Right. Yeah. Okay. What's a periapt?"

"This," a prune-faced agent with no teeth said, pointing at a large chest. "It's the law. Everyone wears one in case the effulgence goes out. Take your pick."

"Effulgence?"

"The glowing stuff on the walls."

"That sounds faintly obscene."

The agent's fleshy lips curled into a smile. "If you think that's obscene, you should see where it comes from."

"No, thank you!" Sorin said, grabbing a vial and strapping it to his upper arm.

Landon selected a glowing pendant, and Thea took a delicate circlet. Even Reinier got a collar.

"What about him?" Sorin asked, pointing to Anslim.

The prune-faced agent closed the chest. "He's already got one."

The journeymen pulled a brooch-like pin out of his pocket and fastened it to his cloak.

"They aren't very bright," Sorin said.

"Neither are you! Now, get moving!"

"Yes, sir!"

Once inside the tunnel that led to the center of Moors Hollow, Anslim reminded everyone that Thea needed to rest.

Now that he thought about it, Sorin realized the usually talkative cleric had been strangely silent since they'd climbed into the hole. "We all do," the archer added, suddenly feeling exhausted. He moved to lean against the wall, but the journeyman stopped him.

"You don't want to get that stuff on you. Most of the time, it stays up high, on the ceiling, but now and then it slides down the walls."

"What's the big deal? Is it poisonous?"

"Let's just say, it likes to grow on things. Especially living things."

"Can't you just scrub it off?"

"Not once it takes root."

"Ew. Nasty." Sorin reflexively rubbed his hands. "Why use it if it's so dangerous?"

"I'd like to see you try to scrape it off."

"Point taken."

Landon cut into the discussion. "Sorry to interrupt your scintillating conversation—"

"Trying out a new word, are we?" Sorin asked.

The woodcutter's eyes narrowed, and the archer stepped behind Thea. "—but do you know a place where we can sit down, Anslim. Preferably safe from getting that stuff on us?"

The journeyman winked. "Follow me."

24 DREAMS OF GRANDEUR

Landon tried to focus, but the muscles behind his eyes refused to cooperate. Next, he attempted to yawn, but even that proved to be too much effort. Instead, he lay there thinking about the dirty wooden planks workers had laid across the heavy beams holding the ceiling in place ages ago.

Like much of Moors Hollow, the hostel Anslim had led them to was rather unique. From the front, it looked like any other two-story wood building, but once inside, a person found themselves in a cavernous space that had been built right into the wall. This meant the dorms were a mix of wooden construction and dirt caves, as well as every conceivable combination of the two. Luckily, the room they'd let was of the wooden variety. That didn't mean it wasn't dirty, but it didn't have the ubiquitous moldy ceilings that had come to symbolize the subterranean village to Landon and his companions. Where light was concerned, the woodcutter much preferred oil lamps and candles to bioluminescent slime.

The previous evening, Landon had drawn the long straw, giving him the pick of the watch shifts. Unsurprisingly, he'd chosen first watch, much to everyone's chagrin. Being on first watch meant he'd get a whole night's uninterrupted sleep, while everyone else had their slumber disturbed at the beginning of their shifts. At least, that was the theory. In practice, Landon didn't benefit from his luck because he continued to be plagued by dreams of epic feats, the result of which was waking up even more tired than when he'd gone to bed.

He had to admit it wasn't all bad, though—wiping out whole armies with a single stroke of the Glyphblade was exhilarating in the moment. However, when he woke up, lying on the floor of a tavern in an underground village, he was left with a deep-seated feeling of inadequacy. Maybe if he recovered the sword and learned to use it, he'd feel differently, but for now, he was just a woodcutter-wannabe-scribe from Brownwater. Actually, he wasn't even that anymore, now that the Leering Ones had burned his village. Groaning with despair, he rolled over.

"Are you okay?" Reinier's raspy voice asked.

Landon stiffened. He wasn't sure he'd ever get used to hearing the dog speak. That's why he didn't turn to look at the wolfhound. Instead, he remained facing the wall in an attempt not to run screaming from the room. "I'm not sure."

"Me either."

This caught Landon by surprise. "How so?"

"I'd always imagined our reunion as a joyful event."

"Reunion?"

"Do you not remember?"

"I'm sorry. I'm not sure what you mean."

"When you were a boy," Reinier said, "I used to play with you when your mother was away."

Landon craned his neck to look at the wolfhound. "No, no. That was Rainy."

"Precisely."

The connection clicked in his mind, but instead of making him feel better, his stomach did a flip, and he rolled back over. "Oh," he moaned.

Woof.

Landon knew that sound. Putting his misery aside, he sat up. Reinier only sounded like that when something was wrong. Craning his neck, he saw Sorin snoring in a corner of the room.

Reinier followed his gaze and woofed quietly.

"Agreed. It's the first time I've been happy to hear Sorin sawing logs."

On the other side of the small room, Thea remained asleep on the straw bed. They hadn't drawn lots for that honor. Everyone had insisted that the exhausted cleric take it, and she hadn't argued. It appeared casting spells was much harder than Landon had initially thought, and she hadn't recovered from their battle with the Leering Ones yet.

Forcing his gaze away from the bed, Landon accepted what he'd already known would be the case. There was only one other person in their party: Anslim. The journeyman had drawn the short straw, meaning he had the last watch, but he wasn't here. He'd left them defenseless in their sleep!

Jumping to his feet, Landon crossed the room to see where Anslim had gone. This woke both Sorin and Thea, but before he had the chance to explain his behavior, the door swung open, and the journeyman stepped in.

Beaming from ear to ear, Anslim announced. "Breakfast is served!"

"Wow!" Sorin exclaimed, rubbing his eyes and staring at the oversized tray of food their companion had carried into the room. "Let's eat. I'm famished!"

Thea untangled her long, golden hair. "You're always famished."

"Hey, what's wrong with you?" the archer asked, noticing the strange expression on Landon's face. "Aren't you hungry?"

Yes, the woodcutter was definitely hungry. The kitchen had been closed by the time they'd gotten to the hostel the previous night, so they'd had to make do with what little they carried. But the mix of emotions he felt—his discussion with Reinier, fear at finding Anslim gone, and guilt for jumping to conclusions again—made him feel queasy.

Thea's stomach growled loudly.

"I didn't know clerics had such noisy tummies," Sorin said, reaching for a slab of bacon.

Anslim slapped the archer's hand away. "Ladies first."

"Don't mind if I do," Thea said, pulling off a hunk of bread and cutting a slice of cheese. "Thank you, Anslim."

"My pleasure. Dig in, boys!"

Landon stopped Sorin a second time. "Wait a minute."

"Oh, come on! I'm starving!"

The woodcutter put up a finger, and Sorin piped down. Then, he fixed a plate of meat and eggs, but not for himself. Instead, Landon offered it to Reinier, who barked loudly and wagged his tail furiously.

"Now, can I eat?" the archer asked.

Anslim nodded. "Go for it."

Sorin grabbed two handfuls of food and unceremoniously shoved them into his face. Even Landon laughed.

"What?" the archer asked through a mouthful of eggs. "I told you, I'm starving. I can't live on bird food alone. I need sustenance."

"Don't worry, there's more where this came from," Anslim said, sitting down with a large sausage skewered on the end of his knife.

As they ate, the journeyman's toe began to tap. After a while, he hummed a little tune. Then, he started to sing, *"How many drinks should one man drink?"*

Sorin raised a fist full of bacon and responded, *"One if he wants to be warm in his bed."*

Landon added, *"Two, if he doesn't mind the floor instead."*

"Three, if she didn't lock the stable that night," Thea chimed in.

Sorin thought it was hilarious that the cleric knew a drinking song and leapt to his feet, prancing around as he sang, *"Four if he makes it home before first light."*

"I've got the next one," Anslim said, also standing. *"Five if he doesn't plan to leave the pub."*

Everyone sang together, *"Seven if he, wait, was he up to six? Nine is fine if eight didn't wait."*

Anslim threw out his hands, and everyone stopped. *"I think we've lost count. What should he do?"*

Everyone responded, *"Drink some more!"*

"I said, what should he do?"

Feet stamped and voices bellowed from the adjacent rooms, "DRINK SOME MORE!" and they burst out laughing.

"I love that song!" Sorin said, tearing off a large piece of bread.

Their lighthearted mood lingered as long as it took to finish breakfast and get washed up using the room's basin. Luckily, several warm jugs had been left by the door, making their baths far more pleasant than if they'd had to use the same, dirty water. They even had their own towels to dry off, a luxury they hadn't experienced in quite some time.

Once they were done, Landon plopped onto the side of the bed and said, "I guess it's time to find Braydn."

Sorin sat beside him. "It was nice not to have to think about that stuff for a little while."

Thea joined them on the other side, and Reinier put his head on the woodcutter's knee.

"I don't think I can do it," Landon said earnestly.

Sorin shifted uneasily. "Do what?"

"Even if we get the Glyphblade back, I don't see myself being able to wield it. I'm not like the person in my dreams."

"Don't worry, Landon," Thea said in comforting tones. "The Light doesn't make mistakes. It chose you for a reason."

Reinier woofed in agreement.

"That's all well and good, but it would be nice if the Light told me *why* it chose me. And, more importantly, what it expects of me."

Thea laughed. "You and me both."

For the first time, the woodcutter truly understood the struggle Thea faced every day as she sought to stay on the path of the Light. He reached his arm around her. To his surprise, she didn't resist. Instead, she placed her arms around his waist and hugged him back.

"Hey, don't leave me out," the archer said, wrapping his arms around the two of them.

Reinier barked and nuzzled his way in between.

After a few seconds, Sorin looked around the room. "What about Anslim. Shouldn't we invite him, too? Hey. Where did he go?"

That broke the moment, and they separated.

"Sometimes he really gets under my skin," Landon said, grabbing his things. "He's so slippery."

Heading to the door, he flung it open with more force than he'd intended.

Anslim was standing in the hallway, blocking the way. "I agreed to travel with you, with the understanding that you were committed to seeing your quest through."

Landon stood dumbfounded with Sorin, Thea, and Reinier peeking around him.

"Is that not the case?" the journeyman asked.

Somehow, Anslim's demeanor ignited a fire inside Landon. It wasn't as much anger or revenge as it had been before, but of intent. He still didn't fully believe in himself, but he did believe in his friends, and it was time to get back to work. "If I have anything to say about it, Volgreth's days haunting Kahr'anis are numbered.

"That's more like it. And what about you three?"

Reinier barked.

"Good."

Sorin stepped from behind the woodcutter with his bow at the ready.

"And what about our cleric?"

Thea fixed the journeyman with a stare so intense, her blue-gray eyes looked like gemstones. "You never have to ask where my loyalties lie."

"Excellent." Looking at Landon, he said, "Don't give me reason to doubt you again."

25 THE GLOWN

Together, Landon, Sorin, Thea, Anslim, and Reinier ventured deeper into the underground caverns of Moors Hollow. It was exactly what the woodcutter had expected and entirely alien to him at the same time. A musty scent clung to his nose, triggering an occasional sneeze, and the odd, undulating mold played tricks on his mind. Having experienced more than his fair share of non-flame-related ways to make light—most notably the Lunar Glow spell—he knew he shouldn't have been bothered, but he was.

The more he thought about it, the more it wasn't the light itself but how the glow moved under the organism's surface. It was alive, there was no question about that, but in what way, he didn't understand. Then again, it did an excellent job of chasing away the shadows, so he did his best to tolerate it; however, he did keep glancing at it to make sure it wasn't dripping onto his head.

"The only thing worse than Volgreth showing up in your bedroom would be getting attacked in a hole in the ground," he mumbled.

The way Reinier whined, he knew the wolfhound felt the same.

As they descended farther underground, the party passed a beggar tucked into a recess in the cave wall. A faint glow emanated from under his patchwork of ragged robes.

"Hello, Friend," Anslim said, stepping over to the man.

The robes shifted, as if someone had tilted their head, but he remained entirely covered.

"That's so strange," Sorin said, peeking over Anslim's shoulder. "He must be wearing lots of periapts. I can see the glow coming out from everywhere."

Anslim turned toward the archer. "He doesn't need such things."

At that, the beggar got to his feet and removed his hood.

Sorin jumped back, trying to pull Anslim with him. "Be careful! He's infected, like you said!"

The man's smooth skin glowed with the same mold that covered Moors Hollow's ceiling. He kept his hands clasped in supplication and bowed his head as if this kind of reaction to his appearance was all too common.

"Calm yourself, Sorin. He isn't contagious."

"But you said—"

"I said it's impossible to remove if it takes root, but once it has, it lives inside a person's body, and is no longer a danger to anyone." As if to demonstrate the veracity of his claim, Anslim cradled the beggar's hand in his own. "This," he continued, "Is Ramsifal, my friend."

Ramsifal's skin was entirely translucent. Even his teeth, eyes, and tongue glowed with the mold.

Sorin stared at the organisms moving along vein-like mycelium under the surface of his skin. As Anslim had said, it was entirely inside the man's body, and the archer relaxed.

Thea was fascinated by the light emanating from Ramsifal's body. "Your Light is beautiful."

"It is my constant companion," Ramsifal said in a dry, whispery voice.

"Wait, I don't get it. If it doesn't hurt you, then why don't we all let ourselves get infected?" Sorin asked. "Then, we'd make our own light and never have to worry about the Shadehaunter."

Thea looked at the archer like he had two heads. "You're a simple man, aren't you?"

"I'm just asking."

"Isn't it obvious?" Anslim asked. "Even here, the *Glown* are ostracized. What do you think would happen if you strolled into Endog looking like that?"

"That's a good point."

Thea shook her head and turned back to Ramsifal. "Are there many like you?"

"Some," the beggar whispered. "But most who carry the *Legacy of Hahl* live solitary lives as he did."

Sorin perked up. "Ooh, that sounds like a story. I love a good story."

"We know," Thea said, rolling her eyes.

Sorin was used to Thea's reactions to the things he said, and he didn't let it stop him from asking, "Who's Hahl?"

Anslim took a more polite tack. "Will you share a meal with us, old friend?"

"Not here, but if you'll come with me, we can sit a while, and I'll tell the story your friend is so eager to hear. Maybe if more people hear it, they won't be as afraid of the Legacy."

Anslim and Ramsifal led the rest of the party out of the main tunnel and into a side cavern where Ramsifal lived. There was a pile of straw, several broken tables and chairs, and a lantern with a cracked globe. Once inside, Sorin immediately noticed that something was amiss in the space: there was no mold growing on the roof.

"It's a trap!" the archer exclaimed, triggered by the shadowy darkness.

Anslim lit the lantern with a flint as Ramsifal handed the others dips, which he lit with a thin stick.

"He glows, remember?" Anslim said, taking one of the dips. "He doesn't need extra light to be protected from the Shadehaunter. He carries it with him."

"Oh, yeah. Right. I forgot myself for a minute." Still uncomfortable, Sorin sat with his back against the wall, holding his candle out, just in case.

"Unlike most of the Glown," Ramsifal whispered, "The fungus didn't infect me. I was born this way."

The archer leaned forward. "Whoah."

"My mother and father were both of the Glown, and they passed it to me. This is very unusual, as most of my kind choose to lead solitary lives, but when the mold began to grow within my mother, my father stayed by her side. So, you see, they chose to carry the Legacy."

The wolfhound whined, and Landon touched him on the back.

"I believe Reinier understands the burden you carry," Thea said, looking pointedly at the woodcutter.

Landon lowered his eyes but didn't remove his hand from Reinier's back, who shifted closer to his master.

Sorin looked like he wanted to ask a question, but the cleric shushed him, allowing Ramsifal to take the time he needed to tell his tale.

After a pause, the beggar continued. "Long ago, when the Shadehaunter first appeared in Kahr'anis, a man named Hahl traveled to the valley to seek his fortune. He was a miner by trade, and he hoped to discover a deposit of gold or platinum. For many years, Hahl dug in the mountains until he was an old man, but he never found the precious metals he'd given his life to obtain. He did, however, find something far more precious.

"Like all Anisens, Hahl feared the Shadehaunter, and when he discovered a mold that glowed so brightly that it cast away shadows, he was elated. He tried to show it to people and even sell it, but they believed it to be cursed and wouldn't allow him into their homes.

"Unsurprisingly, it wasn't long before Hahl himself became infected. Everywhere he went, he was cast out as having been cursed by Volgreth. He tried to explain that it didn't make any sense for the sorcerer to make him glow, being a monster of darkness, but no one listened."

"That's horrible," Sorin said, resting his head on his knees.

"Resigned to solitude, Hahl wandered the plains. That's how he found this place, though it was much smaller back then. Hollans have excavated many new passageways and caverns since the founding of the city."

"Did Hahl have any followers?" Thea asked.

"No, it wasn't like that. He was entirely alone. But right until the end, he hoped to share his discovery with those who would accept it. That's why he wrote down his story before locating a comfortable cavern where he could rest eternally. His sepulcher still exists, but it was sealed off long ago."

The cleric looked moved by the story. "I wish I could see it. I'll pray for him nevertheless."

"As one would expect," Ramsifal continued, "when he passed, his body returned to the soil, as did the mold. It's the very same mold you see over your heads most places in Moors Hollow because every time a new tunnel was excavated, a small piece of the fungus was rooted in the ceiling to provide Hollans with the light they needed to survive."

"So the light is actually the remnants of a dead glowing dude? Weird," Sorin said with a shiver. "I guess I should be glad of it. I'd never be able to find the way out of here without it."

Reinier barked, as if to say, *You might not be able to, but my nose will guide us to the exit.*

"Good boy," Landon said, hesitating only momentarily before stroking the wiry hair on the wolfhound's back.

The party spent the rest of the day with Ramsifal, listening to his stories, though Thea was so fascinated by the light emanating from his body that she monopolized the conversation.

She knew it was more biology than faith, but it was light, and to her, that meant it had to be good.

There was one question that Landon managed to slip into the discussion: did Ramsifal know a person named Braydn, and was he here?

When Ramsifal answered *yes* to both questions, Anslim and Sorin had to keep Landon from rushing out to find the rogue.

"In time," Anslim said, when the woodcutter calmed. "In time."

• • •

The next day, after they said their goodbyes to Ramsifal, Landon got his wish when Anslim led the party through Moors Hollow in search of Braydn and the Glyphblade. They doubled back so many times that no one had any idea where they were going, but it didn't take long to arrive at their destination.

"We're here," Anslim said, stopping in front of a heavy wooden door. "Remember, we're the foreigners."

"What's that supposed to mean?" Sorin asked, trying to peek around the journeyman to see where *here* was.

"Keep your arrows in your quiver."

The archer chuckled. "Nice one."

"No, I mean it. You're in a hole, remember? Don't make trouble."

Sorin stopped laughing and gulped.

Anslim opened the door into what was obviously a tavern. The sound of clinking tankards, laughter, and hearty slaps on the back poured into the hallway from the room beyond.

A sign overhead read: *The Leaky Bunghole. Three-time winner of the Golden Nozzle award! We've got much more than a butt load of beer!*[2]

---

[2] BUTT LOAD: A large cask or barrel containing 126 imperial gallons (or two hogsheads) of wine, beer, or other liquids.

"This is my kind of place! Where's the steak and ale?" Sorin asked.

Thea looked incredulous. "You just had breakfast."

"Nuts do not a proper breakfast make."

26 THE LEAKY BUNGHOLE

The familiar smell of stale ale, unwashed bodies, and greasy food greeted the party as they entered the subterranean tavern. A wood stove in the center of the room ensured the space felt warm and dry, but the shifting smoky hues overhead, illuminated by the ever-present mold, gave the space an unnatural feel.

Sorin leaned back. "Trippy."

"Keep moving," Landon said, finding the colors playing across the patrons' faces disconcerting.

"How about a pint? It'll help us fit in, you know?"

Thea snorted, showing her displeasure at Sorin's thinly veiled attempt to justify drinking.

"It may look like everyone is having fun, but keep your guard up," Anslim whispered.

"So what you're saying is: This place is like every other bar I've ever been to?" Sorin asked with a wry smile.

"Hardly."

Without warning, Landon's demeanor shifted with the force of tectonic plates colliding. "I can't believe it. He's actually here."

Sure enough, Braydn was seated at the bar, cradling a half-empty mug of beer with both hands.

"You!" the woodcutter yelled.

The rogue turned to see his former companions heading toward him. "Landon, buddy. Good to see you. Pull up a stool."

Landon didn't sit. "Where is it?"

The low grumble emanating from Reinier's throat set everyone's teeth on edge, and the din of the tavern quieted.

"Where's what?" Braydn asked, swaying a little as he spoke. "Why don't you have a drink with me, and we can figure out what you're talking about?"

"The Glyphblade, you fool! Give it to me!" Landon demanded, grabbing Braydn's tunic and yanking him off the barstool.

"Easy there, lad," the barkeep said, displaying a single-handed crossbow. She looked like she meant business.

Sorin put up his hands in a show of submission. "Okay, let's everybody settle down."

"Tell your friend to take his hands off my customer, or he's going to leave here with an extra hole in his body."

"You might want to do what she says," Sorin said out of the side of his mouth. "She looks like she's shot folks before…and enjoyed it."

Landon didn't budge. "Not before this thief gives back what he stole."

The barkeep cocked the bolt and raised the crossbow, but Braydn waved her off. "Don't worry about it, Jo. I've got this."

She lowered the weapon but didn't put it down.

"It's right over here," the rogue explained, pulling a long burlap bundle from under a bench so worn by the ages that it bore indentations in the shape of someone's bottom.

Landon took the bundle from the rogue and ripped off the covering. There it was, the Glyphblade.

"That was too easy," Anslim said, his hand shifting over the hilt of his dagger.

The relief Landon felt at recovering the sword quickly gave way to anger at what Braydn had done. "Bastard!"

"Calm down," Thea said, moving closer to the woodcutter.

"Calm down? After what he did?"

"There will be another time."

Sensing things were about to turn ugly, several patrons slipped out the door.

The barkeep was none too pleased, and she raised the crossbow again. "You've got what you came for; now go. You're bad for business."

Braydn reached for his things, but Landon got there first. There was a tense moment as the woodcutter held Braydn's belongings far too close to Reinier's muzzle for Braydn's liking, but Landon relented and handed over the bag.

"Thank you. I'll be going, too," Braydn said with a wave. "Put it on my tab, Jo. Oh, and as for the rest of you, do say hello to Loric for me. I see he isn't with you. Is he off doing wizardy stuff?"

It was the wrong thing to say.

"Loric's dead," Landon hissed. "Because of you."

For the briefest of instants, Braydn's face registered shock, but he instantly regained his composure. "I'm sorry to hear that. I liked the old man. And I hate to disagree with you, but whatever happened couldn't have been my fault. I wasn't there. Remember?"

The woodcutter's heart pounded with such intensity that he was sure the cleric could hear it.

"Easy," Thea whispered.

No. There would be no *easy* where Braydn was concerned.

And though Landon didn't perceive the arcane whisper leaving Braydn's lips, he noticed the Glyphblade shimmer and sensed the deception. That's why he wasn't surprised when his hand closed around the Glyphblade's hilt and he found himself grasping an ordinary stick instead.

"He's tricked us again!"

In a swish of his green cloak, Braydn swooped out of the tavern into the maze of Moors Hollow.

Much to his companion's surprise, Landon didn't run after him. Instead, he smiled.

"What are you waiting for?" Sorin asked, nocking an arrow.

"He thinks he's smarter than us," Landon said coolly. "That he can outwit us at every turn and never be caught."

"Yeah. What's your point? He'll be right if we stand around here doing nothing."

"Oh, we aren't doing *nothing*," the woodcutter said with a gleam in his eye. "And Braydn isn't the only one who knows how to play a game. In fact, Reinier and I love to play games, don't we, boy?"

The wolfhound cocked an eyebrow.

"Did you get the scent from his bag?" Landon asked.

The dog's indignant woof sounded so much like *As if you have to ask!* that even Sorin understood.

"Good boy." Turning his attention to Sorin, Thea, and Anslim, Landon said, "I hope you're feeling up for a little exercise."

Sorin smiled. "Always."

"Excellent. Reinier? Fetch!"

And off they went.

27 Moors Hollow

Landon's feet kicked up clouds of dust as he did his best to keep pace with Reinier. He'd never been able to run faster than the wolfhound, but that didn't keep him from trying.

"Come on!" the woodcutter yelled, still clenching Braydn's stick in his fist. It wasn't a sword, but if he got close enough, the rogue would regret not leaving a coin instead.

Reinier barked, and they made a sharp turn.

"Down that alley!" Sorin said, pointing to the right.

The party moved as one as they pursued Braydn through the village's many tunnels and caverns. Now and then, they caught sight of his green cloak as it disappeared around a corner with Reinier close behind.

"Into the glass shop!" Thea yelled, and everyone followed.

Snaking between cases and stands that held delicate handmade globes and other glassware, Landon raised his stick. "We have him."

Braydn's ragged breathing sounded strained as he backed against a display of delicate crystal bells.

"What are you doing in here?" a lady with frizzy gray hair and a worn leather apron asked. "Put that stick down, you big oaf. You're going to break something."

Landon ignored her, afraid that if he took his eyes off the rogue, he'd escape again. "There's nowhere to go. Give us the sword, Braydn."

"Oh, Landon. Is that the best you can do?" With a wicked smile, he grabbed a tall display case and tipped hundreds of tiny figurines onto the floor.

A cascade of shattering glass filled the air.

Landon shielded his eyes, and when he looked again, the rogue was gone. "Reinier, don't move!" he commanded. To prevent the wolfhound from cutting his paws, the woodcutter hoisted the dog across his shoulders. "Would you stop kicking me? Don't worry. I've got you."

"I'm not kicking you," a gravelly voice responded.

Landon turned to see the shopkeeper beating on him with her fists.

"I'm sorry, ma'am," he said, "but we have a scoundrel to catch."

"You're the scoundrel!" she bellowed, reaching for a broom, not to clean up the mess but to whack Sorin in the back.

"Ow! Hey!" the archer said, stumbling through the door. "I'm not the one who knocked it over!"

Once they were outside, Landon placed Reinier on the ground. "Can you pick up the scent?"

The dog barked and was off like a shot. They did their best, but Braydn navigated the narrow alleys of Moors Hollow with maddening ease, always slipping away before they reached him.

Thea tripped on the edge of her robe, and Anslim was forced to stop and help her.

"Go, go!" the journeyman yelled when Landon slowed to make sure Thea was okay. "We're right behind you."

"All right. Sorin, let's keep moving." Landon didn't have time to admire the wooden buildings built into the cavern walls, or the ever-present fungi, which turned the underground village into a surreal maze of shimmering, prismatic colors. And he certainly didn't notice the crowd of residents gathering behind them, either. How could he? The only thought in his mind was: *Catch Braydn.*

Bursting through the doors of a clothing store, they followed the rogue between headless mannequins and an open display window back onto the street.

This time, however, it took a few seconds for Reinier to regain the trail, and a sense of desperation settled over their party. Maybe they wouldn't catch the traitor after all.

"We're losing him," Sorin said, keeping pace with the woodcutter. "We need to find a way to slow him down."

"If you have any ideas, I'm all ears."

"As a matter of fact, I do."

Sorin skidded to a halt, nocked an arrow, and let it soar.

Landon watched it embed itself in a door Braydn was about to open, pinning it shut. With his escape route cut off, the rogue turned and slipped into a tanner's workshop.

"Nice shot," Landon said, changing direction. "But next time, take him down."

Sorin almost stumbled. Landon meant business!

A blur of angry faces and shouting voices were directed at them as they passed through the tannery. Sorin tipped over a vat after being hip-checked by someone trying to tackle him. A foul-smelling liquid gushed onto the floor, forcing everyone to scramble out of the way. It was the distraction they needed, allowing them to escape out the back door into cavernous tunnels hidden behind the marketplace.

That's when the trail went cold.

"DAMN...Damn...damn..." Sorin's voice echoed through the shimmering grotto.

"Shh," Anslim said, putting a finger to his mouth. "These are the *Old Ways*. Most of the exits have been blocked off, but we still might lose him."

Reinier paced in figure eights, trying to figure out which direction the rogue had taken.

"I can hear you," Braydn's mocking voice came from nowhere and everywhere at once. "Are you tired, Landon? You're breathing so heavily. Maybe you should take a break."

Sorin spotted him first. "There he is! That tunnel over there." But it was a ruse. The rogue had once again deceived them.

Each of the party's periapts switched places with a worthless trinket—a feather, a tin coin, a pebble—and, after hanging in the air for a moment, they all dropped to the ground.

"Braydn's substitution spell," Landon hissed, but the realization came too late. The damage was done.

The rogue briefly appeared behind them, and he tossed glittering dust at the ceiling. The instant it touched the mold, the fungus dried up, and its glow went out. Seconds later, they were surrounded by darkness, and the shadows sprang to life.

"It's the Shadehaunter!" Sorin yelled. "Quick, someone find a candle. Thea cast a spell. Hurry!"

Spectral hands shot out of the gloom from all directions, seizing their arms and legs and covering Thea's mouth, preventing her from praying to the Light.

Landon whacked at them with his stick, but it passed right through, yet they continued to hold him tightly. "How do we defend ourselves against something that has no substance?"

Ghostly voices chanted unintelligibly, rising and falling with terrifying singularity and echoing into the void.

"I can't get my arm free," Sorin said, his body encircled by ever-tightening sepulchral limbs.

Suddenly, a light so bright they had to close their eyes filled the tunnel.

"Ramsifal," Anslim said, showing more relief than they'd ever seen from the journeyman.

The beggar threw off his robes, allowing the light of his body to fill the space. With shrieks born of being denied their prey, the shadows scurried back to the evil that had sent them.

One by one, Landon, Sorin, Thea, Anslim, and Reinier collapsed to the floor, free from their phantasmal bindings.

"Thank you, my friend," Anslim said, using a flint to light a torch. "But how did you know we were here? Did you follow us?"

"No, but when word reached me that topsiders were running rampant through the marketplace, I stationed myself here in case you found yourself led astray."

"You saved our lives," Sorin said, fumbling through his messenger bag for a candle.

Landon checked on Reinier before dusting himself off. "That was too close."

"You aren't out of danger yet," Ramsifal said, slipping the hood of his patchwork robes over his head. "Complete whatever business you have here and leave Moors Hollow as quickly as possible. I fear you are no longer welcome."

Landon didn't have to be told twice. "Understood."

The woodcutter rushed after Braydn, leaving behind the only person he'd ever met who wasn't afraid of the dark.

28 TIME TO GO

When they emerged onto the underground street, Landon's breath caught in his throat. A massive group of locals carrying pitchforks and torches was marching in their direction. "Ramsifal was right. Our time has run out."

"Don't give up yet," Sorin said, grabbing the woodcutter's arm. "Look!"

On the other side of the marketplace, Braydn was pinned against a stone wall between the oncoming Hollans and a fortuitously placed vendor's cart.

Approaching as carefully as one could while trying to avoid being seen by an angry mob, Landon led their party over to the rogue.

Sorin raised his bow.

"Okay, you've got me," Braydn said, locking eyes with Landon.

"Hand over the sword. And no tricks."

"Are you honestly still on about that? I think we have more pressing issues to deal with," the rogue said, nodding toward the Hollans, who were forming a wide arc around them.

Several guards, brandishing pike staves and swords, pushed their way to the front.

"You've caused enough trouble, topsiders," one of the guards said. "Lay down your weapons."

"The sword," Landon insisted, pointing the stick at Braydn.

"Fine. Take it!"

The rogue tossed a stone at Landon, who reflexively caught it in mid-air. When it touched the woodcutter's skin, it instantly turned into the Glyphblade. He finally had it back!

"He's got a sword!" a second guard yelled.

Landon spun around, finally taking in the full breadth of their predicament. "Now what?"

None of the dreams he'd witnessed ended like this. As wielder of the Glyphblade, he was supposed to triumphantly regain the sword and banish Volgreth from Kahr'anis forever, not be arrested by a bunch of tool-wielding subterranean villagers. Didn't they realize what he and his friends were fighting for?

"At the ready!" the guard commander bellowed. "This is your last warning: Put your weapons down. I won't ask again."

He didn't have to.

Someone in the crowd let an arrow fly right at Landon.

Sorin yelled, "Look out!" but Landon's arm was already moving.

Glyphblade swung around and batted the arrow out of the air. Then, it burst into flames, shooting jets of fire in every direction at once.

Screaming in terror, the crowd scattered. Even the guards dove for cover.

Thea grabbed Reinier's collar and commanded, "Get us out of here!"

Anslim hooked an arm around Landon, who was holding the sword away from his body so as not to get burned. "Sorin, help me."

"But what about Braydn?"

The journeyman shook his head. "He'd already gone."

"That guy's as slippery as a wet noodle."

Dazed, Landon asked, "Did I do that?" as he was dragged out of the marketplace.

"Yes! You did," Anslim said. "Now move your legs before the Hollans regroup."

Reinier led them straight onto the elevator platform, but they saw no way to make it move. There was no lever like the one the hatch keeper had used to lower them into the earth, only the dangling rope.

"What do we do now?" Sorin asked, scrambling around trying to locate the up button.

Thankfully, with one last puff of smoke, the sword stopped burning.

Landon quickly sheathed the sword and stepped forward. It was the first time he'd felt truly useful since beginning their trek north. Taking the thick rope in his hands, he hauled on it, and the platform rose toward the entrance.

Sorin was thunderstruck. "I knew you were strong, but that's amazing."

The moment they reached the top, Reinier leapt into the air, changing into her human form and landing on the ladder. Startled by a naked woman throwing herself at him, the gate-keeper stumbled back and fell on the mechanism that opened the secret door to the outside.

The party clambered past him as quickly as their feet would take them.

Landon saw the man's pole reach for the latch, and he slashed at it with the sword. That bought them enough time to throw themselves onto the plains before the hidden door slammed shut behind them. With a sharp bark, Reinier changed back into a wolfhound and led them away from the entrance. Luckily, there was no need to rush because it appeared the people of Moors Hollow were even more shy about revealing themselves than shapeshifters, and soon they slowed their retreat.

Thea shivered uncontrollably.

"What's the matter?" Sorin asked, his senses on high alert. "Do you sense something?"

"Yes, the chill in the air."

"Oh, yeah," he said, lowering his weapon.

Landon stared at the Glyphblade, both excited by its power and terrified of what it had done at his behest.

"Put that thing away before you hurt someone," Anslim snapped. "I doubt I'll ever be welcome in Moors Hollow again after that stunt."

"But we have it," the woodcutter said, sounding more confident than he had in days. "We have a weapon strong enough to challenge Volgreth."

"And kill us if we—and when I say *we*, I mean *you*—aren't careful with it."

"Enough, you two," Thea said, stopping the argument. "What's done is done. The Light has returned the Glyphblade to us, and our numbers haven't been further reduced. For that, we can be thankful."

Anslim didn't look impressed. "But once again, we're out in the open."

"And Bradyn got away," Sorin added.

Thea ignored both of their protestations and started walking. "We can deal with Braydn later. I suggest we find shelter."

When Landon didn't follow the others, Reinier padded over to his side. "Aren't you coming?" he growled.

The woodcutter looked between the sword and the dog. Then, appearing to come to a decision, he nodded his head. "I go where you go."

Reinier woofed, and off they went.

29 MANGALA

The lack of anything of note as the party crossed the plains did nothing to improve their mood the rest of the day. A tree would have been lovely. A break in the fog would have been better, but neither was likely on the dessicated wasteland, and they knew it, or they thought they did. In a surprising turn of events, they stumbled—as in literally fell—into a particularly dense patch of scrubgrass. From the outside, the area looked like the rest of the plains, but in actual fact, there was a depression in the ground, meaning the grass grew taller than it appeared. It was by far the safest camp they'd ever made on the plains, but that mattered little after their near-capture in Moors Hollow, losing Braydn again, and Landon's inability to control the Glyphblade. A rift had formed between the travelers so wide that after they made a suitable clearing in the grass, they sat with their backs to each other, surrounded by their own sets of candles.

The only sound beyond the faint whispers of Thea's prayers was the nearly inaudible rustle of the reeds.

"What's that?" Sorin asked, pointing to plumes of smoke rising from the plains.

Anslim glanced in the direction of the archer's finger. "Emergency ventilation."

"It's because of us, isn't it?"

"Yeah. One of us, at least."

Landon didn't react. He didn't need to be reminded that he'd nearly killed everyone.

He also knew that he'd changed a great deal since leaving Brownwater, and he didn't like the person he'd become. Life had been simple before the Leering Ones attacked: Get up, cut wood, deliver wood, run around with Reinier, and go to bed. Now his days were filled with fear, loss, and death.

He'd been humbled once before, when he'd jumped to conclusions about Loric, but that didn't make what he said next any easier. "I owe you all an apology."

"What was that? I didn't quite hear you," Sorin asked, scooching around on his bottom.

Anslim remained where he was. "I think what Landon is trying to say is—"

"Thanks, but I've got this," Landon said, cutting the journeyman off. "Put plainly, this isn't me."

"Then who is it?" the journeyman asked. "Because this is the only Landon I've known since meeting you."

That stung, but Landon knew it was true. "Someone who wasn't made for this kind of thing."

The woodcutters' sincerity got through to Anslim, and he turned around. "Who is?"

"Knights? Nobles? People born to be leaders? I don't know, but woodcutters studying to be scribes certainly aren't. I'm not saying that I'm not still angry with Braydn. In fact, I'd be pleased to see him in stocks with people throwing cabbages at his face."

"That would be a waste of good cabbages," Sorin mumbled.

Landon chuckled. "True. What I'm saying is: I think I used him as a reason to be mad. I focused my anger on him, but he wasn't necessarily the reason I was angry in the first place. Does that make sense?"

Reinier put his head on Landon's lap. The dog's golden eyes looked up at the woodcutter.

"I was especially mean to you, my friend," he said, patting the wolfhound. "I hope you can forgive me."

Sorin got a twinkle in his eye and said. "Hey, what about me? Don't I deserve a pat on the head? You were mean to me, too."

Thea chuffed. "You deserved it."

"Hey!"

"The fault is not entirely your own," Thea continued. "As you say, you weren't trained to seek out a quest. However, one was laid at your feet nevertheless. That is the way of things. I wonder if hearing a story about someone who faced a similar challenge would help? Someone you have glimpsed in your dreams."

"That sounds like a great idea," Sorin said, always ready for a story.

"I wasn't talking to you."

"I know, but I was afraid Landon might say no."

Landon eyed the cleric. "You never told me you understood the reason for my dreams."

"I didn't want to get in the way if it was the Light trying to teach you, but now, I think an explanation is in order."

"I'm up for anything if it will help me get some sleep," the woodcutter said, leaning forward. "Anslim, will you join us?"

The journeyman gave a long drag on his pipe. "Of course. Especially if it'll keep you from turning me into a human torch."

Sorin grimaced. "That's a terrifying image."

"My point exactly."

After everyone settled themselves around the fire and redistributed their candles in a wide circle, Thea began.

"Loric—Light rest his soul—had the right idea in telling you the story of the Glyphblade. How can someone be expected to wield it if they don't understand what it is or where it came from?"

Landon shrugged.

She pointed to the ground. "If you'd be so kind, please place it where we can see it."

The woodcutter unsheathed the sword and placed it at their feet. The blade was deadly thin with a series of runes etched into the steel that glimmered in the firelight.

Reaching forward, Thea pointed to the first rune. "Loric told you the story of the Moon God."

Sorin nodded, as if she were speaking directly to him.

She slowly moved her finger down the blade to a rune that looked like a circle with an arrow sticking out of it, aiming toward the North-east. "I do not claim to know the lore of our world as well as he did, but I do know the story of this rune: *The Pride of Mangala.*"

"This is going to be good," the archer whispered.

"After defeating the Moon, our hero became famous. Everywhere he went, people lavished on him. They showered him with gifts, threw parties in his honor, and organized parades in his name. But this wasn't the natural order of things. People were supposed to celebrate the gods, not one of their own. And the more celebrated he became, the more upset the gods grew, especially Mangala. At first, she laid traps for our hero, but he always managed to outwit her. Unsurprisingly, this resulted in making him more revered, further infuriating the prideful god.

"Now, instead of telling stories of his remarkable feats when he came to town, he told stories about Mangala that made villagers laugh at her expense. Unable to stop our hero, she turned her attention to hurting people. She sent dust storms and lightning, pestilence and plague, but instead of cowering at her might, people yelled at the sky, cursing her and destroying temples and statues erected in her honor. It was in this way that Mangala was defeated, by taking away the one thing that the Gods hold above all else: pride.

"It seemed so easy to our hero. No great battle. No confrontation. Just the slow erosion of people's need, until all that remained was apathy, the most potent weapon against the narcissistic. However, taking someone's pride is a terrible thing and it comes with a price, weakening the winner as much as the defeated. Mangala understood this, and just before she was banished forever, she stole the one thing that meant the most to our hero, his name.

"Instantly, there were no parties or parades. No one sang songs about him or told stories about his triumphs. When he arrived in towns, no one greeted him, and when he left, they said, 'Who was that? I didn't catch his name.' Although this would have crushed most people, our hero persevered and, in the process, discovered his true purpose." Thea paused before asking, "Do you understand?"

"That's brutal," Sorin said with a whistle. "That must have made him so sad."

The cleric looked displeased. "Is that all you took away from the parable?"

"No. I mean, there was a lot to unpack there. Like, how do we know about him if the world forgot his name?"

"That is a story for another day."

"Shoot."

Ignoring the archer, Thea turned back to Landon. "Do you understand what I'm telling you?"

Landon thought about it for a while before responding. "I think so. It's something to do with pursuing glory and losing your temper, right?"

"You're on the right track. When people get angry or prideful, they act rashly, doing things they wouldn't normally do. They lose their way."

"Mangala acted like that," Sorin interjected.

"Yes, she did, but so did our hero."

The archer looked perplexed. "I don't get it."

"Instead of focusing on his mission, our hero developed a need to be celebrated. That meant he became like the gods he was fighting, including being vulnerable to the same tactic our hero had used against them. It took the loss of his name to realize that his true quest was not self-aggrandizement, but to help all people, whether they supported him or not. Understanding this gave him the strength to face Shukra's trickery."

The archer perked up. "Can we hear that story, too?"

"No."

"Dang it."

"Friend Landon," Thea said sincerely. "There is much sorrow and anger in you, but you are not the only person who suffers. Until you realize this, it won't only be Volgreth we have to worry about striking us down."

Landon looked at the runes traveling down the length of the weapon's blade. Thanks to Thea, he knew what two of them meant, but what did the others represent? "Will learning about the sword help me understand how to use it?"

The cleric shook her head. "Only you know the answer to that question. Don't fight the dreams. Give yourself over to them. Maybe they are trying to show you the way."

"There she goes again, sounding all woo-woo," Sorin said, restringing his bow.

"Then maybe I have two quests," Landon said, putting the sword away, "I must also learn to control my anger, because if I don't do that, I won't be able to stop Volgreth."

"Now that," Anslim said, puffing on his pipe, "is one of the most sensible things I've heard from you, woodcutter."

Not knowing what else to say, Landon apologized again to his companions. "It won't happen again."

Thea scoffed at this. "Do not make promises you can't keep."

"I've heard that before."

"It wasn't intended as a slight. A better promise would be to say that you will practice with the Glyphblade. Any promise greater than that would be fallacious. Remember, it needs to learn about you as much as you need to learn about it."

Landon touched the sword's hilt. "You speak as if it's alive."

"It is of the Light, and all things that walk in the Light are promised life," she said, pulling the spare robes she'd previously offered Reinier out of her sack. "Would you like these?" she asked, presenting them to the wolfhound.

Reinier looked at Landon.

"I…um…It isn't up to me. I'm sorry for not respecting that earlier."

The wolfhound wagged his tail and remained a dog for now.

30 FIRST WATCH

Landon's hands trembled so much that he crossed his arms to conserve what little body heat he had left. Huddled around a sputtering fire, Sorin, Thea, and Anslim did the same.

Sorin had commented for days about how thick the fog was, but when it condensed into full-on rain, he'd stopped complaining because Thea had made it abundantly clear he was treading on everyone's last nerve. Furthermore, if he ignored her warning, she couldn't be held responsible for turning him into a wombat. Like Landon, Sorin didn't know if such a thing was within the cleric's power, but he made the decision not to find out.

Lying alongside his master, Reinier whimpered. The incessant rain had overpowered his wiry coat, which lay in dark streaks, matted against his shivering body.

"It's not coming down that hard," Sorin stuttered, pressing his jaw against his shoulder to prevent his teeth from chattering so much. "But it never ends."

"Indeed," Thea agreed, her stormy eyes clamped shut. "There's more to this rain than a passing cloud. I can feel it."

Reinier whimpered again, and Landon used the lower part of his cloak to shield the dog. It didn't do much to keep the rain off, but Reinier appreciated the gesture.

The woodcutter struggled with the knowledge that their plight was his fault. If he hadn't overreacted so badly, maybe they'd be relaxing in their hostel room in Moors Hollow, but probably not. He had a feeling their group would have moved on either way, but that didn't make him feel better.

He stretched out a cramping leg, accidentally knocking over one of the candles. Luckily, the jar they'd used to protect it from the rain did its job, and he returned it to an upright position without issue.

When they'd first met back in Endog, Landon had wondered why Anslim carried such a big pack. Now, he knew. Without the jars he'd brought, they wouldn't have had the protection of candles in this kind of weather. And thanks to their experience in the shadows of Moors Hollow, everyone remained keenly aware of how tenuous their predicament was.

"Perhaps you should practice with the Glyphbade," Thea suggested as if directly responding to Landon's thoughts.

Ever since Thea had told the story of the sword, Landon had slept better, knowing the images he saw were in some way trying to teach him, or at the very least show him what to do. However, uncontrolled jets of fire still burned brightly in the woodcutter's mind. "Are you sure that's wise? I might hurt myself or one of you."

"If you don't try, how will you learn to harness its power?"

Landon wished he had a cunning retort, but he knew there was no point in arguing. Thea was right. It wouldn't teach itself. Or maybe it could? That would make things easier. The trouble was, he felt cold, miserable, and exhausted, so instead of agreeing, he said, "Maybe later."

"I have used that excuse myself on occasion."

"It's not an excuse!" His denial came out more forcefully than he intended, and he apologized.

Thea crossed her arms tightly in front of her. "It's okay. I often feel the same way."

"You do?"

"Of course. Do you think it's easy always feeling inadequate?"

Sorin looked up. He'd never heard Thea open up this way before.

"Inadequate?" Landon asked incredulously. "I can't imagine you ever being inadequate at anything. We've all seen you do remarkable things."

"Trust me, I have much to learn. And so do you, or the next time you use the Glyphblade, the same thing will happen again...or worse."

"Worse?" Anslim asked. "What could be worse than being trapped in a flaming hole in the ground? I say put it away and forget about it."

"I'm with him," Sorin added, though it came out in fits and spurts because his teeth were chattering so much. "That sword needs to stay right where it is. Start waving it around, and who knows what will happen."

"I see. You think losing control when we're facing Volgreth is a better idea?" Thea asked.

The archer shook his head. "Who me? Nope. No way. I didn't say that."

"I thought not. The more Landon wields the Glyphblade, the stronger their connection will grow. And stronger is better where the Shadehaunter is concerned, but do as you wish. I need to pray."

Sorin leaned his head on his knees. "Yeah, like I was saying. Thea's got the right idea. You'd better practice with that thing, Landon, or things might get *worse*."

"Okay. Okay," the woodcutter said, slapping his sluggish muscles and getting up.

Reinier whined when his master's cloak slipped off his back.

"Sorry, b—" Landon stopped himself. Calling Reinier, *boy*, didn't feel appropriate anymore, but *girl* wasn't right either.

That raised an interesting question in Landon's mind: Why had Reinier chosen to be a boy dog? Was it for his benefit? Probably. And if that was the case, what else had Reinier sacrificed for him? Training by her order? A life of her own? Landon's head hurt. It was too much to reason out in his current state.

"Maybe move a bit farther away," Sorin suggested. "I'd rather you didn't grab the light from our candles."

"If I do, I'll be in the dark, myself," Landon protested.

Thea shook her head. "No, you won't. The Glyphblade will light the way."

Landon didn't know if being a consummate know-it-all came part and parcel with being a cleric or if naivete was a prerequisite for being a woodcutter, but either way, it was frustrating, especially considering how often Thea was right. Of course, she'd been wrong about the lights in the fog, but that was more the exception that proved the rule. Besides, the ploy had been pretty clever: find a cleric who worships the Light, let her stumble around in the dark until she gets desperate, and then show her what she's been praying for. Though now that he thought about it, maybe *clever* wasn't the right word. *Sinister* sounded more appropriate.

Tired of thinking, Landon begrudgingly sloshed across the muddy ground, holding the sword out before him. As soon as they left the circle, it started to glow.

His frustration mounted as he repeatedly failed to channel light with the sword. It glowed. That was good. And the runes along the length of its blade did their thing, too, but that was the extent of it.

"Come on! Show me your power. Blow something up. Do some damage!"

Landon swung the weapon wildly, making Reinier dart out of the way.

Heavy raindrops pelted his upturned face, and he screamed at the sky, "Even if I wanted to, I couldn't. There's no light to channel!"

Reinier let out a sympathetic howl.

Back at the camp, the rain had made Sorin's combination of self-recrimination, frustration, and anger at how much harder—and dangerous!—Braydn had made their travels, fester into a roiling pit in his stomach. It took a lot to get the archer mad, but Braydn had successfully tipped him over the edge. "I can't believe Braydn was sitting there chatting and drinking like he hadn't left us to die."

Anslim nodded in agreement. "He certainly didn't prove himself to be a worthy companion."

"That's putting it mildly."

Thea calmly wrung the water out of her golden hair. "It's most regrettable that he chose the path of darkness. It would be best if we didn't see him again."

"Never would be too soon, as far as I'm concerned," Sorin said, clenching his shaking fists, "but something tells me we haven't seen the last of that trickster. He gave up the Glyphblade too easily."

"Easily?" Anslim asked. "For all we know, we destroyed the marketplace."

"Sorin might be right. I'm beginning to think nothing with Braydn is what it seems," Thea suggested.

"Wait, did you hear that? She said I was right."

"I said, you *might* be right. The point is still open to debate."

"That's good enough for me. I'll take it."

The sound of Landon's boots making squishing sounds in the mud drew their attention as he returned from practice.

"I'm done for the night," he said, flopping onto the ground.

Thea opened her pack, pulling out a thin blanket. It was the last thing any of them had that was dry.

"Very well. It's time for us to get some rest anyway. Come. We'll drape this over our heads. It isn't much, but maybe we can find enough peace to sleep."

"I'll take the first watch," Sorin offered.

"Good, but first, let's set a few more candles. I'll ask the Light to join their flames so nothing can sneak through, but everyone take care. If the circle is broken, we'll be vulnerable."

The others watched as the candlelight formed a shimmering dome over them. When it was ready, Landon, Thea, and Reinier pulled the blanket over their heads, and Sorin set the first watch.

Thea motioned to the journeyman, who was still sitting on the other side of the sputtering fire. "You, too, Anslim. We'll share our body heat and keep the rain off our heads for a while."

"Thank you," he said, moving closer. "I wasn't sure you trusted me enough for that yet."

The look in the cleric's eyes belied her wariness, but the invitation was sincere.

As the night wore on, Sorin stopped playing with his ring and inspected the jars. The candles inside weren't the fancy ones ladies placed on dining room tables—elegant tapers or multilayered pillars carved and peeled into wax sculptures. These were stubby, tallow nubs that looked grotesque as they slouched into amorphous blobs. Esslla had given them a few beeswax candles, but they hadn't lasted long. Neither had the oil lanterns. They'd planned to replenish them in Moors Hollow, but that hadn't been possible in the end. So, it was back to the cheap stuff because cheap meant many, and when it came to candles in Kahr'anis, the more you had, the safer you were.

Unfortunately, in his preoccupied state—still fretting about Braydn and his role in bringing him into their party—Sorin failed to notice one particular candle guttering as it clung to life.

After he finished messing with the candles, the archer contented himself with grumbling about Braydn. He mumbled about traitors, swords, bars, and crossbows for a while, but even that got tiresome, and his eyelids grew heavy.

He told himself to hold on a little longer...let Thea sleep... but his eyelids won, and he unwittingly dozed off.

31 THE TREACHERY OF VOLGRETH

The neglected candle flickered as it reached the end of its wick. Each time it sputtered, Thea's shield faltered, and menacing shapes appeared in the shadows. As if understanding the importance of its job, the little tallow candle tried to stay alight, but, like all candles, it was born with a predetermined lifespan, making it destined to fail.

As the last vestiges of wax oozed from beneath the jar, the candle briefly glowed brighter, as if in singular defiance to the darkness waiting in the shadows. Then, the inevitable happened. Gloom swallowed the candle, masking its last gasp of life from view—a wisp of smoke trapped by its glass protector.

In the end, it would have been better if they'd left the candles scattered about as usual because the instant the candle went out, a gap in the dome appeared, and the inky blackness beyond congealed into an ominous form. Volgreth, the Shadehaunter, had come.

Trapped within a skeletal frame, the gaunt sorcerer stepped out of the night with a malicious smile playing across his face. His black robes billowed, as if blown by some unseen, spectral wind, adding to his fearsome presence, but it was his eyes that were most terrifying. In the deep sockets where they should have been, two glass globes glittered in the firelight. One stared fixedly at Landon while the other shifted between his companions. A lowly woodcutter, a dog, a would-be champion archer, a novice cleric, and...another. A puzzle. Volgreth didn't know what to make of Anslim, but he didn't care either. It pleased him to watch them sleep, vulnerable and utterly unaware of his presence. With dark energy pulsating through his spidery veins, Volgreth lifted a cadaverous hand.

The malevolence looming over Landon turned his dreams into nightmares, and he stirred.

Just as the sorcerer was about to strike the woodcutter down where he lay, Sorin's eyes snapped open, and he yelled, "Watch out!"

Without any concern for himself, Reinier used his powerful haunches to launch himself between the Shadehaunter and his master. Distracted by the commotion, Volgreth's spell didn't take full effect, but it was enough. The wolfhound yelped, collapsing limply on top of Landon.

"No!" Landon screamed, cradling Reinier.

Thea sprang from the ground with her arms spread wide, lifted by the Light within her. "Back, denizen of darkness! You are not welcome here!"

Both of Volgreth's eyes snapped to where she stood. It was the distraction Sorin and Anslim were hoping for, but the Shadehaunter proved to be far more cunning than they expected.

With a wave of his hand, Thea was thrown to the side. At the same time, his eyes shifted, one to the left, staring at the knife Anslim had hurled at him, and one to the right, fixed on the arrow Sorin had let fly.

With a click of his fingers, the projectiles changed direction, embedding themselves in the hard ground at his feet.

"Next time, Hero," Volgreth said, his voice dripping with malice and sounding like an eerie echo as if spoken from the depths of an abyss. Then, he stepped back into the shadows and was gone.

"Stop!" Anslim said, preventing Sorin from losing another arrow. "Don't waste them."

"That…that…was…" the archer stuttered.

"The Shadehaunter," Anslim finished, helping the archer sit down.

"How did he get past our defenses?" Thea asked, groaning as she pushed herself into a sitting position.

Everyone's eyes lit on the one candle that had burned out.

Anslim tossed a new one to the cleric from his pack, and she quickly replaced it. "How did this happen?"

Sorin buried his face in his hands. "I'm sorry. I must have dozed off."

"There's no time for that," Anslim said. "Reinier's hurt."

Unable to hold her animal form, Reinier had transformed back into a woman. She lay limply across Landon's legs, burned, broken, and breathing irregularly.

As the unrelenting rain continued to fall, Landon tried to cover her with his cloak. "Don't die. I beg of you, please, don't die."

Thea's face was tense with concentration. "Light, give me strength." She chanted healing prayers, but try as she might, she couldn't undo the shapeshifter's wounds. "They're too severe. I don't have the strength."

"But look," Landon said. "Her burn marks are gone."

"Some wounds can't be seen," Thea said, tears welling in her eyes.

"Please. You must."

Sorin panicked, his voice rising much higher than usual. "We can't let her die!"

"She needs help beyond what I can provide. I can do no more."

"I know of a place," Anslim said. He was off to the side, preparing to leave, as if he knew this would be what happened next.

The others looked questioningly at him.

"There's a healer. She takes care of those cursed by the dark. She can help," he explained. "I'll take Reinier there."

"I'm coming with you," Landon insisted.

"It doesn't work that way, and you're needed here."

"What do you mean? If she goes, I go!"

"And risk what happened in Moors Hollow? I think not."

"How dare you throw that in my face with Reinier hurt. She's watched out for me almost my entire life. It's my turn to help her."

"Yes, by staying here and finishing what you started," Anslim said resolutely.

"Fine! If you want to leave like Braydn did, go!"

As quick as a flash, Anslim unsheathed one of his daggers and placed it across Landon's throat. "If you ever say anything like that again, they'll be the last words you ever speak."

Sorin raised his bow, but Thea moved to block his shot.

"Calm yourselves. We're all worried about Reinier," she said. "Anslim, maybe you should explain what you mean. Why can't we accompany you?"

"Like I said, it doesn't work that way. She knows me. She'll listen to me. If I approach with a party of adventurers, she'll shut her doors, and Reinier will die of her wounds." Then, his tone got very serious. "Know that I would accompany you to the Unwrought Tower, if I could. The gods know I have unfinished business with Volgreth, as do all who live in Kahr'anis, but I'm the only one who can save Reinier. Let me go. I give you my word, I will do everything in my power to help her and return to you."

The silence that followed was deafening as everyone contemplated the implications of breaking their party.

"I told you that I would travel with you, but the time has come for us to part. Let me go."

Landon let out a sigh. "Do what you must."

"We'll meet again," Sorin said, gripping Anslim's arm.

"Say your goodbyes, Landon," Thea told the woodcutter.

"I did. I just told him to go."

"Not to Anslim."

Landon's eyes grew wide. "Oh no! Reinier is going to be fine. Anslim said—"

"I never said she'd be fine. I said I know of a healer."

"We mustn't waste any more time," Thea insisted, also preparing to leave. "Wrap her in this, Anslim." She handed him the spare robes.

Landon approached the journeyman.

Anslim didn't know if the woodcutter planned to speak to him or strike him. He was ready for either.

"Get her to the healer," Landon said, reaching out his arm. "Do you hear me? Get her there in time."

"By my life, I promise to do all I can, but I will promise no more, as there is no more I can give."

Landon let go and bent to kiss Reinier on the forehead. "Be well, my friend, and return to me." With that, he spun around and stormed off.

Sorin and Thea also said their goodbyes and hurried after him.

Anslim watched them go. "Let the Light be with you, always," he said earnestly. Then, he lifted Reinier's delicate body off the ground and strode in the other direction.

32 A VOW, RECLAIMED

"Who would have thought the rain stopping would be worse than when it was coming down?" Sorin asked, failing to avoid stepping in another puddle. The path had become treacherous because it was nearly impossible to tell solid ground from the river's sluggish waters.

Landon grunted in response.

After the front had passed, the fog had lifted a little, and the sky had brightened (as much as it ever did in Kahr'anis). At first, they were thankful, but that was before the weather changed from cold and miserable to humid and dismal.

Landon's cloak was so weighed down with dampness that he had to carry it over his shoulder like a body from a fire. Thea's fine robes, once a pristine symbol of the Light she worshiped, clung uncomfortably to her body. Both were all caked with mud from the knees down.

Sorin was the only member of their party who didn't look rode hard and put up wet, as the stableboys liked to say. But that was only because he'd removed his shoes and pants, explaining that his legs were easier to clean than his clothing.

Secretly, Thea thought he probably had the right idea, but she had no intention of traipsing across the plains without her robes on, not that the wet, translucent gray they'd become left anything to the imagination. It was enough to see Sorin's butt jiggle through his saggy braies as he marched along the muddy path in front of her. That being said, if she weren't a cleric, she'd have been forced to admit the image was rather silly, but clerics never wasted energy thinking about such inconsequential things.

Interrupting Thea's distracted reverie, Landon said, "Nope, not another step!" and stopped short.

Ever at the ready and still on edge from Volgreth's attack, Sorin whipped an arrow out of his quiver. "What is it?"

To the archer's surprise, Landon didn't warn them of some impending doom. Instead, the woodcutter said, "Turn back. I'll not risk putting you in further danger."

"You're joking, right?" Sorin asked, relaxing his stance. Then, he turned to Thea. "He's joking, isn't he?"

Thea gave him a quizzical look.

"My father's dead. We've been betrayed. Loric was possessed, and Reinier has been injured. This quest of ours is going to be the death of us, and if that's the inevitable conclusion of our journey, let it be mine alone."

"Now I know he's joking. You've been smoking something, haven't you?" Sorin asked, replacing the arrow. "Maybe a little touch of the 'shroom, eh? You might share it to help this journey a little less miserable."

"No. I mean it. Kahr'anis would be a far less hospitable place without the two of you in it. Find Anslim and Reinier and get as far away from here as possible. Find your fortune to the east or west, just don't go north. Go. Leave me to my fate." Landon turned to continue alone, but Thea barred his way.

"Just exactly who do you think you are talking to us like that?" she said, wagging her finger in his face.

Sorin rolled his eyes. "Now you've done it."

"After all we've been through, you think you can cast us aside like dirty rags?" the cleric continued. "If it weren't for us, you'd be rotting in the dirt. What is it? Big Landon has a shiny new sword? What do you plan to do with it? Chop down a tree or something? Because you certainly aren't going to use it to rid Kahr'anis of anything. You haven't even figured out how to use it yet!"

"Ooh, that hurts. But didn't you just yell at Anslim for saying something like that?" Sorin asked, pointing in the direction they'd come from.

Thea's sharp eyes darted to Sorin, "Zip it, arrow boy!"

The archer took a step back and whistled. "Things are *worser* than I thought."

"And as for you, Mister High-and-Mighty Woodcutter, what gives you the right to speak on our behalf? Didn't you learn anything at Esslla's?"

"Please, Thea," Landon begged, his voice wavering. "I've lost so many people already. I couldn't bear it if something happened to you or Sorin."

"Me and Sorin? Me and Sorin? What about you? How do you think we'd feel if you got dead?" she asked, waving her hand at Sorin to make him join the conversation.

Wide-eyed, the archer pointed to the cleric and mouthed, *What she said.*

Landon rolled his eyes. "Come on. All I'm saying is—"

"Nope! I'm not going to stand here while you mansplain how you're the chosen one and we should be good doobies and listen to what you say. *Run along home. You'll be late for supper.* Don't even open your mouth because that isn't going to happen!"

Not having the wherewithal to think of a response, Landon tried to sidestep Thea and found himself face to face with Sorin, though the archer had to stand on his toes to look the woodcutter in the eye.

"Did you honestly think we'd let you saunter off to garner all the glory for yourself? Let's see..." the archer said, counting on his fingers. "I saved you from Leering Ones, pulled you from the river, prevented you from being burned alive in Moors Hollow, and have been forced to sleep next to you in the rain? Give me some credit!"

Landon looked at Sorin, then Thea, and back again. Realizing there was nothing he could do or say to change their minds, he relented. "Okay. I was only trying to protect you."

"We love you too, you big lug," Sorin said, punching the woodcutter on the shoulder. "Now, can we get moving? I'm not wearing any pants."

"Not so fast," Thea said, still seething. "From this point forward, we pledge to live or die together. None of this do-ing-it-on-your-own hero stuff. This is not a quest of, or for, one. We walk together in the name of all who live under the shadow of the Unwrought Tower." Reaching out her hand, she added, "For Reinier, Loric, and all who've suffered by Volgreth's evil will."

"For father and mother," Landon said, placing his hand on hers.

Sorin put his hand on top. "For good ale and dry socks."

"He'll never change, will he?" Landon asked, shaking his head.

Thea sighed. "Not likely."

"We're off to Cragfall Mountains to meet our destiny!" Sorin announced, marching ahead.

"I can't take him seriously without his pants on," Landon said.

"I can't take him seriously, period," Thea agreed, the faintest hint of a smile playing across her lips.

PART III

CRAGFALL MOUNTAINS

33 LEAVING THE PLAINS

High above the valley, the wind whistled through the trees of Cragfall Mountains. It had taken longer than they'd hoped to start their climb, but things had picked up after happening upon a well-worn animal path. Landon hoped bears hadn't made it, but a deer would be nice. Behind him, Sorin and Thea plodded along as they followed the meandering track northward.

"What an inhospitable place," the archer mumbled, not used to the feeling of wind on his face. On the surface, one might have expected it to be refreshing after such a laborious trek across the plains, but it wasn't to someone who'd spent their life on the stagnant plains. And *spent* was an apt term for it, considering the cost of living was so high. Few people made it to an age of wisdom, and those who did shriveled like dried apples, sapped of any identifiable human traits.

"It's not so bad," Landon said, pulling his cloak around him and setting down his sack. "At least it smells better than the Brownwater."

"Yeah, well, Esslla didn't give me a heavy cloak like you, remember?"

Landon remembered. He still felt strange about it, but was thankful nevertheless. "At least the wind has dried our clothes."

"Thank the gods for small mercies," the archer said, not sounding the least bit thankful.

Thea didn't speak. Her garments did little to protect her from the rain and even less against the chilly wind. Thankfully, the Light within her provided the strength she needed to carry on, but she was thankful for the break. That, and the hem of her robes required mending. It had gotten caught on a sharp stick, and she wanted to fix it before it got worse.

Sorin set to work arranging rocks into a circle. When he finished, Landon stacked a pile of dry twigs he'd collected in the center, and it wasn't long before they had a small campfire to warm their cold hands as they ate lunch.

Moving away from a rock that was digging into his backside, Sorin looked at the mountains stretching into the distance. "How much farther do you think it is?"

Thea paused her sewing. "You must be joking. Are you in that much of a rush to face Volgreth again?"

"Not at all. I just want to get inside. I'm freezing."

"The last thing you're going to find in Nacturm Keep is comfort," Landon said, turning toward the archer who was twirling something between his fingers. "How many times does Thea have to tell you to stop messing with that thing before you listen to her?"

Thea didn't bother to look up. "I'm done wasting my breath. It's his funeral."

"Relax," Sorin said, holding it up. "It's only a piece of metal. A shiny gold one, true, but still just a bit of metal. See?" He slipped it onto his finger. "I've worn it plenty and nothing has happened."

"Something happened," Landon reminded him. "You moved that die, remember?"

"Yeah, I've thought a lot about that."

"And?"

"It didn't happen."

"What are you talking about? Anslim couldn't stop talking about it."

Sorin held the ring up to admire it. "Must have been a fluke because I've tried to do it again and nothing ever happens."

"Maybe it only works on dice?"

"Possibly. It certainly doesn't work on you."

"What?" Landon asked, checking to make sure the archer hadn't done anything to him. "Oh, you're just messing with me."

"Nope. I'm trying to move your bag right now. See? Nothing."

"Hey, don't go messing with my sack."

"Okay. I was just making a point." Sorin put his arm down but left the ring on.

Thea finished mending her hem and put the needle and thread away. "Yet."

"What did you say?"

"Nothing has happened *yet*."

The archer laughed. "Always cautious. You should try letting your hair down once in a while."

Thea's eyes narrowed, and she hissed like an angry cat. "I never put it up."

"It's a figure of speech. Oh, never mind."

"Never mind, nothing. Magic can be mercurial. You need to treat that thing with respect."

"Oh, I respect it, all right. I'm hoping it will fetch a good price in the marketplace."

Landon was about to voice his support for Thea when he heard something and raised his hand. The three of them stopped talking and listened.

The rustling didn't sound like the easy brushing of leaves moved by the wind. It sounded deliberate. Before they could take cover, someone appeared out of the undergrowth.

"You!" the archer hissed, drawing his bow.

"Did you miss me?" Braydn asked, a wild look in his eyes. "I've come to reclaim my property."

Landon unsheathed the Glyphblade. He may not have figured out how to wield its magic yet, but it was still a weapon no flesh could best. "Possession is nine-tenths of the law, as the catchpole likes to say."

"Yes, and the tenth percent is the profit I was promised."

Sorin came a hair's breadth away from letting go of the bowstring, but who should he shoot? Dozens of Bogeyfiends had ambled out of the bushes from what seemed like every direction.

They were grotesque, animalistic creatures covered with a patchwork of matted fur and scales. Most walked on two legs, though some crawled or slithered on the ground. Sharp horns protruded unnaturally in places no appendages should grow, and although they only stood a couple of feet high, the horror their beady, red eyes invoked almost made Sorin run away screaming.

Landon, Sorin, and Thea took a defensive pose by putting their backs to each other.

"More of Volgreth's monsters," the cleric said between prayers.

What had become the cleric's familiar dome-like protective barrier sprang up around them, leaving Braydn to pace around the edge. The sound of his laughter made the hair on the back of their necks stand on end.

"That's it, cleric. Call upon the Light, but you and I both know, you don't have the strength to keep your spell in place for long. I can see the bags under your eyes. You're exhausted like your friends. Speaking of which, where are Anslim and Reinier? Have you lost them, too?"

"Shut your mouth!" Landon said through gritted teeth. "Your tongue is not worthy to speak Reinier's name."

"Touchy, touchy."

One of the creatures attempted to penetrate Thea's protective barrier. The second it came in contact with the Light, Thea heard its thoughts, and she recoiled. Somehow, the spell had made a direct connection between them.

The snarling Bogeyfiend pushed back, and Thea screamed, "Light help me!"

"What's wrong?" Sorin asked, frightened by the sight of the cleric grasping her head with both hands.

The memory of Esslla's voice whispered in Thea's ear. *In time, you will be able to see into the dark no matter where it exists—even into the hearts and minds of men and beasts where the darkest of the dark often resides.*

A sinuous line of Light appeared between herself and the Bogeyfiend. Thea recognized it as the manifestation of their connection. With all her might, she pushed the Bogeyfiend's thoughts back, but she went too far and entered the beast's mind.

Sorin tried to get her attention. "What can I do to help?"

"I can hear their thoughts," she moaned, struggling to hold the connection.

"How awful! What are they planning?"

"It's not like that. It's more of a sensation or a feeling."

On the other side of the dome, a particularly hideous Bogeyfiend snarled and bared its jagged teeth.

The archer instinctively pushed his friends back in an effort to put as much space between himself and the monster as possible. "I'm pretty sure I don't need to read their minds to know their feelings."

The harder Thea focused, the more tangible the connection grew until she was in control enough to open her eyes. Instantly, the Bogeyfiend stopped and dropped to the ground, clawing at its head.

"Go!" she commanded.

"Where?" Sorin asked. "We're trapped."

"Not you! It."

Confused by what was happening and unable to think for itself, the creature clambered to its feet and scurried away on all fours.

"Wait! Did you do that?" the archer asked, wide-eyed.

Thea nodded, reaching out to other Bogeyfiends.

"Do it some more! Do it some more!" Sorin encouraged.

Numerous lines of light wormed through the air, connecting the cleric to many of the beasts. Several turned tail and ran, but one stopped, snarled, and turned back around.

"I think I just found the extent of my powers. Start shooting!"

The archer drew the bow and froze, his muscles quivering with the strain. For the first time in his life, Sorin didn't act on instinct because his instincts had been entirely overwhelmed. "Not me!" he yelled, thinking Thea had taken over his mind, too. Moving awkwardly to the left, he stepped wrong and tripped. The nock slipped from between his fingers, and the arrow shot wildly into the air before changing direction and striking the Bogeyfiend he'd originally been aiming at. "Did you see that?"

No one answered.

Making sure he wasn't dreaming, he fired another arrow in the wrong direction, directing it to its mark with his mind. Arrow after arrow found their target, not because of his impeccable aim but because he willed it to.

Thea watched an arrow change direction and follow a Bogeyfiend as it scurried up a tree. "How did you do that?"

"Do what?" Landon asked, swinging the sword back and forth to fend off the creatures in an attempt not to be bitten or scratched. "I hope you're doing better than me. I can't hit anything."

"Then chop them!" Sorin said, calling an arrow back to himself and catching it in midair.

"Chop them? Like a log?"

"Like an axe!"

"Oh! Yeah!" Landon immediately switched from jabbing and slashing to cleaving, bifurcating one of the monsters. The

Bogeyfiend attacking him never had a chance, falling to the ground, divided into two equal parts.

Sorin laughed. "Now that's what I'm talking about. Do that some more!"

But no matter how many Bogeyfiends the cleric turned, Sorin shot, or Landon split, more came.

Thea dropped to one knee. "It's no good. There are too many of them."

Looking supremely confident, the archer smiled. "Not for me. I figured out how I'm doing it. I forgot to take my ring off." He held it up, the arrow etched on top glowing brightly.

"What does that mean?" Landon asked.

"It's like the dice. They do what I want them to do. Watch!"

Sorin shot an arrow in the wrong direction and made it turn and strike one of the beasts.

"What in the world?" the woodcutter said, dispatching another Bogeyfiend.

Thea shook her head. She couldn't understand how the archer kept it all straight in his mind, shooting one instant and calling the arrow back the next.

Even so, it wasn't enough.

"My spell is faltering. Landon, use the Glyphblade," she commanded, acknowledging that they'd soon be overwhelmed.

"Are you sure that's a good idea?" Sorin asked, nocking two arrows and letting them fly at once. Now, he was showing off.

Landon huffed. "Thanks for the vote of confidence."

A Bogeyfiend broke through and rushed the archer, whom he killed by stabbing it with the arrow he was holding. "I changed my mind. Do something. Fast!"

This time, when Landon raised the weapon, the runes along the blade glowed. "It feels different." The weapon tugged at his hands, and he turned. "It's searching for something."

"Point it at the campfire."

Landon did as instructed, and flames leaped into the air. "Look out!" he yelled as a jet narrowly missed Sorin and set a tree on fire.

The archer dove out of the way. "Hey, I'm on your side!"

"Oh crap," Landon said as the sword pulled flames from the campfire *and* the tree.

Every time a new source ignited, the sword immediately drew the fire to it. The campfire and three trees. Now eight sources. Sixteen sources. In seconds, fire engulfed the surrounding forest and was growing exponentially. So much fire swirled over their heads that it sucked the oxygen out of the air.

"I can't stop it!" the woodcutter screamed.

The archer covered his head. "No kidding."

"Sorin, why aren't you helping him?" Thea asked, desperately holding onto a protection spell to keep them from being burned alive.

"How?"

"Direct the Light!"

"You want me to give him my ring?"

"No! Use your ring to guide the flames like you do the arrows or the dice."

Sorin had no idea how to do that, but he raised his arm and tried to visualize the Light striking a Bogeyfiend. It didn't work. "I can't."

"Use your arrows, then," Thea said, the smoke making her cough.

That made even less sense to the archer, but he figured he had nothing to lose—except his life, of course, if he didn't figure out how to make it work quickly.

He aimed at a Bogeyfiend and paused. Then, he turned and aimed directly at Landon.

"It's not my fault!" Landon yelled, misunderstanding what the archer intended to do.

Sorin whispered, "Trust me," before letting go of the bowstring.

As if in slow motion, Landon watched the arrow shoot straight at his chest before veering past the Glyphblade, taking the sword's Light with it. As the arrow streaked through the air, it weaved in and out of the undergrowth, lighting Bogeyfiends on fire as it flew.

"I don't believe it," the woodcutter said.

In seconds, the battle was over.

Allowing the last of her strength to be drained from her, Thea called on water in the air, ground, and even the plants to condense. There was a tremendous whoosh, and the fire around them was snuffed out. Exhausted and confused by her connection to the Bogeyfiends, the cleric fell forward onto her hands and then collapsed to the ground.

Sorin jumped up and down, yelling, "Whoooooeeeee! Did you see that? I mean, oh yeah!"

"Where is he?" Landon asked, running to the edge of the smoldering forest.

"I saw him slip away when the Bogeyfiends attacked," Sorin said, reaching out a hand and grabbing an arrow out of the air as it shot back toward him.

"Don't be cross," Thea said, weakly pushing herself into a sitting position. "I imagine he'll think twice before trying something like that again. The question that should concern you is, why did Volgreth's minions help Braydn?"

"There can be only one answer to that question," Landon said, seething with anger. "He's in league with the Shadehaunter.

Sorin almost leapt out of his skin. "What?"

"Landon's right," Thea said, regaining some of her strength. "It's the only answer that makes sense."

"That means he wasn't trying to steal the sword for himself. That's a good thing, right?"

Landon lifted one of the fallen beasts and placed it on a pile he was making. "What do you mean?"

"Because if Volgreth wants it, he either thinks the sword is powerful or that it's a threat. Either way, he's afraid of it."

"I admire your confidence, Sorin, but until we figure out how to use it, I think it's just as much a threat to us as to him," Landon said, continuing with his work. "I still don't understand what just happened."

Sorin joined him in collecting the Bogeyfiends. "It looked like you figured it out to me."

"I agree. You summoned the Light, and Sorin used his ring to guide it to our evil enemies," Thea said, matter-of-factly.

Landon stood with one half of a Bogeyfiend dangling from each hand. "I get that, but how?"

"Does it matter? It worked," Sorin said, taking a moment to inspect his quiver for broken arrows. "Yuck. I hope we find some water soon. I need to wash up. There's Bogeyfiend goo on everything."

The expression on Landon's face showed that he agreed with the archer. "Did you really control their minds?" he asked the cleric.

"That's a hard question to answer. It was more like the Light shining on their thoughts was too bright for them to handle, so when I told them to run away, they did."

Sorin whistled. "All that praying must be paying off. Remind me never to make her angry."

"You've asked me to do that before, and it hasn't stopped you yet," Landon said, tossing the last carcass on the pile.

"True. True."

Thea did her best to move her matted golden hair away from her eyes. "You don't have anything to worry about. I don't think I'm strong enough to control a person. The Bogeyfiends were more base. More animalistic, for lack of a better way to describe it. They don't think the way we do, so I thought for them."

"Even so, I'm not going to push my luck."

Landon pointed at the grotesque mound. "Someone else is going to have to light this. I've had my fill of fire today."

Sorin obliged and then sat down on a rock facing away from the pyre. "It's more than they deserve."

"Maybe," the woodcutter said, wiping down the Glyph-blade, "But it's better than leaving them lying around."

"No doubt."

Thea sat nearby, deep in thought.

"Uh, oh. I know that look," Sorin said, noticing her. "Thea's up to something."

"Not at all. I was just thinking that combining your abilities to direct the Light makes you a powerful adversary. If I may be so bold, we might have finally figured out a way to stop Volgreth."

Landon sheathed the sword. "I wouldn't go that far. I still don't know how Sorin made the fire follow his arrow."

Sorin elbowed him in the side. "I don't either, but take the compliment when you can get it."

"And why didn't Braydn use that spell of his and take the Glyphblade? He's done it twice before," Landon asked, puzzled that Braydn didn't take advantage of the Bogeyfiend's distraction.

"Because he couldn't," Thea explained. "I've been praying for the Light to prevent Braydn from casting spells on us since the night Loric died. My prayers must have been answered."

"Wait, does that mean he can't take my ring either?"

"As long as the spell holds."

Sorin reflexively covered the ring with his other hand. "How long is that?"

Thea looked at him blankly. "As long as the spell holds."

"Ah, yes. I totally understand now. Clear as crystal," he said, rolling his eyes.

Landon looked at his friends. They were tired and cold but also, in a way, rejuvenated by their newfound abilities. "Do we have to wait for that to finish burning? I don't want to risk setting the forest on fire again."

"No way. I can't take the stench," Sorin said, getting up.

Thea collected her things. "It'll be fine. I've asked the Light to watch over it."

"Then let's leave this place," Landon said, picking up his sack. "Best we keep moving," which they did, accompanied by Sorin chatting incessantly about his ring.

34 UNEXPECTED BEAUTY

As Landon and his companions hiked farther up the Cragfall Mountains, their muscles ached with the effort. All were in good physical health, but after spending a lifetime on the flat plains far below, they weren't used to climbing steep inclines. Adding to their difficulties, the air felt thin, making it hard to catch their breath.

"You sound like a bull in heat," Sorin wheezed. "Leave some air for us."

It surprised Landon that the archer could make a joke despite the grueling climb.

Thea smiled despite the pain. The clerics she studied with at the *Cloister of Eternal Light* never made jokes. They were unerringly kind, of course, but that was less due to their disposition and more because their order mandated it. The condescending way they spoke to each other never comforted her when she was lonely or made her feel better when she was sick.

"Whoa," Landon said, stumbling to a halt.

Sorin peeked around the woodcutter's broad shoulders, and his jaw dropped. Nestled in a valley between majestic snow-covered peaks was a tranquil lake that stretched as far as the eye could see. "Is it a mirage?"

"I don't think so."

A calmness washed over Landon as he breathed in the crisp air emanating from its pristine waters. It almost made the murky gloom of the Kahr'anis plains feel worlds away...almost.

The clouds parted, and a ray of sunlight glinted off the lake. It skipped across the water's surface in a long, golden stream that led right to his feet. On either side, towering evergreens stood nobly along the shoreline, inviting them to lie on their beds of soft pine needles.

Just to make sure he wasn't dreaming, Sorin pinched himself. "Yup. I'm awake."

"Have you ever seen anything like this?" Landon asked Thea, forgetting the exhaustion that had plagued him seconds earlier.

"Not in this lifetime. Let us take a break from our journey and rest here for a while."

"My thoughts exactly," Sorin said, pushing past Landon and heading toward the water's edge.

The woodcutter followed, but Thea stopped to prepare a small fire.

When Landon caught up to the archer, he was flat on his back, reveling in the soft green grass that grew close to the water before giving way to a white sandy beach.

"This is the life," he said, tilting his head and looking at Landon upside down. "You should try it. It's a sight better than the scrub grass and mud we're used to."

Landon knelt and touched it with his hand. It was cool and silky smooth. In front of him, the lake shimmered like a sheet of polished glass. "I honestly didn't know places like this existed."

"Stories are full of this kind of thing."

"Yeah, but those are stories. This is real."

The archer hopped to his feet and walked along the water's edge, scouring the ground for something. He found what he was looking for and said, "Watch this."

Flicking his wrist, he sent a flat stone skipping across the water. Using his ring's power, he made it change direction and jump into the air, where it did several loop de loops before disappearing, leaving ever-expanding rings on the placid lake's surface.

"Show off," Landon said good-naturedly. "I'm going to explore a little."

Sorin stood up from a deep bow to see that his audience had disappeared. Then, thinking a bath would be a good idea, he stripped off his clothes.

"What are you doing?" Thea asked.

"Taking a dip."

"It's freezing. Besides, I don't want to have to look at your butt."

"Actually, it doesn't feel as cold up here for some reason. Maybe it's the sun. Anyway, I'm rather fond of my buttocks, thank you very much. Gaze upon this paragon of beauty."

Thea turned her head. "I'd rather not."

"Suit yourself." Sorin leapt into the air, but the second his pinky toe touched the lake, he let out a yelp that echoed through the valley. There was a tremendous splash, and out of the middle of the erupting water, Sorin sprang back out again, running toward Thea.

"Foolish man. I told you it was freezing. Sit down and warm yourself by the fire."

"Th-th-thank-k-k. Y-y-you."

Later that evening, after Sorin had finally stopped shivering and Landon had bedded down for the night, Thea sat quietly by herself, staring at the moonlit ripples in the water. Recent events had caused many ripples in their lives, and although as the days had passed, the surface of the water had begun to clear for Sorin and Landon, it hadn't for her—metaphorically speaking, of course, as all clerics liked to speak in riddle, instruct in simile, and think in analogy. Truth be told, they invested a great deal of time practicing these skills, though most of the people they conversed with wished they hadn't.

Unfortunately, even after endless hours of contemplation, she was no closer to figuring out her place in the world than when they'd begun their trek across the plains. "I pray and feel my powers growing, but cannot see the path of the Light. How can I hope to achieve High Priestess if I don't understand the role I'm supposed to play in the coming battle with Volgreth?"

Was she to be a healer? No. She could mend light wounds, but her skills hadn't developed enough to be much help in battle. The incident with Reinier had proved that.

Protector? No. Her Light shield was strong enough to repel the shadows but not most corporeal beings. Even the tiny Bogeyfiends eventually managed to push past her defenses. They would have been overwhelmed in seconds if she hadn't discovered the ability to change their minds about attacking.

Mind control? Absolutely not! She was barely able to persuade the little daemons to flee. Controlling a powerful sorcerer like the Shadehaunter was out of the question.

Turning to her faith, Thea prayed. "I beg of you. Show me how to walk in the path of the Light."

To her surprise, a voice came to her floating on the wind.

Patience, my child. All who walk in the Light are shown the way.

"Esslla?" Thea asked, looking up.

The voice didn't answer. At first, she worried it might be a trick again, like the will-o'-the-wisps, but she shook off the feeling. The presence hadn't felt malicious, and neither did this place.

Comforted by the experience, she curled beside Landon and prepared to rest, but not before praying for protection. It wasn't because she didn't trust the archer who had first watch; his mistake had been an honest one. But ever since Volgreth's appearance, she'd focused as much energy as she could spare to devise a spell to warn them if evil appeared out of the shadows. The trouble was that shadows, by their very nature, were indistinct, making it hard to get the sensitivity right.

This night, she wasn't too worried. The full moon cast a bright light over the lake, the fire burned brightly, and they'd set up a circle of candles around them. Satisfied they were reasonably safe, she let sleep take her.

35 PRACTICE MAKES PERFECT

Early the next morning, Landon stood a safe distance from camp, staring at the candle he'd lit. It stared back at him in singular defiance of his attempts to channel its light using Glyphblade. Gripping the sword so tightly that his knuckles turned white, he commanded the flame to come to him.

Nothing. Neither the stone nor the sword did anything.

Narrowing his eyes, he pointed the blade at the candle flame and whipped the sword in the other direction.

"Whoosh!" he commanded.

Not even a flicker.

He knew it was silly, but what other word was he supposed to use? That's what the fire sounded like when it shot from the blade in *The Leaky Bunghole* and in the forest. If only he'd gotten a ring like the archer—something that relied on intuition rather than skill. That would have been much easier.

For the next hour, Landon continued to try to force the sword to respond to his wishes, but he simply couldn't tap into the magic that had flowed so effortlessly when they were in battle.

"Wait!" he said, getting an idea.

Attempting to relive the terror of the Bogeyfiends' ambush, he lifted the blade. A jolt ran through his body, and he cracked an eyelid to peek at the candle.

Did it twitch?

No. It must have been a gust of air.

It flickered again.

That wasn't the wind.

Suddenly, the runes along the sword's blade pulsated with an ephemeral light. Concentrating with all of his might, Landon willed the flame to him, and it leapt from the candle to the blade.

"Yes!"

Then, he panicked because now that he'd captured the flame, he didn't know what to do with it.

"Un-flame! De-fire! Anti-burn!" he commanded, but the blade remained ringed with flames.

Running down to the water's edge, he thrust it into the lake. There was a splash and a whoosh, but it didn't put the blade out! Under the water, it continued to burn with a magical intensity that illuminated the surrounding area. Pulling it out again, he waved the sword around, making streaks of fire in the dusky morning sky.

A commotion caught his attention, and his excitement at calling the flame to him and the fear of being unable to put it out evaporated. Without hesitating, he sprinted back to camp, holding the flaming sword over his head. What had happened? Leering Ones? Alderbeasts? Bogeyfiends?

"I'm here!" he yelled, bursting into the clearing, but no monsters had attacked his friends. Instead, he saw Sorin attempting to wrangle a fish flapping around his feet.

"I caught a fish!" the archer said, smiling broadly. "With my bare hands! Well, almost. It's a slippery bugger. Hey, you got the sword to work."

Coming to his senses, Landon panicked again. "I can't put it out!"

Thea walked over to him and said, "Calm."

The woodcutter instantly relaxed, and the flames disappeared. "How did you do that?"

"The Light calms me, so I assumed it would do the same for you."

"I guess you were right."

"Perhaps. But maybe you had something to do with it. Much can be achieved when we trust each other. When you heard me speak, maybe you believed that you could be calm, and you were."

"What if you said *focus*? I need help with that, as well."

Thea chuckled. "That's something everyone struggles with. Keep practicing. You'll learn."

"Did you two hear me?" Sorin asked as the fish wriggled out of his hands again. "I caught breakfast!"

Landon and Thea shared a glance, and then they went to see what Sorin was on about. To their delight, the fish turned out to be surprisingly large! However, before Thea would let them clean Sorin's catch, she insisted on blessing the fish and thanking the Light for such a wonderful gift. Their stomachs rumbled in anticipation of a real meal—no dried mystery meat and nuts today!

Working together, they gutted the fish and scraped off its scales. It wasn't the most pleasant of jobs, but they smiled and laughed as they worked. Thea foraged for herbs, and Landon found some aromatic hickory wood for the fire. Sorin used a broken arrow as a spit, resting it on top of two Y sticks, and soon the air filled with the mouthwatering aroma of fresh meat as it cooked. No fish had ever been more appreciated.

The meal lifted their spirits in a way they hadn't thought possible, camping high in the menacing Cragfall Mountains. How they'd stumbled on this beautiful oasis, they'd never know, but they were thankful for the respite from their journey.

Later that day, as the sun slipped below the horizon, the trio watched the clouds overhead turn bright hues of red, orange, and yellow—all of which were reflected in the lake's still water.

"By the Light," Thea gasped, awestruck by the sunset's beauty. "We are truly blessed."

"It's hard to believe we're so near Nachturm Keep," Sorin said, breaking the moment's serenity. "Why does Volgreth get to see stuff like this while we spend our lives surrounded by fog?"

"Shh," Thea scolded him. "Don't speak the Shadehaunter's name in such a pristine place. There's time for thoughts like that later. Right now, bathe in the beauty of the world."

Sorin raised his replenished waterskin. "Cheers to that."

As the last vestiges of daylight faded into twilight, the trio sat shoulder to shoulder, thankful that they had each other and dreading what evils tomorrow was sure to bring.

36 REUNION

The wind whipped Landon's cloak, making it billow behind him. The good feelings he and his companions had shared at the lake were but a distant memory, having been replaced by a deep sense of foreboding as they approached Volgreth's lair, the Unwrought Tower. Landon's chest felt tight, and his hands dripped with sweat despite being cold. Back in Brownwater, the decision to face the Shadehaunter had been born of raw emotion and loss. Now, he wondered if he'd been too hasty.

The woodcutter had come to the conclusion that every new skill they acquired, or ability they achieved, didn't make them more powerful but instead revealed how much they didn't understand about the world. And if he and his friends had progressed this far in such a short time, what did that mean for an evil sorcerer who'd been honing his skills for generations? Could they honestly hope to outmatch Volgreth? They were about to find out.

Landon glanced at his companions. Their grim determination told him they were thinking the same thing.

They'd finally made it to their destination: Nachturm Keep. Everyone in Kahr'anis knew where it was, nestled in the highest reaches of the Cragfall Mountains, mainly because it was impossible to miss the Unwrought Tower sticking out of the center of it. Everyone sensed its presence, even if their eyes weren't strong enough to see it or the weather prevented them from peering into the highest reaches of the mountains.

Here, in the northernmost parts of Kahr'anis, people shielded their eyes when they walked outside, even though the sun didn't shine. It was known as the *plains wave,* and it wasn't a greeting or to let someone know you were leaving. It was because no one willingly looked to the northwest.

In defiance of this tradition, Landon, Sorin, and Thea walked right up to the keep's front gate.

The most unsettling part of their arrival wasn't the rotting curtain wall or looming tower. It was that the gate was wide open with no one guarding it. There were no hordes of Bogeyfiends or Alderbeasts. No army of evil henchmen, Leering Ones, or other foul creatures. All they saw was a gaping hole and darkness, the scariest thing in all of Kahr'anis.

"What do we do now?" Sorin asked. "Waltz in as if we aren't entering the ninth circle of hell?"

"I think we need to be a little more cautious than that," Landon said, expecting to see the Shadehaunter emerge from the gloom at any instant.

"He won't attack us out in the open," Thea said as if reading the woodcutter's mind. "We're playing his game now."

Landon didn't like the sound of that, and neither did Sorin, as evidenced by his furtive glances and unwillingness to lower his bow.

"Are we going to stand here waiting for something to happen? What's our next move?" the archer asked.

"First things first," Thea said, lighting a candle and praying to be shielded from evil. She knew the spell wouldn't fully protect them, but anything was better than nothing. "Do we have any of those torches left, Landon?"

The woodcutter checked his sack. "No. Plenty of candles, though."

"If only Loric were here to cast that spell of his," Sorin said before almost choking on his tongue.

To their horror, a skeletal figure emerged from the shadows. It was emaciated, its life having been drained but deprived of eternal rest. The ghoul wore tattered robes that hung loosely from its bony frame, and where its eyes should have been, there were two impenetrably deep, dark holes.

"Loric," Thea gasped, her voice trembling with grief.

The twisted creature's movements were mechanical and unnatural as it turned toward her. His face was expressionless, and his eyes…his eyes…

"Don't look!" Sorin said, forcibly turning Thea's head.

She struggled to shake off the sensation of falling into a darkness that had almost overwhelmed her. "Light help me."

The trio remained glued to the spot. They'd watched helplessly as Loric had been turned into a Leering One, but they'd never expected to see him again.

Landon gripped the hilt of the Glyphblade. "Volgreth will pay for what he's done."

In response, Loric raised his hands. There was a sudden flash, and he unleashed a gust of wind directed at the three of them.

"How can he still be a wizard?" Sorin asked, tumbling out of the way. "Leering Ones are just dead zombie things infected by Volgreth's shadows."

"Obviously not," Landon answered, unsheathing the Glyphblade. "We have no choice."

"Choice? To do what?" Thea asked, dreading the answer.

"Kill him."

"Light, forgive us."

The wide-eyed look on Sorin's face revealed how they all felt, but he knew they had no other choice. If they were going to have any chance at stopping the Shadehaunter, they had to get by Loric first.

With one last glance at each other, they attacked.

Using the power of his ring, Sorin directed his arrows to their mark, but the wizard turned them back with gusts of air. Time and time again, the archer tried, to no avail.

"He's too strong," Sorin said, rolling out of the way and getting to his feet.

Thea whispered. "No, he isn't. If he wanted to, he could have killed us by now. Something is holding him back. I think Loric's still in there somewhere."

"With me!" Landon yelled, and he ran directly at the wizard.

The cleric threw up her arms and prayed, "Fill Loric's eyes with Light!"

Bright jets burst from her hands, and the wizard stumbled back, blinded by the onslaught of Thea's purity.

"She's doing it," Sorin said, loosing arrow after arrow. Each time one skidded off the wizard's shield of wind, the archer deftly called it back before letting it fly again.

Landon pushed his way toward the wizard, his hair and cloak flailing wildly in the wind. It was less of an attack now and more a release of energy to keep them at bay. Step by step, the woodcutter inched closer. Then, it happened.

One of Sorin's arrows breached Loric's defenses, piercing the wizard's arm. Loric screamed, not of pain but fury, but it wasn't the debilitating cry of the Leering Ones he'd previously heard. Loric was weakening.

Buffeted by the wind, Landon whispered, "Forgive me, friend," as he placed the tip of Glyphblade against the wizard's chest. The air crackled with magical energy, and time slowed. Landon felt tears streaming down his face as he advanced, but he did not falter.

The glowing sword penetrated Loric's magical shield, and the weapon's sharp tip pierced the wizard's chest. The creature that was once their friend howled, but he was powerless against the sword's righteousness. Landon thrust his arms forward until the guard prevented him from pushing the blade farther into the wizard's body. Then, as terrible as it was to do, he wrenched the blade back, and Loric collapsed to the ground. Light burst from the point of impact, destroying the writhing shadow within.

Thea rushed to Loric's side, sobbing with grief as she pleaded for the wizard's salvation. "I beg of you, please release our friend from this torment!"

A golden aura radiated from her body, fully enveloping the wizard.

Thea prayed harder and harder, pleading for the darkness that had taken their friend to be cast off and that Loric be accepted into the Light. "Grant him peace. Let him find comfort in your embrace."

Loric's gaunt features slowly began to take on a healthier appearance.

"It's working," Sorin said, lowering his bow.

The black holes disappeared, and the wizard blinked his multi-colored hazel eyes. "You have saved me," he said, taking a deep breath. "Thank you. Thank you all."

Thea kissed him on the forehead. "Forgive us, Loric."

The old wizard smiled. "There is nothing to forgive. All who walk in the Light find redemption," he said with the last of the air in his lungs. Then, Loric passed from the earthly plane.

For a moment, there was complete silence. Landon, Sorin, and Thea stared at their fallen comrade, grief-stricken and broken by the reality of what they'd done.

Landon held the Glyphblade at arm's length. "I killed him. I killed Loric."

"No, Landon. You set him free," Thea said, laying Loric's head on the ground.

Sorin struggled to control his emotions as he looked at the shattered vessel that was once his friend's body. "We can't leave him here."

Before Thea had the chance to respond, a terrible laughter echoed from within the Nacturm Keep. Cruel and unhinged, it burrowed into their minds, raising goosebumps across their bodies.

"Volgreth," Landon hissed. "Show yourself, Shadehaunter!"

The dreadful laughter grew louder, reverberating against the stone walls. It surrounded them, coming from everywhere and nowhere at once.

"We need to keep moving," Thea struggled to say, recognizing the laughter for what it was: a spell of confusion. "Take hold of the blade!"

"What?" Landon asked, unable to hear her above the sorcerer.

Thea pulled the woodcutter's hand toward her and gripped the sword with him. Then she did the same with Sorin's hand, and together, they held the Glyphblade high. It grew brighter and brighter until it shone like the sun, dispelling the gloom surrounding them and breaking the evil sorcerer's spell.

"Amazing," Sorin said. "Is that all we have to do to defeat him?"

Thea shook her head. "Hardly. That was a simple spell. I'm sure he has many more powerful spells waiting for us. That was a test."

"Which means he knows we aren't to be trifled with," Landon added.

"Yes. The next time we meet, it won't be as easy to stop him."

Sorin tried to move but tripped over his own feet. "I'm all right. I'm all right. Just in case you were wondering, not that you were."

"Get a hold of yourself," Thea said, not in the mood for jokes. "We'll lay Loric to rest. Then, we'll send the Shadehaunter back to the darkness where he belongs. He will have no peace. He will have no rest for all eternity."

37 THE UNWROUGHT TOWER

"Ow! Blasted steps! Why are they so uneven?" Landon said, slipping and landing on his knee with a sickening thump.

"To make attacking the castle harder," Sorin said, deftly avoiding the woodcutter's other leg.

"What do you mean?"

"They spiral clockwise, and the stairs are at different heights to make it harder for intruders to advance."

"Well, it's working!"

"Shh," Thea admonished. "I can't hear with you two bickering."

Sorin helped Landon back onto his feet. "We weren't bickering."

"Shh!"

"Okay, okay."

After burying Loric's body and passing through the castle's outer curtain wall, they'd followed a corridor into the keep itself. From there, they'd moved stealthily through the hallways, encountering nothing more than the sound of their footsteps echoing off the glistening stone walls.

Much to their surprise, everburning torches had been hung at intervals along the corridors, making navigating the castle easier. Their light flickered off pools of frigid water, which the party avoided as much as possible. Light had been the last thing they'd expected to encounter in a castle inhabited by the Shadehaunter. Thea surmised it was from before Volgreth took over the castle and built the Unwrought Tower, but that was only a guess.

One area was completely flooded, and they were forced to wade across. Luckily, no drop-off into oblivion was concealed by its reflective surface, and nothing beyond a few leeches lurked in its depths. After stopping to inspect each other to remove the blood-sucking creatures, they'd continued on their way.

Only once did they open a door to peer inside. Its rusty hinges screeched so forlornly that they decided not to look for anything more than the way to the tower because even though the halls seemed deserted, they knew that wasn't the case. Somewhere in this evil place, the Shadehaunter or his evil minions awaited their arrival.

Luckily, it wasn't long before they found what they were looking for: the entrance to the Unwrought Tower. Aptly named, as the tower looked like a cancerous tumor growing vertically out of Nacturm Keep, it stretched high into the sky toward Volgreth's workshop and lair. It was the terminus of their journey, but hopefully not the end of their lives.

Landon led his friends up the treacherous staircase, holding the glowing Glyphblade before him, both for protection and light, as there were no torches here except the two Sorin and Thea had liberated from the lower keep's walls. He knew they were playing into the sorcerer's hands, but what other option did they have?

As with the keep, there was no shortage of rooms in the tower, though most looked like cells. If Anslim and Braydn were still with them, they would have been forced to stop along the way to check for treasure, but Anslim had his own quest to contend with—saving Reinier—and Braydn...

Landon spat.

"Hey! What'd you do that for?" Sorin asked.

"Bad taste in my mouth."

After turning the last corner, Landon saw the stairs stopped at the edge of a dimly lit antechamber. On the other side, two enormous metal doors barred the way. The shimmering, arcane symbols covering them made it clear that they'd reached the last stop of their journey.

"Welcome, weary travelers," Volgreth's voice echoed through the tower. "I'm glad to see you have finally arrived. As people say, my home is your home, though they probably don't mean it as permanently as I do."

The sorcerer laughed, and Sorin put his fingers in his ears, in case it was a confusion spell again.

Thea shook her head, mouthing, *Not that kind of spell.*

The archer lowered his fingers, but he kept them at the ready.

Landon had heard stories of sorcerers going in for a bit of flair with everything they did, but he was in no mood for banter. "Enough. We aren't here to play games."

"So serious!" Volgreth's evil voice boomed. "Must we dispense with niceties so soon? Are you sure this is what you want?"

The doors opened with a crash, and a swarm of bats flew out. Landon, Sorin, and Thea shielded their heads, but they'd seen too much to let something as contrived as a colony of bats shake their confidence. The cleric prayed for Light, and the animals flew away down the steps.

"He's toying with us," Landon said, preparing to charge into the room.

"Don't act rashly. That's what he wants," Thea whispered. "Play the game, for now. Our time will come."

Landon stepped toward the open doors, struggling to control his anger.

"Come, come. Don't dilly-dally," the sorcerer said condescendingly. "Accept your fate."

Landon took another step. "It's time for you to leave Kahr'anis, Volgreth."

"Is it? Don't you like what I've done with the place?"

Unable to listen to the sorcerer a second longer, Landon rushed into the room, swinging the Glyphblade wildly, but Volgreth wasn't there. He'd been tricked, just like Thea had warned. There was the wrenching sound of metal on metal as the doors closed, and the others rushed in, not wanting to be separated.

"Nice one," Sorin said, patting Landon condescendingly on the back.

"Ah, and here are your friends," the disembodied sorcerer's voice mocked. "To come all this way for naught. It must be disheartening."

The space around them was filled with tables and shelves covered with the sorcerer's mischief. Cauldrons bubbled and glooped; glass jars preserved all manner of disgusting things, and the musty smell of old books hung in the air along with the heavy scent of incense and scorched herbs.

"Did you honestly think you could challenge me? Tell me, what was your plan? Did you even have one?" Volgreth emerged from the shadows without warning or sound.

Sorin was ready. He shot an arrow, but the sorcerer disappeared again, leaving it to clank against the stone and fall to the stone floor. The archer didn't bother calling it back as the shaft had shattered on impact.

Here and there, Volgreth appeared and disappeared, making Landon, Sorin, and Thea waste energy preparing for an attack that never came. Losing patience, Landon raised the Glyphblade.

"No, don't!" Thea yelled before diving for cover.

Surrounded by dark energy, the blade channeled fire from several places in the room and shot it in every direction. Even Landon was forced to drop to the floor to avoid being hit.

Volgreth laughed again. "You are making this too easy, Mucklucker!"

Landon was stunned. Did the sorcerer know that much about him?

"Look out!" Sorin yelled.

Inky black shadows groped for them. Tendrils reached out from under tables, and evil shapes slid out from behind bookcases. Thea begged for more strength, but she was no match for the sorcerer.

"Face it, Shadehaunter!" Sorin yelled, trying to taunt the sorcerer into the open. "You've wasted away in your tower for too long. You're nothing but a shadow of your former self."

"What are you doing?" Landon asked.

"That!"

Just as the archer had hoped, the shadows gathered together, morphing into the sorcerer.

"Insolent fool!" Volgreth raged, one glass eye staring at Landon and the other fixing on the archer. "Do you think your pitiful play on words is enough to trick me into making a mistake so catastrophic as to give you the upper hand? You are a naive child not worth my time!"

The Shadehaunter released a blast of energy that passed through Thea's protective shield unhindered and swept Sorin off his feet. Landon watched as his friend was flung across the room, and the contents of tables and shelves were sent crashing to the floor.

"Sorin!" Landon yelled, but the archer didn't respond.

Thea let the shield fail.

"Thea, why?"

"I must find a better use for my strength."

The walls of the Unwrought Tower shook violently as Volgreth unleashed the full force of his dark magic. The air vibrated and became heavy, pressing on them, making their ears throb painfully. Thea was the first to fall, whisked off her feet, and thrown across the room. She was soon followed by Landon, who was tossed against a shelf stacked with books.

Shaking his head, he looked up to see Volgreth advancing toward him. Through the haze of pain, he saw Thea crumpled against the base of a massive iron cauldron. Her breathing was shallow and labored. Sorin remained motionless against the far wall.

Scrambling for something to help him, Landon grabbed a book. Inside were curious symbols and arcane writing he didn't understand. Hopefully, he thought, they held some unseen power.

Volgreth grabbed Landon and lifted him as if he didn't weigh anything. "Many more worthy than you have challenged me," the sorcerer said, raising a hand. "But I am not without respect for the attempt. I will give you a choice: Take your friend Loric's place in my legion, and I will let your friends go, or refuse and watch them die where they lie."

"Never."

Volgreth brought his arm down like an axe, but Landon caught it in the open book. The Shadehaunter shrieked when something oozed out of its pages, congealing around his hand. Forced to defend himself from whatever evil had been released at his touch, he dropped the woodcutter.

Landon fell hard to the ground, but he didn't care about his own pain. Scanning the floor, he was overjoyed to see that Sorin was okay. Dragging a foot behind him, the archer had an expression of razor-sharp determination on his face as he fired arrow after arrow at the Shadehaunter. Then Landon was overjoyed to see Thea move. They weren't defeated yet!

Chanting words no ears should ever hear, Volgreth managed to dispel the grimoire's incantation and adroitly deflect Sorin's arrows, sending them toward Sorin. Back and forth they flew. Soon, the room was filled with arrows zinging this way and that.

The woodcutter marveled at Sorin's ability to keep so many in the air at once. Suddenly, one turned toward him, but Sorin made it curve away and race back toward the sorcerer.

Realizing this was the opportunity he'd been waiting for, Landon raised the Glyphblade and charged.

Volgreth smiled wickedly, but before he struck the wood-cutter down, Sorin made an arrow stop midair, spin around, and shoot straight down at the Shadehaunter from directly over his head. The Shadehaunter was forced to look up, and Thea ran into Landon with as much force as she could muster.

"Go!" she yelled.

Landon stumbled backwards, throwing himself against the door and following his friends out of the room.

Volgreth waved his hand, and all of the arrows shot toward Landon. Grunting with the strain, he pushed the metal door shut in time to hear them ricochet off the other side.

Thea grabbed Landon's hand. "Don't stop! Find someplace to hide."

"This way!" Sorin said, favoring his leg as he descended the stairs. On the next level down, he located a door that wasn't locked. "I really, really hope there aren't any boobies."

Not taking the time to check, he pulled on the handle.

38 ANCIENT SECRETS

The door's rusted hinges let out a frighteningly loud squeal, sending a shiver down Landon's spine. He reflexively stuck out a foot to stop it from moving.

"Like none of us saw that coming," Sorin grumbled, letting go of the handle. "Of course, the creepy old door in a haunted tower creaks."

Landon pushed him out of the way and jabbed the glowing Glyphblade into the room.

The archer put his hands on his hips. "Excuse you."

"What? Do you want to risk any shadows where Volgreth can suddenly appear?"

"Nope. Not me. I don't want that at all. After you."

Before the woodcutter could enter, it was his turn to be pushed out of the way. Thea stepped between her companions and prayed for light. Anything shiny in the room began to reflect some unseen aura, illuminating the space.

Landon and Sorin were dumbfounded.

When the woodcutter regained his power of speech, he said, "Wow, I've never seen you do that before."

"The more I call on the Light, the more wondrous it becomes."

"I'd say."

The terror of the moment broken, Sorin leaned pensively against the black stone wall. "Does anyone else think it was strange that Volgreth didn't kill us?"

Instantly, tensions returned to their previous high.

"Hold your tongue!" Thea hissed. "We don't know that we're alone yet."

"But he didn't even follow us."

"Volgreth is sadistic. Ever seen a cat play with a mouse it's caught?"

"Yes."

"I imagine our despair is more satisfying than killing us outright. It prolongs the game."

Sorin followed his companions into the room, plopping into the first dusty chair he saw. "Okay, that's enough. I get the picture. He's the cat. We're the hairball."

"What are you doing? We don't have time for a rest," the cleric said.

"It's my leg."

She knelt to inspect it.

"Ow! Stop poking it."

"Hold still, you big baby. Nothing's broken."

"In that case, poke away," Sorin quipped. "Hey! I didn't mean for you to actually do it. Don't you know sarcasm when you hear it?"

"Clerics never use sarcasm."

Landon and Sorin froze, not knowing how to react to such a ridiculous claim.

"It was a joke," she said, shaking her head.

Sorin sighed. "Whew. I thought you'd lost touch with reality for a minute there."

"Oh no. I still know this hurts," Thea said, poking Sorin's leg.

He yelped but didn't protest. The cleric had just tried to use humor to make him feel less anxious. That was a big step for her, and he appreciated it.

"Any better?" Thea asked, completing her prayers.

Sorin tested the leg. "Much. Thanks."

Satisfied they were safe, for now, Landon said, "I think this is Volgreth's study, or was at one time."

Tall bookshelves loomed overhead, but they weren't like the ones in Volgreth's workshop or back at the fortress in Bleeding Tree Forest. The books here had been carefully preserved, though they hadn't been touched in years. Most of the tomes had pieces of rotting parchment sticking out of them as if someone had marked the most important parts for their research. In addition to books, relics were scattered throughout the room. There were warped mirrors, tarnished silver containers, strange instruments fashioned from bone, and a variety of colorful stones, most of which glowed with Thea's spell.

"I don't like this place," the cleric said, crossing her arms as if she were cold. "There's dark magic here."

Landon shrugged. "There's dark magic everywhere in the tower. I'll be glad when we're rid of this place."

"You mean, *if,*" Sorin added.

"I'm trying to think positively."

Thea ran her finger across a stack of books. "I recognize many of these titles. These texts contain forbidden knowledge. My order has always believed that the written word of the dark was destroyed when Light came into the world, but obviously, it has survived."

"Hey, check this out," Sorin said, pulling a capsa from between two dusty volumes. Unlike the other rotting documents, books, and furniture, the tubular case was in excellent condition, finished with sparkling gold and platinum filigree that glowed with Thea's spell. "Now that's treasure."

Landon tried to see what the archer was holding. "What did you find?"

"A scroll holder thingy. I wonder what's inside." Sorin popped off the end and poured the contents into his hand.

"Well, would you look at that? A scroll. What a shocker. I was just saying to myself, *Wouldn't it be cool if the scroll holder thing had a scroll in it?*"

Thea marched over. "Stop playing with that. You don't know if it's dangerous."

"But aren't spells written in some kind of mystical cipher? You know, so lowly archers like me can't read them? Well, I can read this. It says—"

"Don't!" Thea yelled, snatching it from his hands.

"Wait a minute. I found that."

"First, you open it without checking for hidden protections, and then read it aloud? It's like you want to get hurt."

"But that's what I'm trying to tell you. It's not magic. It looks normal. No cipher."

Thea's eyes widened as she inspected the parchment. "You fool! Traps don't only spray acid or make you fall into pits and stuff. Some are far more clever than that. This is a spell to summon a daemon. And since no mage would willingly invoke such a thing—"

"Evil ones would," Sorin interjected weakly, reclasping his messenger bag where he'd intended to put the capsa.

Thea ignored him. "This one is written in such a way that anyone can read it."

"That doesn't make sense. Normal words don't hold magical power. Even I know that."

"That's the trick," she continued. "It's basically self-translating. It appears to the reader in whatever language they speak, even though it's written in runes. Then, some doofus like you comes along and says, 'Oh look, it's not in that magical writing stuff, so it must not be a spell,' reads it aloud, and plop, there's a daemon in your lap!"

"Oh."

The cleric grew silent, and both Landon and Sorin focused on her. Something was wrong.

Thea lowered the scroll. She had a worried look on her face. "This speaks of the Witchingwraith. I wonder…"

Landon tried to coax her into finishing the thought. "Wonder what?"

Instead of answering him, she said, "Try and find Volgreth's notes."

"In this mess?" Sorin asked, grabbing the first book he saw.

"It won't look like the other books. Maybe a small journal or codex."

"What's that?"

"A collection of loose parchments," Landon answered.

Thea looked pleased. "Exactly. It may or may not be bound, and it very likely is written in code."

Sorin gave a thumbs-up. "Got it."

The three of them set to work scouring the study for anything that looked like the sorcerer's notes. The room wasn't huge, but the number of books in it made the search take a considerable amount of time.

Landon understood many of the titles and even the texts inside, thanks to the lessons his father had taught him, but nothing seemed relevant until he accidentally knocked a small leather notebook to the floor. He was about to open it when the cover caught light reflected from a nearby platter, revealing a symbol he didn't recognize. "Thea, I think you should take a look at this."

The cleric peeked her head over the top of the desk. "That might be it. Let me see." After making a rather obvious show of checking it for traps or protective spells, she opened the cover and looked inside.

Sorin rolled his eyes. "Just in case you were wondering, that little demonstration was for me," he told Landon.

"I wasn't wondering. You might have noticed that I didn't open it."

"Yeah, yeah. Good for you, *Mr. Teacher's Pet*."

"It *is* written in code," Thea said, thumbing through the pages.

"Can you read it?"

Lifting her robes, she removed a small leather pouch strapped to her leg. It contained a mirror. "I can now. The writing is backwards."

"You are full of surprises," Sorin said, remarking on the hidden pouch.

"What exactly are you looking at?" she asked.

His face turned bright red. "Oh, right. Sorry." Putting his hand to his mouth and clearing his throat, he added. "Nice leg."

Thea let go of the hem of her robes and used the mirror to reflect the writing. "It says here that Volgreth sought to harness the Witchingwraith's power. He believed that if he bound the wraith, he could use its power to undo the damage he did to Kahr'anis, converting the plains into farmland and fixing the Brownwater."

"Uh-uh. No way. I refuse to believe that evil monster ever had good intentions," Sorin said dismissively. "Maybe he convinced himself that he had Anisen's best interests at heart— that I'll buy—but not the whole, *I'm a misunderstood wizard who can fix the world if you'd just give me the chance* act."

Landon cut the archer off. "Are you finished? I want to hear what Thea has to say."

"Whatever."

"Go ahead. He'll be quiet."

Thea continued to flip through the pages. "It looks like he spent years trying to contain it, but it proved too strong."

Sorin chuffed. "Shocking."

Thea read aloud...

The Witchingwraith cannot abide light in any form. It cannot pass it, nor can it extinguish something as simple as a candle flame. Consequently, it (and its daemons) inhabit a human host to protect it from the light, removing the person's eyes so that no light can get inside. It's a truly hideous fate.

I have exploited this weakness by filling my castle with ever-burning torches, spending my days searching for signs of shadow and extinguishing it with light. However, I fear I have expended too much energy in my quest to contain it, for I believe the Witchingwraith has escaped. Last night, an unnatural fog engulfed the plains, blocking out the sun.

I sense the wraith beyond the edges of my sight.

It longs to walk in the light unfettered.

It longs for a host.

It longs for me.

She paused.

"Is that it?" Sorin asked, obviously shaken. "Does it end there?"

The cleric shook her head and continued. *"The shadows are deepening. I am afraid. I am afraid of the dark."*

Landon looked thunderstruck. "It possessed him, didn't it? Like Loric."

"It's a reasonable assumption," Thea said, putting the book down. "This complicates things."

"What do you mean?" the archer asked. "This is a good thing, right? We released the shadows from the Leering Ones and even poor Loric. Doesn't that mean we can get the Witchingwraith out of Volgreth?"

"Possibly."

"Come on. Give me a little credit."

Thea didn't answer immediately. She was too deep in thought. "I have an idea."

Sorin looked worried. "That sounds ominous."

"I'm afraid we'll only get one chance, though."

"You'll have to be more specific."

Landon put a hand on Sorin's shoulder. "She means, either we walk out of this tower alive or Volgreth does."

"That's what I was afraid of."

After listening for movement in the hall, they prepared to leave the study, but not before Thea put the scroll back in the capsa and hid it under a pile of papers.

Sorin was none too pleased. "Aren't you going to bring that with us? I'm sure it's worth something."

"It's far too dangerous. I don't want that dark magic anywhere near us."

Landon also looked unconvinced. "It feels irresponsible to leave it here. What if someone else finds it? They might be tricked like Sorin was and invoke a witchy thing."

"I don't think it's likely that anyone else will be poking around in here any time soon. We need to focus on Volgreth. We can deal with the rest later."

"Why don't we burn it and take the container?" Sorin asked, displaying his flint.

"Because that might release a poison, or maybe that's part of the trick. The spell caster knows the reader will see what it is before they invoke the daemon, so they build in a fail-safe: burn the scroll and release the monster. I don't know. We've made the mistake of looking at it. Let's leave it at that, okay?"

Landon opened his mouth to protest, but Thea cut him off. "It's not coming with us," she said resolutely.

Understanding the conversation was over, he and Sorin said no more.

As they crept out of the room, the woodcutter pined for the simple days of chopping wood. Back then, he didn't have to worry about scrolls that made daemons jump out at you. The worst that usually happened was someone cut off their foot, or a splinter popped their eyeball like a gooey balloon. Neither sounded fun, but if that happened, you got a cool peg leg or an eye patch, not to mention a great story to tell at the pub. The one thing you *didn't* get was a daemon possessing your soul. That was bonkers. With a deep sigh, he said, "Come on. Let's get this over with."

"After you, big man," Sorin said, following the woodcutter up the stairs.

39 My Light is Your Light

A massive explosion rocked the Unwrought Tower, showering Landon, Sorin, and Thea with bits of rock and debris.

"Save yourself! We're going down!" the archer screamed.

"Hey!" Thea yelled. When Sorin turned, she slapped him across the face to stop his hysterics. "No, we aren't. But Volgreth is up to something. There can be no doubt about that."

He stood there for a few seconds before realizing what had happened. "Ow! And thanks. I don't know what came over me."

Landon peeked around one of the tower's many misshapen corners. "It's too dangerous to stay here. We can go up or down. Which will it be?" He knew there was only one possible answer, but it felt leaderly to ask.

"I wish down was an option," Sorin said, readying his bow.

"Then up we go."

Step by step, the trio ascended the tower. Thankfully, Landon didn't slip like he had the first time, and the limp he'd earned wasn't much more than a scuff of the foot now and then.

Upon entering the antechamber this second time, they were surprised to find the twisted remains of the doors to Volgreth's workshop torn from their hinges.

The woodcutter navigated his way through the wreckage. "Watch your step."

Sorin followed close behind, picking up any arrows that hadn't been damaged in their previous fight. "Do you think he blew himself up?"

"We should be so lucky."

"More like he no longer needed this place," Thea said, surveying the damage. "Time may be running out for us to stop him."

"*Them*, you mean," Sorin corrected, referring to the fact that they now had to deal with the Witchingwraith, too.

Landon headed toward an overturned table. "Look for clues as to what happened and where he might have gone. And watch your back."

"Watch for shadows, too," Sorin added as if anyone in Kahr'anis needed that particular reminder.

Although the explosion had blown out the candles and lamps, small fires burned in every corner of the space, providing more than enough illumination for them to conduct their search.

Sifting through a pile of broken pots, Thea gasped.

Sorin looked up. "Did you cut yourself?"

"No. No. I was startled. Everything's okay." But that wasn't strictly true. She'd stumbled upon a collection of clerical items, many of which she recognized as having belonged to mystics who'd gone missing over the years. Saying a prayer for them, she carefully moved things around until her fingers stopped on a broken set of prayer beads.

She knew it was dangerous to possess a magic item without understanding its power—something she wished Sorin would take more seriously—but she had to risk it even though anything lying around had likely been corrupted by Volgreth's dark magic. She lit a candle and prayed for guidance.

Esslla's voice spoke in her mind. *No evil can come of the Light.*

"Great." Another riddle. Thea hesitated briefly, hoping Esslla meant the beads hadn't been corrupted, and placed them in her pocket.

On the other side of the room, a series of scratches on the floor caught Sorin's attention. He knew what that meant: a secret door. Getting to work, he pulled on books, shoved the shelf, and grabbed anything he could reach to see if it would open the door, but no luck. He was about to give up when his eyes landed on an ancient candle holder. He looked to the other side of the shelf. There was a candle holder there, too, but it had cobwebs on it.

"It can't be that easy. That's the oldest trick in the book." Taking hold of the brass fixture, he pulled, and the bookshelf swung open.

Landon and Thea turned at the sound.

The archer whistled. "Jackpot."

Concealed behind the case was a narrow set of wooden stairs.

"I thought we were already at the top," he said, pointing up.

Thea looked at him blankly. "There's always the roof."

"No. You don't think."

"Only one way to find out."

As if in response to the cleric's observation, the distant echoes of a bellowing voice filtered down the steps to them.

Sorin scowled. "Or there's that way. This isn't going to be fun, is it?"

Thea lit a candle. "Give me a moment to pray."

This time, when they met Volgreth, there was no welcoming banter, only swirly magical energies. Before the party even had time to exit the stairs onto the tower's roof, the sorcerer screamed, "Your journey ends here. Or should I say, down there!"

With that, the magic coalesced, and Volgreth sent all three plummeting off the roof toward the jagged stones of Nachturm Keep far below.

And then they were back.

"What?" Volgreth asked, looking perplexed. Then, assuming he'd somehow missed, he tossed Landon, Sorin, and Thea off the roof a second time.

Almost instantly, the trio appeared where they'd been standing.

Landon's head spun like a top. "What's happening?"

Before anyone answered his question, he fell again.

Sorin felt sick. "Make it stop."

"I cast a spell before we climbed to the roof. He can't knock us off. We'll just keep popping back to where we were."

Landon and Sorin exchanged a glance that said, *She's getting very powerful!* before they found themselves sailing through the air again.

"Impossible!" Volgreth yelled, furious that he couldn't get rid of the interlopers.

When they appeared on the roof this time, Sorin, who was panting and doubled over, put up a finger. "One second, please, while I catch my breath."

Thea was as shocked as everyone else that the spell worked so well. "Thank the Light," she said, collapsing on the ground.

Landon regained his footing first. "You won't defeat us that easily!"

"Very well," Volgreth said, raising his arms. "There's more than one way to end you!"

"Landon! The sword," Thea yelled.

The woodcutter lifted the Glyphblade, but the runes didn't glow. "It's not working." Then it dawned on him. There was no sun. No fire. No candles. No cleric spells reflecting light in objects. Just clouds shrouding the sky. No wonder Volgreth had led them up here. It was to negate the power of the

Glyphblade. The woodcutter locked eyes with Thea and shook his head. "No dice."

Volgreth laughed. "Now you see. You can't defeat me!"

Then Thea did something perplexing.

"Why are you smiling?" Landon asked.

"Because I understand now. I have found my true purpose." Raising her arms, she said, "Landon, take the Light of my faith."

Sorin panicked. "What? You can't be serious. There has to be another way."

Glowing from head to toe, Thea Starheart floated near an embrasure between two merlons, her white robes and golden hair billowing around her with some unseen magical force. Right where her heart was, the glow was so intense that Landon and Sorin had to avert their eyes.

When next Thea spoke, she sounded distant, like many voices calling from afar. "You must act quickly, Landon Quilson, son of Jardon and Marda, *Daughter of the Light*. Channel my Light and free Kahr'anis."

Landon didn't know why he was screaming, but he couldn't stop himself. Sorin was screaming, too. So much pain. So much suffering. So much love.

Raising the Glyphblade, Landon yelled, "I am Landon Quilson and I command the Glyphblade."

"Seek the Light for it seeks you…"

"What? Who's that?" Landon asked, before remembering his vision back at Esslla's earthen home.

"Do you know who you are?" the voice asked.

"I still don't understand."

"Then Kahr'anis is lost."

"No, it is not lost!" he bellowed. "We've come too far to fail now." Landon looked at the tower roof beneath him. "Where the ground is not the ground." He stared at the horizon. "And where the land meets the sky. It is here, where I will meet my true self."

"Landon!" Thea yelled again. "Hurry!"

"But I still can't control it."

"The Light will guide you."

"As will my ring!" Sorin said, raising his hand to display the shimmering arrow.

Landon held the sword over his head with both hands and screamed, "For Father! For Mother! For Kahr'anis!"

The Glyphblade vibrated with an intensity he'd never felt before as he called the cleric's Light to the blade.

"Sorin, now!" Landon yelled, and the archer let his arrow fly.

Then something amazing happened. The stone he'd found back in Endog became transparent, and the arrow passed straight through it—through the sword—taking the *Light of Thea Starheart* with it.

A mocking smile curled the thin lips of Volgreth's gaunt face as he watched the arrow streak toward him, trailing a brilliant beam of light behind it. He nonchalantly raised a hand to stop it, as he had the last time he'd faced the archer, but this time, the projectile did not stop. Volgreth's eyes grew wide with disbelief. "No! That's not possible!"

His smile turned into a grimace as the arrow passed through his defenses, burying itself deep in the palm of his hand. Howling in pain, he grabbed the shaft and pulled the arrow the rest of the way through.

The blinding Light of Thea's faith burst forth from the place where his skin had been pierced. The sorcerer was thrown to the ground, dislodging the globes he wore to cover his lack of eyes. They rolled to the edge of the roof, caught on the parapet, spinning wildly as they attempted to focus.

The force of the explosion also knocked Sorin off his feet, but Landon remained standing, watching in horror as an inky blackness poured out of Volgreth's empty eye sockets. The Witchingwraith had been cast out, stripped of its corporeal vessel.

Regaining control of its shadowy form, it sent tendrils of darkness to consume Landon. The woodcutter fought with all his might, swinging the glowing Glyphblade, hacking the darkness, but he was unable to fend off the evil spectre. Slowly, it pushed him toward the edge of the roof.

Blackness filled the air, but Landon would not yield, determined that if his destiny were to die, he'd take the Witchingwraith with him.

Flailing the sword, he gripped a merlon with his free hand in an attempt to slow his retreat, but still the Witchingwraith came. As Landon's strength waned, he dropped to the ground.

With the hideous wail of triumph, the daemon reared back, preparing for the kill.

"Come, creature of darkness," Thea whispered. "Come to the Light."

The Witchingwraith hesitated.

"Come to me. Come to the Light."

"No, Thea, don't!" Sorin yelled, pulling himself up, but even the nimble archer wasn't quick enough to stop her.

The Witchingwraith let out a gutwrenching wail, turned, and flew directly at the cleric.

She floated in the air, arms out, welcoming the evil daemon with a gesture of uninhibited acceptance.

The wraith enveloped her, and for a moment, it looked like it would possess her as it had done with Volgreth. But that was before Thea Starheart, *Daughter of the Cloister of Eternal Light*, let her Light shine.

"My Light is your Light!" Her words rang out like a peal of thunder, and the Witchingwraith's anger turned to fear, but it couldn't wrest itself from her embrace. Thea glowed brighter. "My Light is your Light!"

Landon and Sorin dropped to one knee, shielding their eyes from the magic emanating from the cleric.

"MY...LIGHT...IS...YOUR...LIGHT!" she shouted one last time, and the Witchingwraith disintegrated, leaving only whisps of smoke and ash blown away by the breeze.

As its darkness dissipated, so did the gloom that had plagued Kahr'anis for generations. The fog lifted and crepuscular shafts of sunshine poked through the clouds, striking the plains.

Even here, high above the valley, the sounds of cheering far below reached their ears, but the joy of the moment did not last.

"Thea!" Sorin screamed as he watched the cleric hover in the air for a few seconds before the Light of her heart faded and she fell.

Scrambling to his feet, Sorin darted across the roof with reckless abandon. Landon had to fall on top of him to prevent the archer from following Thea off the roof.

Sorin pushed his friend away, leaning dangerously over the parapet. "No, Thea…"

"She's gone," Landon said, pulling him back. "She's gone."

The archer lay in the woodcutter's arms, inconsolable at the cleric's loss.

"She did what we came to do. In that, we can take solace," Landon whispered, his heart shot through with grief.

"Who did?" someone asked.

"Our friend, Thea," Landon answered without thinking.

"Oh."

"Wait. Thea?"

There, standing nearby, was the cleric. Her robes were scorched, and she looked exhausted, but she was the most beautiful thing Landon had ever seen in his entire life.

"Are you a vision?" Sorin asked, forcing himself up and taking her hands.

"It's me."

"How can that be?"

"I cast a spell, remember?"

"I know, but…"

Unable to stand any longer, Thea collapsed into Sorin's arms, and his tears changed from sadness to joy.

Leaving his companions, Landon climbed into an embrasure. He'd never seen Kahr'anis in the light, and a strange thought popped into his head—an idea so bizarre that he had to laugh. Kahr'anis was beautiful!

Sorin and Thea looked up at him and laughed, too.

40 THE FALL OF VOLGRETH

From high atop the Unwrought Tower, the Realm of Kahr'a-nis looked like the maps travelers carried—only this was real, and more than that, it was alive. Tufts of grass that used to look sickly swayed gently in the breeze, made golden by the sun's rays. The Brownwater River was transformed, its clear waters glistening as it flowed south, and the many roads that met at Endog fanned out toward countless cities and towns dotted across the valley's vast plains. Far to the south, Bleeding Tree Forest looked wholesome and green, the curse having been lifted with the destruction of the Witchingwraith.

Landon stood there breathing in the crisp morning air. He'd been stifled by the murky fog that plagued the plains for his entire life. Now, there was no sign of it. Was it possible they'd done what they set out to do?

Someone moaned, and he turned to look at Thea, who was still cradled in Sorin's arms. "How bad is it?"

"That wasn't me," Thea responded.

Instantly on guard, the woodcutter spun around, following the mournful sound to its source. There, on the opposite side of the tower's roof, Volgreth was trying to get to his feet.

Landon drew the Glyphblade.

"He's alive," Sorin gasped. "How is that possible?"

Volgreth staggered a few steps, tripped, and fell back to the ground. "Why? Why?" he asked over and over again. "Why?"

The sorcerer's moans hung in the air like a funeral dirge, and his haunted eyes were filled with anguish.

Sorin spat. "He doesn't deserve to feel remorseful after what he did."

Thea shifted in the archer's arms. "No, Sorin. We must help him, or we're no better than the dark magic he wielded."

Landon was surprised that Thea held sympathy for the man, but she was a cleric. Their compassion supposedly knew no bounds.

"But what if it's a feint?" Sorin asked, unwilling to give the sorcerer the benefit of the doubt.

Landon's gaze lingered on the broken man. He didn't know if Volgreth deserved their help, but he couldn't deny that he looked genuinely distraught. Then again, what if Sorin was right? What if it was a ruse? After all, Volgreth had chosen to evoke a daemon. That meant there was evil in him before the Witchingwraith took control. It would behoove him to be careful.

"Leave it to me," Landon told his friends. "You wait here."

This time, they let the wielder of the Glyphblade go.

"Be careful," Sorin said, removing an arrow from his quiver.

The closer Landon got to Volgreth, the more he thought helping the sorcerer was a fool's gambit. He almost turned back when the man spoke.

"I'm sorry."

The weight of those two words pressed on Landon's conscience like a thumb on the butcher's scale. Was it possible to call evil into the world and still be forgiven? To visit unspeakable horrors on people and expect a helping hand? To kill their friend, Loric, and be offered a second chance? Landon didn't think so, but he couldn't turn away.

With these thoughts racing around his head, he took the man by the arm and led him across the roof.

When Volgreth locked eyes with Thea, he stopped moving. Visions of the atrocities he'd perpetrated on the members of her order flooded their minds, and he moaned again.

"No one can undo the past," Thea whispered, but Volgreth couldn't hear her. His torment was too great.

With a sudden burst of strength, he wrenched his arm free of Landon's grasp and hurled himself off the tower. His black robes flapped around him like the evil specter that had possessed him, but they didn't slow his fall. Down he sped, faster and faster, toward the malignant stone of Nachturm Keep. There was a terrific thump, and a cloud of dust leapt into the air.

"No!" Thea said, covering her face.

Landon and Sorin stared in disbelief.

"Why didn't he pop back up here?" Sorin asked, frantically looking around. "Shouldn't he have come back like we did?"

Wiping her eyes, Thea whispered, "I never prayed for him."

41 PRECIPICE OF THE UNKNOWN

Even the dangerous slopes and jutting rock formations of Cragfall Mountains felt more inviting to Landon, Sorin, and Thea as they made their way down to the plains. It had taken several days and many healing prayers for Thea to be able to make the journey, but now they were well on their way.

The first night in the black tower was the most difficult. However, once they were able to get down the warped stone stairs and leave the keep, things got easier. Even so, the hike was taxing, and they kept their eyes open for a place to rest.

"Watch your step," Landon said, taking Thea's hand.

"Funny, the path seemed longer on the way up," Sorin said, standing with his hands on his hips.

Landon looked up. "What are you babbling about?"

"The lake. We made it to the lake. I hope I can catch another fish. Hey, what's that?" There was a rustling in the underbrush, and the archer instinctively nocked an arrow.

Following suit, Landon unsheathed the sword. "Show yourself," he commanded.

He was no longer the naive woodcutter and aspiring scribe of Brownwater. He was Landon Quilson, wielder of the Glyphblade and *Liberator of Kahr'anis,* companion of Thea Starheart, *High Priestess of the Cloister of Eternal Light*, and friend of Sorin, the greatest archer of the freed lands.

"Is that how you greet a friend?" Anslim's voice called out from the trees.

As he stepped into view, Landon saw that he was carrying a string of fish over his shoulder. "Looks like you won't be able to catch any fish, Sorin. He's already caught them all!"

"Anslim!" Thea yelled, stumbling over and giving him a cleric-sized hug.

"She never does that to me," Sorin said, sounding a little put out.

Landon clasped Anslim's arm. "It's good to see you." Then, a flicker of worry crossed the woodcutter's face. "Where's Reinier?" he asked, steeling himself for the worst.

"Well, uh…" Anslim said, looking down.

"Oh no," Sorin said, the smile leaving his lips.

Then, an explosion of slobber, fur, and muscle burst out of the trees, nearly bowling Landon over. The wolfhound reared back, placed his paws on Landon's shoulders, and enthusiastically licked his nose.

Taking the dog's face in his hands, Landon stared into Reinier's golden eyes and said, "You had me worried, old friend."

Thea wrapped her arms around the dog. "Thank the Light."

For many hours, they sat around a campfire, eating and chatting. They even laughed a few times, which was remarkable considering all that had happened. Their hearts were lighter, now that they were reunited, and the setting sun brought with it the promise of a new day, free from thick clouds and evil sorcerers.

The fire in the center of their group crackled and popped, casting flickering shadows around them, and they didn't even flinch. No longer would they have to sit amongst tallow candles to ward off the Shadehaunter—no one would.

"Look at that," Sorin said, pointing to the sky. Above them, millions of stars twinkled.

None of them had seen the night sky so clearly before, and they stared at it in wonder.

"My mother read books to me about the night sky, but I thought it was make-believe. I had no idea it was this beautiful," Landon said, lying on the ground. "That one's called the Great Bear."

Sorin cocked his head to the side. "Looks like a soup ladle to me."

The others agreed.

"It's a reminder of how much we don't know about the world," Thea added thoughtfully. "I hope to explore more of it with all of you."

The sentiment of that statement made everyone pause. Were they a team, or would they soon go their separate ways?

Reinier whined, and Landon said, "Don't worry. We're not going anywhere."

The wolfhound responded by nuzzling the woodcutter's hand.

Sorin reclined against a log. "Yeah, I'm good."

Lastly, Anslim caught Landon's gaze and nodded his head.

Yes, they were a team.

"I'm okay with going anywhere," the archer said, "As long as we don't go back to *The Leaky Bunghole*."

Drawing on his pipe, Anslim grimaced at the memory of Landon setting the underground bar on fire. "Hmm, I don't know. I'd like to go back to Moors Hollow someday. I have some unfinished business there."

Thea raised an eyebrow, but Anslim didn't elaborate.

"That being said," he continued, "I do know of a different place where we'd be welcome."

"Welcome?" Landon asked.

"What I mean to say is, it's a place where people with our skills can find work."

Sorin propped himself on an elbow. "What kind of work would that be?"

"Exactly," Anslim said, with a mischievous smile.

They laughed and settled down for the night.

As Landon was getting comfortable on a bed of soft pine needles, Thea tapped him on the shoulder. "Can I have a moment?" she asked, keeping her voice low.

"Of course. Is there a problem?"

Thea handed Landon a string with polished beads knotted into it. Each one was made from a different precious stone.

He whistled. "That must be worth a pretty penny. Where did you get it? The tower? I didn't think you were interested in treasure hunting."

"I'm not. These are special."

The way she spoke piqued Landon's curiosity. "In what way?"

"They were your mother's prayer beads. All clerics carry a talisman of our faith. I believe you saw mine the day we met."

She removed a skillfully carved tree hanging from a thin cord from under her robes.

"I remember," Landon said.

"When I found your mother's beads, I knew I needed to return them to you. They come with Esslla's blessing, I think."

Landon turned the necklace over in his hands. "They were Mother's? Really?"

"Yes. And now they're yours. Take care of them. If I'm not mistaken, they contain great power as she prayed over them every day, imbuing them with the Light of her faith."

Landon felt the stones' smooth, worn surfaces against his skin. He imagined they felt like the touch of his mother's fingers, and he smiled. Then, he handed them back to the cleric.

"You keep them," he said. "You are far more deserving of such a treasure as this. Use them with good purpose, as my mother did."

Thea was dumbfounded. Had she heard him correctly? When she looked into Landon's eyes, she knew she had. "Thank you. This is a special gift. I will honor your mother's memory and use the beads to bring Light into the world—after I figure out what she used them for, of course."

• • •

As they readied to go the following day, Landon surveyed their group. They'd come far and learned much, but somewhere deep down, he was still a humble woodcutter; Sorin was a talented archer with big dreams; Thea was a cleric devoted to her faith, and Reinier was a Mystic and loyal shapeshifter. That left Anslim.

Landon didn't know what to make of the man as he puffed on his pipe. The journeyman had undoubtedly proven himself trustworthy, but he couldn't deny there was an air of mystery about the man that Landon couldn't quite put his finger on.

"Ready?" Sorin asked, breaking Landon out of his thoughts.

"Absolutely."

"Then lead the way."

Landon put a hand to his chin. "I would, but I don't know where we're going."

"Don't worry," Anslim said. "I'll point you in the right direction."

In his mind, the woodcutter thought, "With any luck, he's telling the truth," and off they went, following the mountain pass down to the plains of Kahr'anis with Reinier bounding this way and that.

Behind them, Sorin heard the soft rustle of leaves. He turned to look, but when he saw nothing, he chalked it up to being overly cautious. It was probably a chipmunk foraging for nuts. Thinking nothing more about it, he kept walking.

When the party of travelers vanished around a bend in the path, Braydn stepped from between the trees. He bore a curious expression on his face, and in his hand, he held a golden capsa that he tapped against his leg.

He'd gotten the treasure he was promised after all, and so much more...

Thank you for reading SHADEHAUNTER!

If you enjoyed reading this book,
please consider leaving a review on goodreads.com.

Would you like to continue the adventure?
Keep an eye out for more Kahr'anis
novels coming soon!

ABOUT THE AUTHOR

When not exploring the Realm of Kahr'anis, R. J. Xander enjoys returning home to New York State, the most magical place in the world, where, with the help of his brilliant wife, two kids, and dog named (you guessed it) Fido, they spend every waking moment plotting their next grand adventure.